How would sh
suddenly swep
declared his lo

Sebastian reached for her hand. "Come on, Miss Wallflower, let's dance."

"How dare you call me a wallflower," Marley said in mock horror. "There are plenty of men here who're just waiting to dance with me."

"No doubt," Sebastian answered and firmly pressed her against his chest as the music turned slow. "I'll just be the first of many. Now relax, you're as tense as a cat in a room full of ferocious pit bulls."

Marley's emotions were at war. It was rare that she got this close with Sebastian. She wondered if he was aware that, even though they saw each other quite often, they kept a discrete distance from one another.

Therefore, this was a surprise. One that she wasn't prepared for.

She felt herself melt inside. It was as if she'd finally arrived where she was always meant to be. It was scary. Scary...and exciting.

Dear Reader,

When I was a girl, my favorite uncle, Fred, worked as a fisher. My family lived inland here in Florida, so we didn't get to the ocean often. But Uncle Fred made sure we sampled all sorts of seafood.

What's more, he wore an eye patch, and to an imaginative little girl who loved tales about pirates, he became even more of a hero to me. He, along with the small town I grew up in, inspired this story. I hope you enjoy it.

Janice

HEARTWARMING

A Family for Keeps

—

Janice Sims

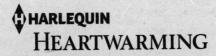
HARLEQUIN
HEARTWARMING

HARLEQUIN®
HEARTWARMING™

Recycling programs
for this product may
not exist in your area.

ISBN-13: 978-1-335-42676-5

A Family for Keeps

Copyright © 2022 by Janice Sims

All rights reserved. No part of this book may be used or reproduced in
any manner whatsoever without written permission except in the case of
brief quotations embodied in critical articles and reviews.

This is a work of fiction. Names, characters, places and incidents
are either the product of the author's imagination or are used fictitiously.
Any resemblance to actual persons, living or dead, businesses,
companies, events or locales is entirely coincidental.

For questions and comments about the quality of this book,
please contact us at CustomerService@Harlequin.com.

Harlequin Enterprises ULC
22 Adelaide St. West, 41st Floor
Toronto, Ontario M5H 4E3, Canada
www.Harlequin.com

Printed in U.S.A.

Janice Sims is the author of over forty titles ranging from romance to romantic suspense to speculative fiction. She won two Romance in Color awards: an Award of Excellence for her novel *For Keeps* and the Novella of the Year Award for her short story "The Keys to My Heart." She won an Emma Award for Favorite Heroine for her novel *Desert Heat*. She has been nominated for a Career Achievement Award twice by *RT Book Reviews*. Her novel *Temptation's Song* was nominated for Best Kimani Romance Series in 2010. Her novel *Safe in My Arms*, the second novel in the Gaines Sisters series, won the 2014 RT Reviewers' Choice Award for Kimani Romance. She was the 2016 recipient of the Francis Ray Lifetime Literary Award from BRAB, Building Relationships Around Books. She lives in Central Florida with her family.

Books by Janice Sims

Harlequin Kimani Romance

Visit the Author Profile page at Harlequin.com for more titles.

This story is dedicated to my sister, Elaine, who said it's hard enough to find true love when you're physically healthy, but impossible when you're not. So I created a heroine who has a physical disability. And to my cousin, Cathy, and Aunt Gladys, who were so excited when I told them about this story that they started talking about the characters as if they were real. Which, to a writer, is a good sign that you're on the right track.

CHAPTER ONE

On a Friday morning in mid-May, Marley Syminette stood in her bedroom, putting on a pair of athletic shoes. She'd already dressed in a pair of jeans and a nice blouse, her customary uniform as a kindergarten teacher. She was aiming to make it to Port Domingo Elementary School by seven. The morning had been peaceful and quiet so far, and she was in a meditative mood—until she heard a shrill scream through her open bedroom window. It had come from the direction of her grandmother's house next door.

Her heart thudded, but she quickly calmed down. She recognized the tone in her grandmother's voice—her grandmother was annoyed by something. However, there was no immediate bodily threat to her, because she was also laughing. More than likely, her cat, Ellery, whom she'd named after the fictional detective Ellery Queen, had gotten himself into mischief again.

Marley sat down on the bed to tie her laces, doing those on her right first. She favored her right leg because it was her bad leg. Today it wasn't giving her too much pain, just a tingling numbness down the back.

She hurried to the kitchen and grabbed the spare set of keys to her grandmother's house from the peg on the wall next to the back door. She'd need them if this was actually an emergency, and her grandmother's door was locked.

Once outside she raced as swiftly as her annoying right leg allowed along the wooden plank walkway that connected the two houses' pergolas in their backyards.

"I'm coming, Eula Mae!" she yelled at the same time she reached her grandmother's pergola that led to the back door. Eula Mae Syminette despised being called Grandma by Marley and her brother, Torin, and her sister, Tandi. She said it made her feel ancient when she was *only* eighty years young.

"I think I've got his attention now. He's following me," Eula Mae called in her heavy Bahamian-with-proper-English accent. She stepped out of the back door making sweeping motions with a broom. She was laughing uproariously at Ellery, her large tawny Maine coon cat who made Marley think of a tiny lion. Ellery dashed past her and hid under the bench in the garden, cowering in fright.

"So, it's true. Cats are terrified of snakes," Marley said, laughing now too because she'd just assessed the situation and found it hilarious.

A three-foot-long, nonpoisonous rough green snake whipped its body across the kitchen door's threshold and wound its way down the back steps. It was the same snake that had taken up residence in her grandmother's garden some time ago. Marley had looked the species up on a website that listed Florida's wildlife. She'd seen the snake on numerous occasions since her grandfather Albert died three years ago. "You should have let me catch it and release it in the woods when I offered," she said to Eula Mae.

Eula Mae, still wearing her pajamas and fluffy pink slippers, frowned, her pretty nut-brown face crinkling. "Albert isn't bothering anyone."

"You know that's not Granddaddy, right?"

Marley asked, unable to stop laughing. She was only teasing. She had no doubt Eula Mae was still in her right mind. In fact, she was one of the sharpest people Marley knew of any age.

Eula Mae walked over and hugged her much taller granddaughter, beaming up at her. She was no more than five-one, whereas Marley was five-eight. "Sorry about the commotion. He caught me off guard, the rascal. Everything's fine now. You can go on to work. Ellery and I will be all right."

Marley glanced at Ellery, who was still cautiously peeking out from underneath the garden bench. He didn't look like he'd be fine.

Meanwhile the green snake had disappeared among the thick flora of Eula Mae's garden. Eula Mae had a green thumb. It was spring, and her garden was flourishing with collard greens, several types of peppers and tomatoes hanging heavy on their vines. To say nothing of the inedible flowering plants like roses and tall sunflowers on stalks that reached toward the sky. The scent of night-blooming jasmine filled the cool morning air. It felt like it was around seventy-five degrees.

Marley hugged her grandmother back and released her. "Okay, if you insist everything's fine, I'd better get going. Don't leave the back door open or 'Albert' might take that as an invitation to come inside again."

"I won't," Eula Mae assured her, but Marley took her promise with a grain of salt. Her grandmother was notorious for doing things her own way and for some reason, she liked that green snake.

"I understand your allowing him the run of your garden, but really, Eula Mae, I draw the line at letting him move into your house."

Eula Mae laughed delightedly. "Even if I'd allow it, Ellery would have a fit!"

Ellery yowled from beneath the garden bench as if he wholeheartedly agreed.

Marley sighed with resignation. "Okay, I'm going to work. Have a nice day."

"You, too, sweetheart," Eula Mae said, turning to go into the house. She gestured for Ellery to follow her and the cat made a mad dash inside ahead of his mistress.

Marley smiled at the sight and left. She still had to go collect her things from her house. She had twenty minutes to walk the quarter mile to Port Domingo Elementary School.

As MARLEY WALKED through her neighborhood of mostly well-kept bungalows and then turned onto the main street of Port Domingo, she couldn't help wondering if she'd see the two Japanese tourists again. She'd noticed them enjoying breakfast al fresco on the front porch of the huge Victorian that was Mason's Bed and Breakfast, the town's only accommodations for visitors. The two gentlemen were years apart in age. One had appeared to be in his eighties, distinguished and silver-haired; the other she'd gauged to be in his early thirties, handsome with dark, wavy hair.

Living in a small town, you tended to notice strangers when your days were filled with viewing the same faces. Not that the population of Port Domingo was monotonous to her. The town, in her opinion, was a microcosm of what a community should be: a mix of races, cultures and nationalities working to make their lives harmonious. Besides the two biggest groups—Black and white native Floridians—there were immigrants from Mexico, Cuba, the Bahamas, the former Soviet Union, Canada, South America, Central America and Nigeria. A true melting pot. Port

Domingo welcomed all visitors with open arms, too.

But as she neared Mason's Bed and Breakfast, she was disappointed to see that the gentlemen were not there this morning. No one was sitting on the wide porch. Mr. Boyd Mason, proprietor, came out of the front door, dressed in a dress shirt with a bow tie, dark slacks and wingtips. He waved at her. "Marley, you're looking particularly lovely this morning."

Mr. Mason was a widower in his midseventies. He was a tall, spare man with thick salt-and-pepper hair and bright green eyes that always had an amused glint in them, it seemed. He had an appreciative eye for the ladies and a compliment always at the ready.

"Good morning, Mr. Mason. You're looking well yourself," Marley called back, smiling warmly. "Did the two gentlemen who're usually having breakfast at this time move on?"

"Oh, no, no," said Mr. Mason enthusiastically. "They assured me that they intend to stay a while. Left quite early this morning, though—for sightseeing, no doubt. But they'll be back."

Port Domingo was predominately known for its good fishing and excellent seafood. The visitors had probably chartered a boat for some deep-sea fishing.

Her phone beeped, denoting a text message. "Well, good for you," she said to Mr. Mason while reaching into her shoulder bag to retrieve her phone, "having such wonderful guests."

Mr. Mason beamed. "Yes, I haven't had anyone stay this long since the festival last year."

"Have a good day," Marley called, continuing her trek down Main Street.

Phone in hand, she glanced down at the message. It was from Sebastian Contreras. A rush of excitement filled her, and she had to take a deep breath to gain control of her heartbeat. She inwardly chided herself. But her heart was treacherous. In spite of her hopeful, romantic feelings for him, Sebastian treated her like a sister. They'd grown up together. Their mothers were best friends. Their entire families were close.

Marley had to remind herself that Sebastian Contreras was not interested in her as a woman, just as a surrogate sister. Sure, they were as close as a man and a woman could get and still be just friends. But it ended there. Besides that, he was the father of one of her kindergarten students, a five-year-old she'd adored since his birth.

Marley loved kids, which was why she was a kindergarten teacher. And it was why she was in the process of trying to adopt a little girl who was in her class. She sighed deeply, thinking of how slowly the adoption process was going.

She forced herself to snap out of her momentary funk and read Sebastian's text.

Good morning. Bastian may be a little sleepy in class today. I had to take him over to my parents' house early this morning. I'm taking one of the vessels out for the day. Be back tonight. Full moon this weekend. Don't go to the cove without me.

Marley guessed he was substituting for a sick employee. He ran his family's commercial fishing business. These days, he usually left the fishing to his employees, but in a pinch he stepped up to fill in wherever he was needed. He'd grown up handling all of the duties on a fishing vessel, from piloting the vessel to scrubbing the deck.

She checked the time of the message: five fifteen that morning. Sebastian apparently had sent the message early because once on the water it was sometimes hard to get a signal.

She fired off a quick reply. Okay, stay safe.

Commercial fishing could be a dangerous occupation. In fact, drowning was still one of the biggest causes of death in Port Domingo, and had been since Port Domingo had been established in the late 1800s. That could be expected when many of the heads of households were fishermen.

Marley put her cell phone back in her shoulder bag and picked up her pace. She passed The French Bakery, the smells of freshly baked goods assailing her, reminding her she hadn't taken the time to eat breakfast. Also along Main Street was the post office, a hardware store, a homey café and a bank. City Hall and the police station were housed in the same building. There was also a lovely park across from the newly built public library where residents took their children and walked their dogs.

Shop owners and other people hurrying to work called good-morning to her, and she cheerfully returned their greetings. But her mind was preoccupied by the last line of Sebastian's message: *Don't go to the cove without me.*

He and Marley enjoyed swimming together on nights when there was a full moon. The cove was their favorite spot. As they floated on the calm waters of the cove, they shared their day, talked about their dreams, worked out problems. They discussed anything and everything. She wondered if those times meant as much to him as they meant to her. But then, he wasn't fated to being unmarried for the rest of his life like she probably was. Sebastian had already been married once, but it hadn't worked out. He'd been blessed with a wonderful son, though.

She sighed as she turned down Douglas Street where Port Domingo Elementary School was located. Her state of singlehood was something she'd have to contemplate some other time.

She began climbing the stairs leading to the huge double-door entrance, but a sharp pain ran along the side of her right leg from knee to hip. *Oh, yes,* she thought as she got her foldable cane from her bag and snapped it fully open. The aluminum clicked loudly as it locked into place. *That's why I'm still single. I come with baggage, a huge amount of baggage.*

A negative experience with a narcissist she'd dated in college had taught her to be cautious. He'd thought he was God's gift to women and believed she should have been grateful he was dating her at all because of her limp. She'd dropped him like a hot potato.

"Good morning, Miss Syminette!" a couple of students chorused as she entered the building. She smiled at them and returned their greetings, her heart beating for a different reason now. It was love, plain and simple. She loved her job, and she loved her students. Who cared if she wasn't a perfect specimen? They didn't.

BONITA FAYE MILLER, a first-grade teacher and the best female friend she had, met Marley at the entrance to her classroom. Bonita Faye was Hawaiian by birth and had the dusky complexion and wavy black hair of her ancestors, a mixture of African, Japanese and

Pacific Islanders. Like a lot of residents of Port Domingo, she had moved there for one reason or another, loved the place and decided to stay. In Bonita Faye's case, she was the widow of a soldier who had been stationed at the air force base in Pensacola, which was only a few miles from Port Domingo.

The two friends greeted each other, then Bonita Faye lowered her voice and asked, "Any new developments on the adoption?"

Marley quickly unlocked her classroom's door and gestured for Bonita Faye to follow her inside. She expected some of her students would be arriving soon. She didn't want them to overhear her talking about her plans to adopt one of their classmates.

Once inside, she said, "No, Mrs. O'Neal promised to phone as soon as she heard anything."

"Well, I hope it's soon," Bonita Faye said exasperatedly. "You've been waiting a long time. I can't imagine what the holdup is for. You'd be a perfect mother."

Marley thought so, too. But she was aware she had several negatives working against her. "Maybe the fact that I'm not married and I have a physical handicap is giving them pause," she suggested.

Bonita Faye made a sour face. "Other single people adopt, and you're healthy as a horse."

Marley laughed. "A horse, huh?"

"A cute horse," Bonita Faye said as she turned to leave. She had to go prepare her own classroom for her students. "See you at lunchtime?"

"Of course. Have a good morning session," Marley said.

She hurried to her inner office to store her things, then went to the blackboard to write today's quote.

Two five-year-olds were already removing their backpacks at the back of the room.

One of the students was Chrissie James, the little girl she was trying to adopt. She was currently living with foster parents who already had their hands full with four other children, two biological and two adopted, and couldn't afford to take Chrissie permanently. The little girl saw her and smiled widely, her dimples showing. "Good morning, Miss Syminette." She was such a shy child that she rarely could maintain eye contact without ducking her head and blushing. Coppery-brown-skinned with mounds of curly black hair, she had golden brown eyes that were huge in her sweet face.

The other child was Bradley Anderson, a confident, playful little towheaded boy with blue eyes who enjoyed making others laugh so much he sometimes got into trouble for disrupting the class. But Marley encouraged individuality in her students and didn't mind his antics as long as there was no meanness behind his behavior.

She walked over to them, cheerfully saying good morning and hugging each of them in turn. That's how they started the day in her class.

CHAPTER TWO

"When it comes to commercial fishing, we're small potatoes," Sebastian Contreras explained to Akira and Daichi Nishimura as he piloted the trawler to their destination.

Sebastian stifled a yawn. He wasn't used to being on the water this early anymore.

He ran a hand over his day-old beard and wondered how Bastian was doing. He was usually the one to take his five-year-old son to school. But he had a reason for being out here so early. They'd been sailing the Gulf of Mexico since five thirty that morning, and the fish finder had recently located a school of snapper only a short distance away. The midsize trawler had a complement of ten crewmen, excluding Sebastian.

"There are commercial crews who go to sea for months at a time, storing fish in specially made freezers until they return to port. That kind of fishing isn't good for the ocean, or for our future. Personally, we're more into sustainability. We fish locally. We supply local restaurants and supermarkets and ship to customers as far away as Louisiana."

Akira Nishimura listened intently, his intelligent brown eyes alight with interest in his tanned face. His grandfather Daichi was sitting beside him on the bridge atop a built-in storage bench. Daichi had a completely absorbed expression on his face.

Sebastian was glad he had their attention. He'd asked Akira Nishimura and his grandfather to accompany him and the crew on this fishing trip because he was trying to stall their bid to buy his family's company.

He hadn't entirely decided how he felt about their proposal. The Nishimuras had offered him a lot of money for his family's fishery. However, he was quite certain his parents would be horrified that he'd even think about selling the family business. They were deeply rooted in the community. Port Domingo was home. Cuba was their homeland, but the United States was the home of their hearts, and he knew it. Therefore, he hadn't shared the news of the offer with anyone. Not even his best friend and confidante,

Marley Syminette. He imagined she would be on his parents' side in the matter.

Akira had walked into Sebastian's office and made the offer two days ago for the Contreras Fishery, a family business that had been in Port Domingo for over fifty years. Sebastian's grandfather, Pedro, had started it after coming to America from Cuba. The Afro-Cuban had been a fisherman all his life, so there really wasn't a question of how he would make his living in the United States. He'd in turn taught his son, Emiliano. It was Emiliano, Sebastian's father, who'd purchased the company's first commercial fishing vessel. Emiliano had grown the business even further after his father retired, and when Sebastian had taken over six years ago, he'd also expanded. Profits grew, their employee roster tripled. Soon, they were the biggest provider of jobs in Port Domingo.

Akira, a man of about thirty, around five-ten, fit, with thick wavy black hair, had come to Sebastian that day ready to negotiate. Dressed in a crisp, tailored suit, he'd painted a vivid picture for Sebastian as to why he should sell the business to the Nishimuras. He had handed Sebastian a business card.

Sebastian had looked down at the beautifully embossed card and glanced back up at Akira. "Nishimura International?" Sebastian had heard of them and was, frankly, shocked that they were interested in buying his family's fishery.

Akira inclined his head, his face devoid of emotion but his eyes shining with purpose. "My grandfather based his business on service. Where there was a need, he filled it. He soon made himself indispensable to some of the wealthiest people in Tokyo. He saved his money and he bought failing businesses and turned them into successes. Born a poor fisherman's son in a village that was destroyed by a tsunami when he was a boy, he is now very successful." He gestured around them. Sebastian's office window offered a lovely view of downtown Port Domingo. Sebastian had gazed out at the picturesque little town with its quaint shops, people briskly going about their business on a sunny afternoon as Akira continued.

"When my grandfather and I arrived in your town, he felt energized again. You see, my grandfather is dying. He has maybe six months—nine at the most—to live. I'm afraid

he has gotten into the habit of acquiring businesses and turning them into something spec-
tacular, and that's how he feels about your
town and your business. He thinks of it as
one last chance to do something meaningful
with his life. To add to his legacy. What he
leaves behind after his death means a lot to
Grandfather."

Sebastian had been stunned. He was sym-
pathetic that Akira was losing his grandfather.
He understood loss. His own grandfather,
Pedro, had passed away nearly ten years ago.
But the effrontery of the speech hit him also.
Why did Nishimura assume they would willingly give up a business they'd built and nur-
tured for over fifty years? Legacy meant a
great deal to them, too.

"I'm very sorry your grandfather isn't well.
Life isn't fair," he said, his tone compassion-
ate. "But what makes you think we need your
help? We're doing fine. Making a good profit
and steadily growing. No disrespect, but your
grandfather will have to find another pet project."

"It would be foolish of you not to hear me
out," Akira insisted, looking into Sebastian's
eyes. "You don't strike me as a foolish man."

Sebastian took a deep breath and exhaled. "Go on."

"You have responsibilities not only for your family but for the families of the people who work for you. By selling to us, you will be able to provide for them exponentially better than what you're doing now. We would never demean your efforts. You are obviously a good, hardworking man who cares for your family and your community. But we might have some suggestions on how you can improve upon what you're doing."

Sebastian's mind had flashed to his son, Bastian. There was so much he wanted for him. Sebastian worked such long hours some days, he got home bone-tired and unable to enjoy the time they spent together. He didn't mean to neglect him, but that's what he did some days in spite of his good intentions.

Hard work, though, was such an integral part of his life—and of the lives of everyone he knew—that he took it as entirely normal and had never bemoaned the fact. He was not the type of man who looked for miracles or something lucky to happen to him, like winning the lottery. Life was hard work, and that was okay with him.

Akira was watching him with an expectant expression, and perhaps a hopeful one; Sebastian couldn't be certain.

"Okay, I'll listen, but I want to take you on a fishing trip, just so you'll understand how we operate. Maybe it'll convince your grandfather of the fruitlessness of his plans for our town and this business."

"You don't know my grandfather," Akira had told him with a smile.

Now, here they were on the bridge, still engaging in a conversation that wasn't getting the Nishimuras any closer to changing his mind. He was adamant about not selling and they appeared to be convinced that, in the end, the fishery would belong to them.

The vessel arrived at the spot the fish finder had indicated, and they dropped anchor. Sebastian could hear the crewmen on deck rushing to ready the industrial-size net that would trap the school of yellowtail snapper.

Sebastian rose and glanced at his guests. "Are you ready to catch some fish?"

He led them on deck but cautioned them to stay back, well out of the way of the crewmen. It was a bright, sunny morning by now and the ocean breeze was brisk. The crew were attired in goggles, rubber jumpers, durable work pants, rubber-soled boots, long-sleeved shirts and sturdy rubber gloves that came to their elbows. The gloves protected their hands and arms from fish fins as they separated the keepers from the throwbacks.

Sebastian smiled at the eager expression on the old man's face. He truly was enjoying himself. The sparkle in his eyes made Sebastian recall his first time on a vessel, fishing alongside his dad and the other crewmen. Yes, there was definitely something exhilarating about being at the mercy of the sea's sometimes treacherous whims.

Suddenly one of the crew yelled, "Whale shark, starboard!"

Sebastian, Akira, Daichi and the other crew members who weren't actively lowering the net ran to the right side of the vessel and looked in awe at the huge, bluish-grayish shark gliding alongside the boat.

"He's got to be at least twenty-five feet long," Sebastian said. He took his phone out of his pocket and snapped some photos. Looking around him, Sebastian saw the other men had had the same idea.

Daichi, his face a mass of smiles, exclaimed,

"I've never been this close to a fish of this size before. This is awesome!"

Akira laughed, squinting down at his grandfather in the bright sunshine. "Awesome, sofu? You've never *seen* a fish this size before, and I've never heard you use that word before."

"Well, it's appropriate," Daichi said, still grinning.

Akira turned to Sebastian. "Are they dangerous?"

Sebastian chuckled. "I've never heard of a whale shark attacking humans. They're filter feeders. They eat plankton and also small fish. They're probably not after the snapper. Or any of us."

Witnessing the emotional exchange between grandson and grandfather and seeing the delight the two men took at encountering a whale shark, Sebastian began to reconsider their offer. These men were not corporate sharks looking to snap up Contreras Fishery simply to add it to their assets. Maybe they would be good to the employees. Maybe they would support the community and be a positive force in Port Domingo.

He decided it was time to inform his parents about the offer and get their input. Although he had the final say in business decisions, he respected his parents' opinions.

"If you two don't have plans already," he said to Akira and Daichi, "I'd like you to come to my house for dinner tonight. I'm sure my parents would be delighted to meet you."

Daichi bowed, which Sebastian had observed was something he did when pleased with a notion. Akira smiled, but didn't bow, which Sebastian chalked up to his being of a younger generation. Akira answered, "It would be our pleasure."

MARLEY'S SCHOOL DAY had been busy and fulfilling. After the end-of-day teacher's planning session, she walked down to the docks where her parents' seafood restaurant sat across from the Contreras Fishery.

Marley's mother, Nevaeh, had texted her to ask if she could fill in at the restaurant for a couple of hours while she helped her friend Isabella Contreras prep dinner at Sebastian's house. He was entertaining some business associates tonight.

Earlier she'd gotten another text from Sebastian saying, Please come to dinner tonight.

I need a date. A few years ago, they'd agreed to be each other's plus-ones. It was an agreement neither of them had ever balked at, although they usually mercilessly ribbed each other about how pathetic they were to not have a significant other in their lives. She was already thinking of some juicy zingers to lay on him later tonight.

But for now she would do her part to help her mother. When Nevaeh and Isabella got together in the kitchen, magic happened.

As soon as she strode into the tastefully decorated restaurant with a nautical motif, shouts rang out across the expansive dining room welcoming her. Marley weaved her way between the tables, returning the hearty greetings and waving to those in the booths at the back. She knew the regulars, and those she didn't recognize she guessed were visitors to Port Domingo. They got their fair share of tourists during spring and summer.

"Girl, what are you doing here? Don't they keep you busy enough at the school?" Diego Fuentes said as she went past him. He was an old classmate whom she'd known since kindergarten. He was sitting at a table with two male friends who were stuffing their mouths so fast she worried they might choke. His arm muscles bulged as he brought a large fried shrimp to his mouth.

She was surprised to see him there after three in the afternoon. He owned a small construction company, though, and could set his own hours. Some project had probably lasted through their regular lunch hour. This time of day, the restaurant's customers consisted largely of senior citizens who ate dinner early.

"Diego," she said happily. "How is Sandy? Are you looking forward to celebrating your tenth anniversary this weekend?"

"You're coming to the party, I hope," he said, munching on the shrimp. "It's not going to be anything fancy. Just a few friends, barbecue and some dancing on the back deck."

"Sounds perfect," Marley said over her shoulder as she continued walking toward the kitchen. "Bonita Faye and I will be there."

"You two are joined at the hip," Diego remarked offhandedly. "I'm inviting some single men to see if they can do something about that."

Marley stopped walking, turned and smiled at him. "Diego, if they put your brain in a bird's head, it would fly backward. Tell Sandy hello for me and enjoy your late lunch." She walked on through the swinging doors of the kitchen.

Behind her, she heard Diego and his friends burst into laughter. Diego had picked on her even as a kid. But she'd known how to defend herself then, too.

Bonita Faye was widowed and childless. Marley had never been married and was also childless. Bonita Faye was twenty-eight and very attractive. Marley was thirty-two and considered herself fairly attractive, yet neither of them was dating anyone. Hence, their friends joked they must be in a relationship and just not divulging their secret. There was no truth in the rumor. But sometimes you couldn't stop gossiping tongues from wagging. She and Bonita Faye simply ignored them.

She wondered why there were no rumors about her and Sebastian. The two of them were together around town much more than she and Bonita Faye. She supposed some people enjoyed innuendo more than facts.

The kitchen was a hive of activity. Her sister, Tandi, who was busy pulling a wire basket out of the fryer, was the first to spot her.

"Hey, sis. Mom just wants you to do the prep work for the dinner crowd, then you're free to get ready for the party at Sebastian's."

Tandi was tall like Marley, but she was five years younger at twenty-seven. Her skin was the color of toasted almonds, whereas Marley had skin like rich milk chocolate with red undertones. Both sisters had plenty of curly black hair, which in Marley's case fell to the middle of her back. Tandi had recently decided she wanted a new look and had her springy coils braided. The braids fell to her chin and her edges were smooth and baby soft. Marley thought her kid sister looked gorgeous.

"Got it," Marley said, heading over to the storeroom to stash her belongings. "Where's Torin?"

"In the office, doing the payroll. Thank God it's Friday!" Tandi laughed shortly and returned to her task. She allowed the wire basket filled with fries to drain for a minute, then poured the crispy fries onto paper specially made to absorb the oil before lightly salting them.

Marley went to the sink to scrub her hands all the way to her elbows, then got busy washing and cutting Idaho potatoes into French fries. She'd leave them soaking in salt water to draw out some of the starch. Next she washed her hands again and began preparing various fresh vegetables for salads. Lastly she shelled, deveined and butterflied several dozen jumbo shrimp. She saved the shrimp for last so as not to get any harmful bacteria on the vegetables, which could make some unsuspecting customer sick.

When she was finished, after collecting her things from the storeroom, she walked across the kitchen and kissed her sister on the cheek. "See you at Sunday dinner."

The whole family got together at her parents' house every Sunday, barring a natural disaster.

Tandi smiled at her, a mischievous glint in her eye. "You gonna tell Sebastian you love him tonight?"

Marley laughed. "Why do you insist I'm in love with him?"

"Because I know you. It's no use running from the truth."

"Where do you get these? You read too many romance novels," Marley lightly accused her.

"Darling sister, you can never read too many romance novels."

Marley laughed again and beat a hasty retreat. Just her luck having an overly observant sister.

IT WAS SIX FIFTEEN. Sebastian had gotten home over an hour ago after bringing the boat to port and saying farewell to Akira and Daichi until later. He'd left his employees to transport the haul to the fishery's freezer, or in one case, to Torin Syminette, who was waiting with the restaurant's van to pick up fresh fish. Sebastian waved to Torin as he hurried inside the fishery's offices to collect his laptop, then he drove over to his parents' house to pick up Bastian.

His dad was watching Bastian while his mom and Auntie Nevaeh were prepping for the party at his house. He regretted being away from Bastian for so long. Little man was his heart. He'd explained to Akira and Daichi that tonight's affair would include family, to dress casually and get ready to eat some of the best barbecue to be found in the South. He wasn't a bragger, but he was a master of the backyard barbecue. Weren't all men?

After he got his son home and into the bath, Bastian said, "Daddy, can I stay up and watch TV tonight? I don't have to go to school tomorrow." Sebastian paused as he dried Bastian off.

"Tell you what," he said. "If, after you have met our guests and had your dinner, you want to curl up in a chair in front of the TV in the den, I'm not going to stop you." He knew Bastian would be out like a light before the first half hour of TV viewing. Then, Sebastian would gently lift him and tuck him in bed.

For now, Bastian grinned up at him, his short, perfectly white teeth showing in his golden brown face. "Thanks, Daddy!"

"But first, let's get your clothes on," Sebastian said, handing Bastian his underwear. A few minutes later, Bastian was dressed in jeans, a favorite cartoon T-shirt and white athletic shoes. Sebastian had showered and dressed himself earlier.

"Okay then, ride 'em, cowboy," Sebastian said. Bastian grinned in anticipation of one of his favorite games then leaped onto the bed and climbed aboard Sebastian's back.

"Giddy up!" Bastian cried, his voice echoing a little too loudly in Sebastian's right ear.

Wincing, Sebastian laughed and, good horse that he was, galloped into the kitchen, where his mother and Auntie Nevaeh were putting the finishing touches on tonight's side dishes. Earlier they'd seasoned the meats he would be grilling, so all he'd had to do was fire up the grill and place the ribs, chicken and steaks on it. The meat was now slowly cooking to perfection.

In the kitchen, he set Bastian on the floor and his son immediately ran into his grandmother's arms. Sebastian took the opportunity to observe his mom and Auntie Nevaeh. They didn't appear worn out from having come to his rescue, thank goodness. He felt guilty for giving them such short notice. But he knew they could handle the task.

The two of them had lots in common: both were no-nonsense women in their late fifties. His mother was Cuban with Spanish ancestors from Catalan. Auntie Nevaeh was Bahamian American with African and British ancestors. They came from different backgrounds but they were as close as sisters.

Isabella scooped Bastian up, kissed him on the cheek and set him back down. He was getting too heavy for her to carry him around.

She eyed Sebastian suspiciously. "So, what's the big secret? And who are the people coming for dinner tonight?"

Sebastian smiled. He eyed the delicious-smelling dishes sitting on the gas stove's cooktop. "Mama, you made spicy rice, beans and fried plantains. And Auntie Nevaeh, you made mac and cheese and… Are those conch fritters? You two outdid yourselves!"

His mother gave him a pointed look. She was well aware that he was avoiding telling them what they wanted to know. He smiled again. "As for who's coming tonight, you'll have to wait until Pop, Augustin, Uncle Aloysius, Marley and Eula Mae get here." He glanced down at his watch. "Which should be pretty soon."

The doorbell rang as if on cue. "I'll get it," he said cheerfully. He saw his mother and Auntie Nevaeh exchange exasperated looks before turning the corner.

"That boy gets on my nerves sometimes," he heard his mother comment a little irritably.

"Be patient, Izzy. Maybe it's something good," Auntie Nevaeh said, always the optimist.

CHAPTER THREE

"So, THEY'RE THE men I've been seeing at Mason's Bed and Breakfast," Marley exclaimed after Sebastian had finished explaining why he'd called this meeting and was entertaining business associates tonight.

He was glad Marley had shown up. She looked beautiful in her simple, yet altogether stunning, jade green sundress. She ought to wear dresses more often. She was sitting in the great room with Bastian on her lap. Sebastian's parents, Emiliano and Isabella, and his brother, Augustin, sat on the long couch. Marley's parents, Aloysius and Nevaeh, and her grandmother Eula Mae sat on the other side.

Sebastian was standing in front of them, wondering why they weren't peppering him with questions. Earlier he'd passed around a slip of paper with the dollar amount the Nishimuras were offering for the company. Everyone must have been as shocked as he had been by the huge number. No one had said a word about it.

"Yes, they're the ones," he answered Marley. "Akira and Daichi Nishimura." He checked his watch. "And they should be here soon."

Suddenly everyone started talking at once. A delayed reaction to his shocking announcement, no doubt. All the voices got jumbled and he couldn't make out what each individual was saying so he pointed at his father to speak. "Dad?"

"But why us?" his dad wanted to know. "I've heard of Daichi Nishimura and he's described as someone who always gets what he wants. Do we need to get a lawyer to defend ourselves from being taken over?"

"No, Dad, I don't think we do at this point," Sebastian calmly replied, smiling at his father. His dad was slow to anger but hard to stop once he got going. "I've already told them that, more than likely, we're not selling."

He could see the relief on his father's face at his statement. His mother's and Marley's, too. She valued family and community as much as he did. And selling the company would be tantamount to giving up on the people of Port Domingo in her and his parents' eyes.

Everyone he loved was in this room. His mother, father, brother and son all carried the Contreras name. His brother was also part of the business, and captained one of the vessels.

And the Syminettes were like family. Their families had a symbiotic relationship. They'd been in one another's lives for as long as he could remember. The Contreras family caught the fish and the Syminettes sold it in their restaurant. His mother and Marley's had been friends since before their births. This decision would affect them, too.

"Then why even invite them over tonight?" his mother asked. "What's on your mind, Sebastian?"

Sebastian smiled wistfully. "I suppose it's because their offer intrigued me. At first I was offended by the way Akira put it. It was as if he thought his company could come in and tell us how to run our business. Then, when he told me about his grandfather's condition, my heart softened and I wondered, why not give the old guy his last wish, after a fashion? He likes Port Domingo. I mean he *really* likes it. Enough to want to spend some of his last days here trying to make the lives of the people better. Plus, to outright ignore the offer wouldn't be wise. We should consider how a huge company like the Nishimuras' might benefit not only the family but the whole community. So, we should give it serious thought."

"It's nice, what you're doing for the elderly Mr. Nishimura," Eula Mae spoke up, her eyes twinkling with warmth. "You want to make his last days enjoyable. You're a good man, Sebastian."

He noticed Eula Mae had said her last sentence while giving her granddaughter a meaningful look. Marley ignored it.

"I don't know," Augustin said. He was twenty-eight, taller than Sebastian's six feet, but not as muscular. He'd inherited his height from their six-foot-two father along with his wavy brown hair, which he wore a bit long. His light brown eyes were more like their mother's, though. "Their offer is tempting."

Everyone voiced their objections and Sebastian raised a hand to quiet their grousing. "Let Augustin speak."

"I understand family tradition," Augustin said. "But on the world stage, how competitive can we be as a fishing business?"

"We have a niche business," Sebastian said,

defending the company. "We aren't looking to rule the world, just our small part of it. We've been successful at what we do. We have happy customers."

"Amen!" Auntie Nevaeh cried, showing her support.

"Yes," Augustin allowed. "I get it. But… Wouldn't it be nice to not have to work so hard for a change? I'm not even thirty and I'm tired. Fishing is hard work. I don't want to do this for the rest of my life. I want to lie on the beach with a drink in my hand and a pretty senorita next to me."

"That's why you got your business degree," Sebastian reminded him. "We've all told you we'd understand if you moved to Miami, as you've talked about. If that's your dream, live it. Nobody should be a fisherman if that's not what he wants to be. But as for me, it's in my blood and I can't imagine doing anything else."

MARLEY HAD TO admit to herself, when Sebastian said his way of life was in his blood, she got choked up. His loyalty to what his family had built over the years was one of the things she loved most about him. She hugged Bastian tight to her chest. She couldn't let a tear fall while sitting in this room. All eyes would be on her and every female would demand to know what was wrong. She was surrounded by strong, nosy women.

The doorbell rang and saved her.

Everyone sprang into action, standing and smoothing their clothing down so they'd make a good first impression.

"Be extremely polite," Isabella ordered them. "We want them to be comfortable. Eula Mae, don't flirt with Mr. Nishimura. He's sick and we don't want him having a heart attack."

Eula Mae, in her colorful outfit, looked aghast. "Who, me?"

They all laughed. "Yeah, you," Marley said dryly.

Taking Bastian by the hand, Sebastian went to answer the door with the whole gang following close behind.

"Welcome, Akira, Mr. Nishimura," he said as he opened the door and stepped back to allow them to come inside.

Akira and Daichi strode in with smiles on their faces, Akira offering up a gift bag with what sounded like bottles of wine inside.

Marley's expectations of meeting the two

gentlemen she'd seen on Mason's porch had been exceeded. Both were smartly dressed in quality attire: slacks, short-sleeved shirts and leather slip-ons in the grandfather's case and expensive athletic shoes in the grandson's. Just right for a casual evening. Akira was extremely fit and vitality exuded from him. His tanned skin glowed and his dark, wavy hair shone. His smile was brilliant as Sebastian introduced him and his grandfather to everyone.

His grandfather, who had a thick head of silver hair, was perhaps a couple of inches shorter than his grandson. To her untrained eye, he didn't appear sick, and she wondered what his ailment was. He was smiling warmly, eyes twinkling with pleasure as though he had looked forward to this gathering. She noticed his expression became even more excited when his gaze rested on Eula Mae. Perhaps he had expected to be the only octogenarian at dinner tonight. Eula Mae must have been a delightful surprise. At least, she hoped so. Her grandmother was mischievous and plainspoken. She prayed Eula Mae would go easy on him.

After everyone had been introduced, the

party moved outside to the patio where there were tables set up near the outdoor kitchen. Marley sidled over to Sebastian and whispered, "We need some background music. I'll go put something on."

There were built-in speakers high on the brick walls of the patio. "Motown, I think," she added. "We have more guests from that era here tonight."

Sebastian smiled at her. "Good idea. Thanks, Ariel." That was his nickname for her, after the Disney mermaid, because after her leg was injured, she couldn't run like she used to, but she could swim and would spend as much time as she could in the water.

Marley grinned at the nickname and turned to go inside to the den, where the stereo system was located. Sebastian went to check on the meat in the smoker.

When she got back outside, strains of Smokey Robinson and the Miracles singing "Tears of a Clown" filled the air, and Sebastian had put the chicken, ribs and steaks on platters in the center of the long dining table. The guests helped themselves to the food. Augustin was manning the bar and provided the guests with their choice of libations.

She noticed Eula Mae and Daichi Nishimura had already gravitated toward each other. They were seated together at the end of the table, heads together chatting and smiling. They had filled their plates, but didn't have drinks yet, so she walked over and offered to get them some.

"Eula Mae, Mr. Nishimura, what can I get you to drink?"

Eula Mae, who looked lovely tonight in one of her boldly colored African-inspired caftans with a matching head wrap, glanced up at her. "Ginger beer for me, dearest."

Daichi seemed reluctant to pull his gaze from Eula Mae. "Ginger beer sounds good to me," he said softly. "Thank you, Marley."

Marley moved away, amused at the vibes those two were giving off—more like teenagers instead of two people in their eighties. Marley smiled as she walked up to the bar. Augustin was handing his dad what appeared to be a short glass of cola. A whiff later, though, proved there was rum in it.

"No more than two of those," Augustin joked with his dad after handing it over. "Or Mom will have to drive you home."

"She's the better driver, anyway," Emiliano said. Then, "But don't tell her I said that."

After Emiliano walked away, Marley placed her order. "Two ginger beers and one Diet Coke, please."

An inveterate flirt, Augustin's dark eyes lowered momentarily and he breathed deeply as though relishing the way she smelled tonight. "What is that scent you're wearing, Marley?"

"It's just Argan oil mixed with a little sweet orange oil. It's completely organic," Marley provided with a short laugh. She'd gotten out of the habit of wearing cologne because some of her students were allergic. Truth was, she didn't even miss it.

"Well, you smell good, girl," Augustin said as he prepared the drinks. To Marley, he looked bored, as usual. She couldn't blame him, though. He was the youngest person here tonight, besides Bastian. Small-town life had never appealed to Augustin, who'd always yearned for the latest thing: news, technology, fashion, cars and women. Sometimes she felt like telling him to go on to Miami, as he'd threatened to do in the past; hence the reason for Sebastian's outburst a few minutes ago.

Sebastian was losing patience with his belly-aching. But Augustin had to be the one to do something about his own dissatisfaction.

He set her drinks on a silver tray, and she smiled at him. "Thank you, sir."

"It's my pleasure," he said, winking at her.

After delivering Eula Mae and Mr. Nishimura's drinks, she gave them their privacy after a pointed look from her grandmother. Then she sauntered down the length of the long table to where Sebastian was chatting with Akira and supervising Bastian's meal. Bastian loved meat but he had to be coaxed to eat his vegetables.

As she sat down and began preparing herself a plate, Akira turned to her and said, "Sebastian told me you speak a little Japanese."

Marley softly laughed and explained, "My friend Bonita Faye speaks fluent Japanese. Her grandmother's from Kyoto. Bonita Faye taught me a few phrases, but I would be lost on a visit to Japan, believe me."

Akira regarded her with interest. She blushed under his scrutiny and pulled her cell phone from the pocket of her sundress. "Let me call her. I did promise to FaceTime her. My grandmother's known for her flamboyant outfits, and Bonita Faye wanted to see what she was wearing tonight."

Marley dialed quickly. The phone only rang a couple of times before Bonita Faye picked up. Her friend had dressed for their video session. Her makeup was perfect, her long black waves shone, and she was wearing a colorful blouse. Bonita Faye had a fear of being caught with her hair sticking up all over the place or any other embarrassing state while video chatting.

"Bonita Faye, say hello to Akira Nishimura, who's visiting from Tokyo," Marley said. She handed her phone to Akira, who confidently took it and began chatting pleasantly with Bonita Faye in Japanese.

With Akira occupied, and from the tone of his voice, pleasantly so, Marley continued putting food on her plate. Out of the corner of her eye, she noticed Sebastian was smiling at her.

"What?" she asked, eyeing him askance. He and Bastian were sitting across from her and Akira.

"Matchmaking, and you haven't been here an hour yet. You're as bad as our mothers and Eula Mae."

"I'm not matchmaking," she denied. "I'm just introducing an interesting man to an equally interesting woman."

"That's the definition of matchmaking," Sebastian maintained.

Akira was clearly enjoying talking with Bonita Faye. She gave Sebastian a triumphant look and he smiled broadly. "You're too much, you know that?"

"No, I'm just enough," Marley told him and bit into a juicy piece of chicken. "Mmm, delicious."

Sebastian's smile got even broader. "Why, thank you."

"Mom and Auntie Isabella seasoned it just right!"

His smile was replaced by an outright guffaw. "You, Mom and Auntie Nevaeh never get tired of razzing me about my cooking, but I've noticed that you three seem to enjoy it immensely."

"That's because Auntie Isabella taught you the proper way to cook meats on a grill and in a smoker. You sear it to seal in the juices, then you slow cook it to ensure its tenderness. You were taught well. But, seriously, can you take credit for actually cooking it by yourself? Auntie Isabella tenderizes and seasons the meat beforehand. That's why we tease you. There's more to barbecuing than just tossing meat on a grill."

Shaking his head in resignation, Sebastian said, "You have a point."

She smiled at him. "But you're still going to brag about your barbecue."

"Of course," he said with a mischievous smile.

"Then I'm going to keep razzing you."

Akira rejoined them, handing Marley her phone. "Bonita Faye wants to speak with you."

Marley took the phone and rose, walking away a few feet so she could speak privately. "Hey, girl."

"He's gorgeous," Bonita Faye enthused. "But I was so nervous. It was like getting thrown into the deep end and I couldn't swim. My flirting skills are rusty!"

"He's smiling," Marley told her. "So, you did great. Hold on." She walked over to her grandmother and said, "Smile, Eula Mae. Bonita Faye's on video."

Eula Mae blew Bonita Faye a kiss. And,

since she knew Bonita Faye enjoyed her colorful outfits, she got up and struck a pose.

Bonita Faye laughed. "Oh, she's beautiful as always. She makes me miss my momma and grandma in Hawaii."

Marley threw her a kiss, too. "All right, girlfriend. I'll talk to you later."

"Bye," Bonita Faye said, and she ended the call.

Marley put her phone in her pocket and went back to join Sebastian, Bastian and Akira at their end of the table. Akira was chowing down. He swallowed and looked up at her expectantly. "Bonita Faye says you're both teachers at the elementary school. Teaching is a noble profession. Being responsible for nurturing children who will perhaps one day lead the world." He smiled warmly at her.

"That's a nice way of looking at it," Marley said. "If I can just help them to learn that they should treat everyone as equals and not be a bully, my job's done. They're smart and curious and, deep down, all of them want to be decent human beings. That's good enough."

Both men were gazing at her curiously. Sebastian with pride and his brotherly love, which she was aware of and cherished, shining in his eyes. And Akira with admiration.

She flushed, not being used to so much male attention.

Bastian yawned widely. His eyelids were heavy, and his head was bobbing close to his chest.

"The sandman has sprinkled sand in somebody's eyes," Marley commented at the adorable sight.

Sebastian got up from the table and picked Bastian up. The little boy didn't protest. Marley knew from experience that when Bastian was ready for bed, you had a tiny window to get him under the covers before he was out cold.

"Want help?" she asked Sebastian.

Sebastian smiled at her and his eyes seemed to linger on her mouth, which was frankly surprising and made her blush again. "No, I've got this. Stay and entertain our guests." And off he went.

Marley watched him leave, her heart all aflutter at his use of the word *our*...as if they were a couple...

WHEN SEBASTIAN RETURNED to the patio, both his parents and Marley's were all up dancing to "Ain't No Mountain High Enough" by Marvin Gaye and Tammi Terrell.

Eula Mae and Daichi were even giving it a shot. However, Marley and Akira were still sitting at the table, laughing at something one of them had said. He moved around the dancers and sat down beside Marley.

He took a deep breath of her inviting scent and let it wreak havoc with the wall of resistance he always had to erect when he was around her.

That wall had become weaker lately, but Marley had been hurt before and so had he. Sebastian had to be sure she was ready to give her heart to him before admitting he adored her. It could backfire—on them both.

Marley and Akira immediately sobered when he sat down, which made him curious as to what they'd been discussing.

Akira smiled in his direction, and said, "Grandfather and I have enjoyed ourselves immensely, Sebastian. Thank you for your hospitality, but I think I ought to get him back to the bed-and-breakfast now." He briefly glanced over at his grandfather and Eula Mae, smiling at one another as they swayed to the music. "He's been quite lonely since Grandmother passed away several years ago. Miss Eula Mae is lovely, and I know he's been flirting with her outrageously."

Marley laughed softly. "They're probably pretty equal in the flirting department."

Sebastian agreed. Eula Mae had a zest for living that exceeded anyone else he'd ever encountered. She was his role model.

The three of them got up and began making their way over to Daichi and Eula Mae. "We've enjoyed having you," he told Akira.

Daichi peered up at his grandson. "Is it time for you to put the old man to bed?"

Akira bowed regretfully. "Yes, it's getting late and you need your rest."

Daichi took one of Eula Mae's hands in his and placed his other atop it. "You are a breath of fresh air, Eula Mae Syminette."

Eula Mae smiled warmly, her brown eyes alight with good humor. "Ditto, Daichi Nishimura. We must do this again soon."

"You can count on it," said Daichi.

Then everyone walked the Nishimuras to the door and bid them good-night.

After the Nishimuras had departed, Sebastian and Marley lingered near the door while the others returned to the patio.

Sebastian looked down into her face. "So, what do you think of Akira?"

"Well," she said cautiously, "he seems very down-to-earth. His grandfather, also. I liked them. But I'll let you know more after our lunch date tomorrow."

Sebastian was stunned. He thought she'd been trying to hook Bonita Faye up with Akira. Sebastian schooled his expression. He didn't want her to notice his confusion. He forced a smile. "He works fast. One woman on the phone and he has a date the next day with another."

Marley laughed shortly. "You make him sound like a player. He's just a nice man, showing interest in two unattached women. Let's face it, Sebastian, the single men of Port Domingo aren't lining up to date me and Bonita Faye. It's good to feel admired and, well, thought of as desirable."

"Desirable?" Sebastian asked, lowering his voice because he didn't want their folks to hear. Was he jealous of Akira?

This feeling was new to him. But then, he'd never been around Marley when she was interacting with another man. "Well, I'm happy for you and Bonita Faye. A man had to come halfway around the world, all the way from Tokyo, to show you hometown girls some attention that we hicks have been too stupid to bestow on you."

"Now you're getting testy," Marley said, teasing him. "I would think you'd be glad that someone finally asked your plus-one out. It's been ages."

She began walking through the house to the patio. Sebastian followed. "I don't suppose you could take time out of your busy schedule and join me tomorrow night at the cove? Remember? Full moon, you and I have our floating therapy session? Bastian will be spending the weekend with his grandmother," he said.

"Floating therapy sessions" was what Marley called their monthly clandestine meetings in the middle of the night at their favorite swimming spot, weather permitting.

"I wouldn't miss it," she assured him, turning to give him a brilliant smile, which went straight to his lovesick heart. He tried his best not to blush.

CHAPTER FOUR

IT WAS NEARLY noon on Saturday when Sebastian parked his blue late-model Ford F-150 at the curb at Miss Evie's house and sat pensively for a moment before going inside. Evie Cramer was his ex-wife Darla's mother and Bastian's grandmother. Once or twice a month, Bastian got to spend Saturday night with his mother's side of the family. Sebastian saw no reason to hold a grudge with Darla's family just because she'd abandoned him and Bastian five years ago. Bastian needed to know his relatives. Darla's family had nothing to do with her decision to leave. In fact, they'd been very supportive when Darla had "run off," as Miss Evie put it. That sweet lady had been profoundly apologetic for her daughter's behavior and as shocked as anyone else when it had happened.

After he thought Bastian had fidgeted enough in the passenger seat, Sebastian unlocked the doors and said, "Now, how are you supposed to conduct yourself this weekend, Bastian?" Just a reminder to his energetic son not to run his grandmother ragged.

"Like a gentleman," Bastian said, turning on a cheeky smile, eyes twinkling merrily. "Like a Contreras man should behave."

"Yes, and show your grandmother some affection. She's been saving for a while to see you and hug you and kiss you. Hug her back."

"Yes, sir," Bastian intoned with an exaggerated sigh as if this speech was so old he knew it by heart.

"And try not to eat every cookie in the house. Your grandmother is a pushover when it comes to feeding you, and you take advantage. We don't want a repeat visit to the bathroom with your face in the toilet bowl, do we?"

Bastian giggled. He apparently thought upchucking was funny. Sebastian gave his son a serious look. "Don't let your eyes get your stomach in trouble, okay, little man?"

"Gotcha," said Bastian brightly. "And let her win at Wii."

Bastian's grandmother was hooked on Nintendo's video games and got a kick out of playing them with her grandson. It was cool with Sebastian as long as they avoided the more violent games.

"Let's not go overboard," Sebastian said as he reached for the door's handle. "She's not going to like it if she thinks you're letting her win. If she's having especially bad luck, it's okay to let her win once in a while, but not every time. She'll get suspicious."

Bastian grinned conspiratorially and nodded his understanding. "But I can beat Uncle Jerry every time, right?"

His Uncle Jerry, Darla's thirty-five-year-old brother, lived with his mother, ostensibly to keep an eye on his elderly mother. However, the rest of the family thought he was a freeloader.

"Your Uncle Jerry's toast!" Sebastian said.

Then he got out of the truck and jogged around to the passenger side to help his son out.

He glanced toward Miss Evie's neat bungalow. She was standing on the porch beaming in their direction, her pretty face lit with love. In her midseventies, she had honey-brown skin and wore her natural hair in a short salt-and-pepper afro. Petite and trim, she was wearing jeans, tennis shoes and a short-sleeved T-shirt in hot pink.

"Good morning," she called happily, clapping her hands with excitement. "Aren't you two handsome!"

She met them on the lawn, their feet sinking into the plush grass. She grabbed Bastian and hugged him. "Grandma missed you so much." She moaned with the hug and Bastian moaned too within her tight squeeze.

She chuckled as she released him. "Sorry, baby, Grandma forgets her strength."

She turned her cheek in Sebastian's direction and he bent to kiss her silky cheek. "Miss Evie, you're looking as fit and fabulous as ever."

Evie laughed shortly. "I'd better. We walked three miles this morning, thank the Lord. The church ladies were in fine form."

Sebastian grinned at the thought of the church lady racewalkers, athletic shoes on their feet and Bibles tucked tightly to their chests as they determinedly sped down the streets of Port Domingo. Young people out for a jog would move out of their paths for fear of getting trampled by the church ladies, the indomitable Miss Evie leading the pack.

He handed Miss Evie Bastian's overnight bag. "Please," he said, concerned father that he was, "don't let him stay up past midnight."

Miss Evie looked aghast. "And have him turn into a gremlin? Never!"

Sebastian smiled at her. Bastian had told him on a number of occasions that he'd stayed up to watch *Saturday Night Live*, his grandmother on the sofa beside him, snoring loudly.

"Okay, I'm off," Sebastian announced. "Have fun, you two."

Miss Evie took Bastian by the hand and they walked to the house. From the porch, they waved as Sebastian pulled away from the curb.

Sebastian let out a contented sigh as he drove. Bastian was in good hands. It was time to pretend he had a social life and find something to do with the rest of his day. Of course, when you owned a home, there was always something to do around the house. But, since he was pretty good about keeping up with chores, there was nothing pressing. Therefore, he had time to drive around town and spy out where Akira might be taking Marley to lunch today. After all, there weren't that many choices.

He doubted she'd want to go to her family's restaurant. There wouldn't be a shred of privacy there. Not with her mother and sister and brother probably all working on Saturday. No, Akira would either take her to the pizza place, Momma Rosa's Pizzeria, or to Kaye's Café. Marley wasn't wild about pizza, so it stood to reason that it would be Kaye's Café. Kaye Johnson was, after all, a high school classmate of Marley's, and she'd want to patronize Kaye's place. Maybe he'd have an early lunch there himself. But, no, it wouldn't look right if he showed up. Marley would be immediately suspicious and call him on the carpet for being a nosy so-and-so. And he would be.

He ditched the whole idea of driving by the café. How would that look? Like he was a lovesick ninny? Of course, Marley wouldn't come to that conclusion. She wouldn't recognize him as lovesick even if he brought her flowers and candy and declared his love for her. She was that oblivious to his feelings.

But Akira might wonder why he'd shown up and start wondering if perhaps Marley meant more to his new American friend than Sebastian was letting on. The fact was, he had no right to behave like a jealous fool because he had no claim on Marley.

He should go home to clean the grout in Bastian's bathroom. That would occupy a good hour of his time, if he did it right. Besides, he was going to see Marley tonight at the cove. She'd tell him all about her "date" with Akira then, anyway. He could wait.

But, really, what was Akira doing asking his girl to lunch? What was his deal?

Since the weather was fine, about eighty degrees and the sky a crystalline blue, Marley chose to walk to Kaye's Café. It wasn't quite noon yet, and Main Street was bustling with Saturday morning shoppers. Practically all the parking spaces were filled in front of the stores. Other cars were circling, their drivers trying to find a space. She was glad she wasn't contributing to the problem.

As she passed the French Bakery, its outside tables filled to capacity, one of their customers yelled, "Marley, you're wearing that dress, girl!"

It was Cassandra "Sandy" Fuentes, wife of her erstwhile childhood bully, Diego, and a good friend of hers. She stopped on the sidewalk, hand on hips, and grinned at Sandy, who was having a coffee and doughnut alone. Marley figured she was on her break. Sandy owned a salon that was just down the street. Saturday mornings were quite busy for her, too, and she didn't linger over breaks.

Playfully twirling on the sidewalk to show off her pale yellow sundress, she said, "Thanks, Sandy. Enjoying a few minutes away from the salon, huh?"

Like most working mothers, Sandy juggled several things at once. Sometimes, Marley would take her two little girls for the afternoon, just to give Sandy a few hours to herself.

Sandy tilted her dark glasses up onto her curly blond head and grinned back. "Yeah, you know how it is. I've got to get away every now and then to maintain my sanity. But I'm not complaining. Business is good, thank God. So, what brings you downtown this beautiful Saturday morning? Shopping?"

"I'm meeting someone for lunch," Marley said.

"Hmm," Sandy said, considering the options, no doubt. "Anybody I know?"

"No, I'm afraid not," Marley said, still smiling.

"Bringing him to the party tonight? You can't miss it. You were there when Diego and I got married ten years ago."

"I won't miss it," Marley told her. "And who said it was a 'him'?"

Sandy laughed and waved Marley off. "Oh, go on with your secretive self. I've got to get back to work and you don't want to keep your mystery date waiting. Have a good time!"

"I will," Marley assured her. "You enjoy the rest of your day, too."

"I'm going to have to tell Diego he can stop trying to set you up with his buddies. You've already found someone," Sandy called, obviously still digging for information.

"Do that, please," Marley said, walking away. "That husband of yours is worse than my mother at trying to fix me up."

Sandy laughed again as she gathered up her belongings to head back to the salon a block away. "He means well," she said.

"They all mean well. Hug Selena and Ariana for me. I miss them."

"I'll be sure to," Sandy replied, and the two

friends waved, letting those words be the last they would exchange for now.

Marley walked on, her steps light and her spirit lifted by her encounter with Sandy. It was nice to know people cared about her enough to take interest in her love life, such as it was. It also felt good to be clear with them that she was in charge and didn't really need their help. That didn't deter them, though.

There were some things you simply had to accept if you lived in a small town. One of them was that people were inevitably going to find out about your personal life. And it was worse if you were a teacher of small children. Parents felt more comfortable if their children's teachers were happily married or at least in a faithful long-term relationship. Marley supposed it was a matter of propriety. Teachers were still held to a higher moral code due to being conveyors of life lessons to their students. Marley guarded her privacy, but in her heart she felt it was only right to conduct herself decently while molding young minds. She had no problem in that respect because her love life was nonexistent.

So, if her neighbors tried to make sure she

was paired with some nice man, she was patient with them, but the truth was she was only interested in one man.

Marley's arrival at Kaye's Cafe was announced by the jingling of the quaint bell above the door. The café was moderately crowded. The atmosphere was inviting with white-linen-topped round tables and a sparkling crystal chandelier hanging in the center, giving the place an enchanting touch of class. There were also booths along the outside and a homey counter for those who wanted to chitchat with their waiter/waitress, which was always welcomed at Kaye's Café.

The enticing aromas of comfort food made her mouth water in anticipation. Soft pop music played in the background, muting the sounds of busy workers in the kitchen. At the long counter, she spotted Kaye Johnson herself pouring coffee for a customer. Kaye, a petite, attractive African American woman in her early thirties, looked up and smiled in her direction. "It's about time you got here." She gestured behind her with a gentle toss of her long black braids over her shoulder. "Mr. Nishimura, who asked me to call him Akira, is at your favorite table."

Marley smiled at Kaye. "Thanks, Chef." Kaye modestly left off the title when referring to herself, but the fact was Kaye was a trained Cordon Bleu chef, with honors, and that deserved some recognition as far as Marley was concerned.

Kaye blushed modestly. "Oh, stop it. I'm just a down-home cook who's struggling to stay relevant."

"And I say we're lucky you gave up France for us," Marley said, smiling, as she continued toward the rear of the restaurant. "Good seeing you, girl."

"Same here," Kaye said, once again giving her customer at the counter her undivided attention.

To her surprise, Marley also spotted Daichi Nishimura at a table not far from where Akira was sitting by the window. He had his head down, reading a newspaper.

Akira glanced up and smiled broadly at her. Marley kept walking past Daichi's table until she reached Akira. Akira immediately stood up and helped her with her chair. She hung her shoulder bag on the back of her chair and got comfortable. Akira was casually dressed in a short-sleeved sky blue polo shirt and a pair of khakis. On his feet, he wore nut-brown leather loafers. The whole outfit gave him the air of a posh rich guy—which, she supposed, he was.

"You look lovely," he complimented her, his brown eyes sparkling with joy. Her heart fell to the pit of her stomach. She was hoping his invitation to lunch was simply a way to get to know some of the people of Port Domingo, and wasn't because he was attracted to her. She wanted his romantic interests to be in Bonita Faye.

Taking a deep breath and releasing it, she said, "You look good yourself." Time to change the subject. "Mr. Nishimura's not joining us?" She glanced in his grandfather's direction. Mr. Nishimura was still engrossed in his newspaper.

"No," Akira said, smiling warmly. "I insisted he come with me because I don't like leaving him alone. He says I coddle him too much. But, we almost lost him to pancreatic cancer not long ago. He's in remission now, but I simply don't like him out of my sight. He insisted on this tour of the US, and my one condition was he had to abide by my rules where his health is concerned. So, he is here, but he insists that you and I should be alone. Besides, he says he has a date himself." His eyes narrowed with suspicion. "However, I have yet to see anyone show up."

Marley briefly wondered whom Mr. Nishimura could have made a date with. It wasn't as if he'd been in town long enough to— Then it dawned on her. A few moments later, Eula Mae waltzed into the café, wearing a very colorful cotton tunic pantsuit and a matching head wrap, her tiny feet clad in electric blue leather sandals. Her grandmother definitely had a flair for the dramatic. Eula Mae waved at her and Akira when she got to Daichi's table. She called, "Hello, children!"

Daichi was busy hastily rising to help Eula Mae onto her chair.

"Mrs. Syminette," Akira said respectfully. He didn't seem in the least surprised that she was his grandfather's date. Marley supposed it was because his grandfather had talked to him about Eula Mae. Her grandmother did make a lasting impression.

"Good afternoon, Eula Mae," Marley called back. "I had no idea you were headed in this direction. We could have come together in my car."

"MYOB," Eula Mae said, her brown eyes alight with mischief.

Marley had to remind herself that the mischief was entirely in Eula Mae's mind. How much trouble could an eighty-year-old get into, anyway?

She smiled indulgently and turned back to Akira. "She wants me to mind my own business," she told him. "My grandmother has a love of intrigue, although I'm comforted by the fact that the trouble she gets into in her head rarely translates to the real world. You'd never guess she was a respectable schoolteacher for years and is the person who inspired me to become a teacher."

"You're lucky," Akira said, glancing fondly at his grandfather. "My grandfather has gotten into some real trouble and age hasn't slowed him down."

Marley was about to ask him for an example when the waitress abruptly interrupted their conversation.

"Good afternoon, welcome to Kaye's Café. I'm Tish. Have you had time to study the menu?"

Marley realized Akira had been looking over the menu when she'd walked in. Being a frequent customer, Marley already knew what she wanted. "Is Kaye's chicken potpie on the menu today?"

Tish, a brunette in her early twenties with short curly hair, was dressed in what served as the café's uniform: a white, short-sleeved buttoned-up shirt and blue jeans with a pair of white athletic shoes. She grinned. "Of course. It's been one of our most requested dishes so far today."

"I'll take that," Marley said. "And an iced tea, no sugar, with extra lemons on the side."

Tish was quickly scribbling on her pad. Finished, she smiled in Akira's direction. "And you, sir?"

"Chicken potpie sounds good and hearty," he said contemplatively. "And, just water to drink. Thank you."

Tish scribbled down his order. She tucked her pen behind her ear and stashed her pad in her apron pocket. Giving them another bright smile, she said, "I'll go place your orders and will be back in a jiffy with hot rolls and your drinks."

She hurried off, the soles of her athletic shoes squeaking on the hardwood floor.

Akira looked at Marley. "You were about to say something before the waitress arrived."

Marley appreciated that he'd been paying attention when she was speaking earlier. He smelled nice, too, like clean linen. She took a deep breath. What was happening here? Was she attracted to Akira Nishimura? Or was it simply the fact that, besides Sebastian, she was rarely alone with a man who wasn't a relative and her social skills were sorely lacking? She was trying to get Akira and Bonita Faye together. Her mission was to direct Akira's romantic interests toward Bonita Faye. So, she smiled warmly and said, "I was hoping you invited me to lunch to find out more about Bonita Faye."

For a moment, she thought she'd put her foot in her mouth because Akira simply stared at her with his mouth agape. Then, he laughed softly. "Am I that obvious? Yes, I do want to know more about Bonita Faye. She fascinates me. But I was going to finesse the information out of you. My smoothness rating has plummeted."

They both laughed at that. Then, she said, "No finessing needed. I'd be delighted to talk about Bonita Faye."

Akira lowered his eyes shyly. "She mentioned she's a widow," he said. "I couldn't help feeling that since it was practically the first thing out of her mouth that I should take it as a warning. That, perhaps, she isn't ready to date yet."

He was very astute. "It's been two years since she lost her husband. You're right. She wonders if she's ready for that step. But there's no harm in making a new friend, is there?"

Akira's deep brown eyes met hers. "Yes, I see what you mean. Phone conversations to begin with, and then dinner after she gets to know me better."

"Sounds good," Marley said. Then, she was back to her mission: finding out more about him to see if he and Bonita Faye might be suitable for each other. She nixed the idea of asking about his grandfather's misadventures, although she was very curious about them. That wasn't important now.

"What do you do when you're not touring the United States with your grandfather?" she said instead.

Akira sat up straighter in his chair and regarded her with a delighted expression in his dark brown eyes, so Marley guessed the subject was a favorite of his. "I am head of mergers and acquisitions for the company. I get to do what my grandfather has always loved doing—find struggling companies and make them better by either incorporating them into our company, or buying them outright."

"It can't be an easy job sometimes," Marley guessed. "Being the target of a takeover probably doesn't sit well with some people."

"Well," Akira said, "if they see it as a takeover then I'm not doing my job. I try to show them the advantages of working with us. Advantages to their company. And, of course, they do have the option of rejecting our offer. But I'm very careful about whom I approach. I do my research and can usually predict whether or not our offer will be welcome. We try not to ruffle any feathers and make the transition a smooth one. Aggressiveness is not something we admire in our company. We want peace above all else. Peace and prosperity for all."

"Nice goals," Marley said. "But appearances can be deceptive. What you saw when you first observed a company might not be what you thought. Take Port Domingo, for example. We're basically a working-class town. We may have a picturesque setting and it may appear to be an ideal place for a summer vacation or just a weekend retreat. Admittedly, we're sitting on some prime real estate being this close to the Gulf of Mexico and with ideal weather conditions. Did you know that Port Domingo, while right next to the ocean, has rarely sustained heavy damages from hurricanes? Some say we're blessed by God and the angels. Some say it's just dumb luck, but most of the old-timers claim it's because of Father Francisco Ortega's blessing."

"Father Ortega?" Akira asked, giving her a questioning look.

Before she could launch into her favorite tale about Port Domingo, Eula Mae walked up to their table, Daichi in tow, both of them carrying their plates and drinks. "I couldn't help overhearing that you're about to tell Akira our town's history." She winked at Daichi. "You don't want to miss this."

She indicated with a nod of her head for Akira and Marley to be dutiful grandchildren and help their grandparents into the two empty chairs at the table. When they were all seated, Eula Mae smiled sweetly at her granddaughter and said in her best retired schoolteacher's voice, "Proceed."

"Your orders were prepared so fast, I brought the rolls and drinks with your food," Tish said breathlessly, balancing a large tray as she strode up to their table. "Oh, I see your party has grown. Hello, Mrs. Syminette."

Eula Mae smiled at Tish. "Good to see you, LaTisha. Please give your mother my best."

"Oh, yes, ma'am," Tish promised as she deftly served Marley and Akira their meals and drinks. Marley couldn't help smiling. Her grandmother knew practically everyone in town. She'd retired by the time Tish was in school, but she'd taught Tish's mother.

Finished with her task, Tish grinned at Eula Mae. "Enjoy your meals!"

Once Tish was gone, Marley waited until Akira sampled his food and she'd taken a bite or two of Kaye's delicious chicken potpie, the insides savory and chock-full of fresh vegetables and tender chicken in a creamy golden sauce and the crust so crispy and delicately flaky, it practically melted in your mouth.

"This is outstanding," Akira said. "I love how simple yet decadent it tastes."

"That's what happens when you've got a genius in the kitchen." Marley complimented her schoolmate's skills.

"Get on with the story," Eula Mae reminded her, then she tucked into her BLT. Daichi was enjoying stir-fried chicken and vegetables over rice.

Marley cleared her throat and took a sip of her iced tea. "In the late 1800s, on this very spot, ex-sailors and ex-soldiers and, let's face it, ex-pirates settled down with their families and decided to make this their permanent home. Most fished for a living, some farmed, but they all saw the wisdom in pooling their resources. Fishermen shared their catch, farmers their crops. There was a daily market at the docks where the trading took place.

"They lived peacefully for years like this, their spot having no name, per se, just a place that was beginning to feel more and more like home. Then, one day, an elderly Catholic priest was found in a boat adrift on the sea. Some fishermen rescued him and brought him with them to what's now Port Domingo. He stayed with a fisherman's family until he was strong again. After that, he would hold church services down at the docks every Sunday morning. People started showing up to hear him. They liked him. Quite frankly, it was the only entertainment these simple people had. One Sunday, a fisherman stood up and said, 'Are we ever going to name our town? Some of us have been here for over five years. Shouldn't we call ourselves something besides a village?'

"So, they had a discussion. Someone suggested they should call their village Port Sunday, since they were definitely by the sea. And while they didn't have a lot of ships come to their docks delivering goods from all over the world, their fishermen brought fresh fish to the port every single day. So, a port they were by definition. And since it was on a Sunday that they'd decided the village needed a name, then why not call it Port Sunday? The villagers mulled that over for a few minutes, and then Father Ortega spoke up. Domingo, he told them, meant *Sunday* in Spanish. Simple folks that they were, their village being called something as fancy as Port Domingo appealed to their hopes and dreams for themselves. From that day forward the village was known as Port Domingo.

"To add gravitas to the occasion," Marley went on, "Father Ortega suggested he bless their new town. He stood before them with his head bowed to God, and they followed suit. 'Dear Lord,' he humbly said, 'bless this town. Let it grow and prosper, protect it from storms and other ravages of nature. Keep the people pure-hearted and thankful for your blessings. Let them always remember to share with their brothers and protect each other. Amen!'"

Daichi smiled. "That's beautiful. But how do you know those were Father Ortega's exact words?"

Eula Mae laughed. "Honey, every time someone tells that story, the words change. But the meaning stays the same. Port Domingo is its people. And the people love and protect each other. As long as they do that, they believe their luck will hold."

Marley grinned. "We're a superstitious bunch."

Akira and Daichi joined in the laughter, and they enjoyed their meals together, the four of them chatting for over an hour.

Later, as she and Eula Mae went in one direction and Akira and Daichi in the direction of the bed-and-breakfast, Marley noticed that Eula Mae was glowing. She attributed that glow to Daichi. Perhaps Marley had underestimated how lonely her grandmother had been since her grandfather Albert had passed away.

She draped her arm about Eula Mae's shoulders as they strode down the sidewalk. "You know, I believe that's your first date since we lost Grandpa."

Eula Mae smiled up at her. "Who exactly do you suppose I can date in this town? Men my age are few and far between. And I'm not interested in becoming a cougar."

Marley laughed. "I'm surprised you know what a cougar is."

"I keep my ears open," Eula Mae assured her.

CHAPTER FIVE

THERE WERE STILL hours to go before Sandy and Diego's party, so when Marley got home she did a few chores around the house, washed and conditioned her long, curly natural hair, giving it a deep conditioning treatment, and gave herself a manicure and a pedicure. As she sat with her feet soaking in the tub, her cell phone rang. She'd left it within reach as she sat on the edge of the tub in the bathroom. She grabbed it to look down at the display. She was surprised to see it was her brother.

"Torin, hey, what's up?" she answered, her voice reflecting her pleasure at hearing from him. He wasn't the type to call for a casual chat.

Torin cleared his throat, and she already knew what he had to say was not going to come easy for him.

After a few more seconds of hesitation, he said, "Can I run something by you, sis?"

"Of course, I'm listening." Her brother was such a self-contained person, she rarely got the chance to say those words.

"I'm thinking of making the air force my career. Do you think I'm crazy for believing there's more for me than being in the reserve and working in the family business? I mean, I love my family and I love my town, and working at the restaurant and being in the reserve makes me happy, but I want more. There's so much more that I could be doing with my life. And what if the woman I'm supposed to spend my life with doesn't live in Port Domingo and will never visit Port Domingo? I would be limiting my options by staying here, right?"

Marley was excited by all of the words coming out of her brother's mouth. He hadn't strung this many words together since…well, forever. She had to make certain her response was not flippant or ill-thought-out because this was obviously important to him. So, she let her heart speak for her.

"Torin, you're strong and brave and considerate and loyal, all the qualities I'm sure the air force would be happy to find in a recruit. You've already done an outstanding job in the reserve. You and your unit saved lives during Hurricane Irma when you went to South Florida to help out. Sounds like you've given this some thought. What exactly are you worried about? That Mom and Dad aren't going to want to give you up? None of us want to lose you, baby brother. We're selfish that way. But, we also want what you want. If you want to make a career out of the air force, we'll support you."

She heard a huge sigh of relief from her brother. "I knew you'd say that, Marley. Now, I've got to get up the nerve to have a talk with Mom and Dad. Thanks for the support."

Marley grinned widely. It felt good to be of help to her usually reticent brother.

"They'll understand," she said confidently.

"From your lips to God's ears," Torin said, not sounding totally convinced, but more sure of himself than he'd sounded earlier. Then, in a playful tone, he added, "From the sound of water splashing, you must be soaking your feet. Make sure you work on those crusty heels."

"Oh, you!" Marley laughed, his teasing taking her back to their childhood when he was always joking around and making her life miserable, as little brothers had a habit of doing. How dare he? She certainly didn't have crusty heels. "Bye!" she cried indignantly. And she hung up on him, still laughing.

Her laughter faded as she wondered if Torin was serious about leaving. It made her sad to think of him out in the world on his own. She knew he was thirty, but the three of them—she, Tandi and Torin—had never lived more than two miles apart from one another, except for when she'd gone away to college. She supposed she'd just have to get used to the idea.

But thinking of Torin leaving made her consider her own dreams. She still clung fiercely to the hope that Chrissie's adoption would come through soon. She wanted to be Chrissie's mother more than anything. Even if her dream of someday being with Sebastian never came true, at least she and Chrissie could be a family of two.

Chrissie's mother, Aisha, had been killed in a car accident three years ago. Marley had met Aisha by chance one Saturday morning when Marley was picking up a few items at the local mom-and-pop grocery store. The store served the immediate needs of the residents, but the basic necessities only. If you needed to do a full week's grocery shopping, then you drove to the nearby town of Destin and shopped at a fully stocked supermarket.

That morning, Marley was bending down to get a carton of orange juice when she heard a moan. Out of the corner of her eye, she saw a heavily pregnant young woman bending to try and pick up a box of cereal she'd dropped. Marley hurried over, scooped up the box and handed it to her.

Smiling, the young woman—an African American with long, curly black hair and prominent dimples in her honey-brown face—said, "Oh, thank you. Lately, it isn't so easy to bend over."

"I imagine not," Marley had said, smiling back. She was a teacher and naturally interested in the welfare of children. Plus, she was nosy as heck, and here was someone she didn't know. That was, in and of itself, a minor miracle. She liked to think she knew everyone in Port Domingo.

"You must be new in town," she said conversationally as the two of them began strolling down the aisle together.

The young woman had smiled in a long-suffering manner, as if she'd heard those words many times before. "I am." She'd lovingly touched her stomach. "We are. I'm usually on the move a lot but now I have to settle down and do a little nesting."

Marley's mind was working quickly at that point. The maternity top the other woman was wearing had seen better days, and her tennis shoes looked about ready to go to shoe heaven, they were so beat up. Marley wondered where she was staying in town. She definitely couldn't afford Mason's Bed and Breakfast. Their prices, while reasonable for most people, were not exactly cheap.

"Visiting relatives?" Marley ventured.

"I'm renting a room at Mrs. Brown's place," the young woman said. Marley was pleased to note the lack of exasperation in the stranger's tone. Even she felt she was being a nosy Nelly.

She was familiar with Mrs. Brown, of course. Gayle Brown was a widow in her sixties who owned a cute little bungalow on the edge of town. She rented her spare room to temporary workers at the fishery, or others who were just passing through. These arrangements were rarely long-term, and Mrs. Brown was often left with an empty room to rent.

But a heavily pregnant woman? Mrs. Brown, whom Marley knew to be a woman with a delicate nervous condition, must be sweating at night, worrying that the baby would come at any time.

Marley stopped in the aisle and fished out one of her contact cards from her shoulder bag, handing it to the stranger. "Look," she said. "My name is Marley Syminette. I'm the new kindergarten teacher at the elementary school, but I've lived here all my life. Port Domingo is a nice place to live. Our church, Santo Domingo Catholic Church, also runs a day care, with rates according to your ability to pay. It's open Monday through Friday from seven in the morning until six in the evening. If it's just you two, I suggest you come to church tomorrow and introduce yourself to everyone. The ladies of the church will be there to support you when you need them."

Seeing the amazed yet delighted expression on the young woman's face, she felt empowered to continue: "I realize I'm being presumptuous. Forgive me if I'm overstepping my place."

Marley, frankly, had never done anything like that before, but her parents had raised her to always be willing to offer help. This young mother-to-be had touched her heart.

There were tears in the stranger's eyes. Whether it was from hormones due to her condition or just the thought that a crazy lady in a mom and pop store would offer such advice, Marley wasn't certain.

Her hand trembled a little as she wiped away tears, and she smiled at Marley. "Thank you. I am definitely in need of some good advice. And my name is Aisha. Aisha James."

Aisha did, indeed, come to church the next day and the congregation welcomed her with open arms. The ladies, many of whom were empty nesters and in need of someone to lavish love and care on, were especially good to her. However, Aisha wasn't just a receiver of gifts, she was a giver.

Marley remembered the first time Aisha sang in church. The parishioners were so stunned by the singular beauty of her voice that some had cried. Aisha blessed them with her presence and sang sweetly for them every Sunday morning from then on.

She and Marley became friends and Aisha

confided in her that she had aged out of the foster care system and had been on her own ever since. She was a hard worker, though, and was able to find waitressing jobs, which sustained her. Marley had been curious about the baby's father, but had not broached the subject, afraid she might offend Aisha. Aisha, for her part, didn't talk about who'd fathered her child.

Two years later, at Aisha's funeral, there hadn't been a dry eye among her church family. For those people truly had been her family. Afterward, when no relative of Aisha's could be located, little Chrissie had gone into the foster care system just as her mother had before her.

Marley tried to keep track of Chrissie, but because she wasn't a relation, it was difficult. She deeply regretted not attempting to adopt Chrissie right after Aisha's death, but she hadn't been as emotionally mature then.

However, almost three years later, by some miracle of fate, Chrissie had been assigned to a family in Port Domingo. Marley was surprised one day when Chrissie's foster mother, Cheryl Koontz, along with the principal, Dr. Lynne Eastman, had stridden into her classroom with Chrissie. Marley had immediately recognized Chrissie and was happy to have her as her student. What's more, although Marley was sure the little girl couldn't have remembered her, she seemed to warm to her instantly.

After school that day, Marley made it her business to find out all the particulars of Chrissie's new life. She'd learned from Dr. Eastman Chrissie's sad situation: though the Koontzes were happy to serve as foster parents, they couldn't afford to adopt her as they already had four children.

Marley had wasted no time in contacting the Florida Department of Children and Families to adopt Chrissie. She'd filled out all of the required paperwork, went through an exhaustive interview and was told she appeared to be a good candidate. But that had been five months ago and she was still waiting to hear the verdict.

"Girl, you need to snap out of it," she chided herself as she lifted one leg at a time from the bathtub and toweled her feet dry. There was no use worrying about Torin. He had a good head on his shoulders, and he would do the right thing. As for Chrissie's adoption, she felt sure that Mrs. Barbara O'Neal, her caseworker, would phone soon with good news. Chrissie hadn't come back into her life for nothing. Divine hands were directing events. All she had to do was have faith. Because if things didn't work out, she would fall to pieces.

Turning her mind to a more positive subject, she wondered what Sebastian had been up to today after dropping Bastian off at his grandmother's house. He'd told her it was Bastian's weekend with Miss Evie, and that later he'd meet her at the cove…

SEBASTIAN WAS WALKING around his house barefoot in an old white T-shirt and well-worn jeans, looking for something else to do after cleaning the grout in Bastian's bathroom. He had music blaring throughout the house and would often dance for a while before pretending to find something else to do.

He opened the refrigerator door and was seriously contemplating removing all of the food items and cleaning it, when he was literally saved by the bell.

He gratefully closed the refrigerator door and jogged through the house to the front door. He paused for a moment to turn the music off, then peered through the peephole. He couldn't believe his eyes.

Yanking the door open, he yelled, "Madre de Dios, it's a miracle. Why didn't you tell me you were coming home?"

His best friend since high school, Miguel Fuentes, stood on his doorstep, grinning widely.

"Well, aren't you going to ask me in?" said Miguel, laughing. "I know you live in a Podunk town, but that's no reason to forget your manners."

Sebastian stood aside and gestured with his right hand for His Majesty to come inside. The two friends had carried on a running argument over the years as to which of them was living the best life. Now, Sebastian supposed, Miguel had come all the way from Chicago with every intention to continue the feud.

After closing the door, Sebastian turned to look at Miguel, who was attired in expensive jeans, a short-sleeved polo shirt with some ostentatious designer logo on the front pocket and Italian loafers that must have cost a thousand bucks, at least.

His friend was a couple of inches shorter than his own six feet and from the pouch around his midsection, Miguel had also put on a few pounds since he'd last deigned to come home.

"So, where is my godson?" Miguel asked, removing his designer sunglasses and gazing around the spacious great room, its pinewood floor gleaming.

"He's at his grandmother's this weekend," Sebastian answered, chuckling. "It's not as if I'm not glad to see you. I'm just surprised. We talked only a week ago, and you didn't mention you were coming home. Did something happen? Are you all right?"

Miguel, familiar with the house, walked toward the kitchen. "I'm parched. Got any tequila and limes? I'd like it over ice, please."

"It's barely after noon. Definitely not happy hour." Sebastian walked behind him, shaking his head.

Something was up. Something serious. Miguel was a workaholic. He was an orthopedic surgeon in Chicago, and he often boasted about all the professional athletes whose careers he'd saved due to his prowess as a surgeon. Why was he in Florida, of all places, looking like a player on the prowl? A quick glimpse outside before Sebastian had closed the door revealed a Porsche, fresh off the showroom floor, sitting in his driveway. Miguel was trying to impress his hometown with his success. Which as far as Sebastian was concerned, was his choice. He didn't preach to people. Live and let live, was his motto. Everybody had their own reasons for their behavior. But it was odd of Miguel to come home so unexpectedly.

Miguel climbed onto one of the high stools at the large island in the kitchen as if waiting for his drink to appear. Sebastian sighed and went to the refrigerator, got a bottle of light beer and offered it to Miguel. "That's the best I can do right now. You know I'm not much of a drinker."

"I know," Miguel lamented. He opened the bottle and took a thirsty chug. "Ah, that's good."

Setting the bottle on the countertop, he met Sebastian's eyes. Sebastian didn't look away. His friend had come to him because he needed to talk to someone who would listen to him without judgment.

He waited patiently while Miguel gathered his thoughts or, perhaps, his courage.

"I'm burnt out," Miguel said with a heavy sigh a few minutes later. His face crumpled, as if he'd never even said those words before, and that the realization of what they meant had just hit him.

Sebastian waited. Even though he wanted to reassure his friend, to say, *No, you're not at your wit's end. The situation isn't as bad as you think. There's hope. All you need is a little rest, time to refocus and allow your body to recuperate.* But he didn't say any of that because this was Miguel's problem, and you didn't just jump in and offer a few platitudes when your friend was suffering. First and foremost you were simply there for them with a ready ear.

Miguel started talking then. And the ferocity with which he spoke told Sebastian that he hadn't confided in anyone else yet.

"I misjudged my ability to work without ceasing. I thought that my body could take the long hours, lack of sleep, lousy food gulped down between appointments. Because the money was coming in so fast and furiously. My reputation as a surgeon was top-notch.

You can't find a better orthopedic surgeon in Chicago. I have a long waiting list with names of the most successful professional athletes in Chicago. But, one day about a month ago, I passed out while in the operating room. Good thing I had a competent surgeon in there with me who completed the procedure while I was being carted out of the operating room. She saved me that day.

"When I woke up, my doctor told me I had diabetes. *Me*. I don't get sick. But, apparently, my body didn't get the memo. Overwork, lack of sleep, stress, terrible food choices. These bad habits all added up, and now I have a chronic illness that could kill me if I'm not careful. My doctor ordered me to take a month off from work and really think about my choices.

"So, I went down to the Porsche dealership, bought a car and got on the road."

"You drove from Chicago?" Sebastian exclaimed. Miguel had once told him that if he had to drive home from Chicago to Port Domingo, he'd never come home again. He enjoyed flying first-class too much.

Miguel smiled. "I figured it would give me time to think about my situation. And, what's more, I didn't tell anyone in my family I was coming. En route, I got a text message from Diego about his and Sandy's anniversary party. I'm going to go tonight and surprise them all."

"That would do it," Sebastian agreed.

"And since I know you're a homebody, I figured you'd be around and willing to let me hide out here until the party tonight," Miguel continued.

He was calmer after his confession, more like his old confident self.

"Not a problem," Sebastian said amiably. Underneath, though, that *homebody* comment rankled a little. It made him sound like someone who rarely went anywhere or did anything exciting, and that wasn't him. However, he did believe home was the best place to be. Home was your haven.

Realizing he'd been standing ever since Miguel had arrived, he sat down on a stool opposite him. "So, how long are you in town for?"

"I don't really know," Miguel said, picking up his beer bottle again and drinking slowly. Lowering the bottle, he regarded Sebastian.

"Fact is, I don't know what I'm going to do with myself for the next three weeks."

"Mama Fuentes will be glad to fatten you up some more," Sebastian said with a mischievous glint in his eye.

"Are you saying I'm getting fat?" Miguel laughed good-naturedly.

"We could all use some extra time in the gym," Sebastian said patting his flat belly.

Miguel laughed. "As hard as you work, you never had a problem with weight gain."

"There's something to be said for blue-collar work," Sebastian teased.

"Blue collar," Miguel guffawed. "You run a very successful company. You're not the average working Joe, and you know it."

"The family company is doing all right," Sebastian admitted. Then, "In fact there's a Japanese company that's interested in buying it."

"What?" Miguel said, brown eyes sparkling with keen interest. "Tell me all about it."

So, Sebastian did.

CHAPTER SIX

"OH, NO, ANOTHER guy is wearing cowboy boots," Marley whispered to Bonita Faye as the two friends stood together watching the dancers on the covered deck out back at Diego and Sandy's party.

It was a beautiful night for a celebration. The sky was clear and the full moon shone brightly. The temperature hovered at around seventy-five, after a day when the temperatures had been in the eighties. There was a nice breeze. Japanese lanterns were hung high all around the huge deck, which was currently supporting at least forty people, but there were also electric lights illuminating the night, so visibility was good. It was still early. Marley suspected not all of the guests had arrived yet.

"Why are you concerned about the number of guys wearing cowboy boots?" Bonita Faye asked curiously.

"You haven't been to one of Diego and Sandy's parties before," Marley said. "But Diego loves line dancing. And he has certain guys he phones up and tells to wear boots, so they'll all look good doing it. It sounds crazy, but wait and see. It never fails. There will be line dancing tonight."

"You don't like line dancing?" Bonita Faye asked.

"I have no problem with the dance, per se," said Marley. "But, depending on the amount of alcohol consumed, things could get lively."

"Lively?"

Marley had confused her friend. "One year a fistfight erupted because some guy stepped on another's foot. And it can get competitive, too. Most of the women just give up and leave the dance floor once the guys start acting nuts."

Bonita Faye laughed. "I can't wait."

Marley suddenly heard a collective gasp over the loud music. Someone immediately turned the music off.

She and Bonita Faye turned to see what everyone else around them was staring at.

Sebastian had just walked onto the deck

alongside Miguel Fuentes, Diego's older brother.

She heard Diego yell, "Ay, mi hermano!" And then Diego and Miguel were hugging, the crush of the crowd moving aside to give them room.

From across the deck, she locked eyes with Sebastian and he smiled and strode over to her and Bonita Faye. Her heart danced happily at the sight of him. He looked so handsome in his short-sleeved white polo shirt and black jeans…and, yes, he was wearing black cowboy boots. His tanned skin glowed against the background of that white shirt. And when he smiled at her, his dimples came out in full force and his white teeth gleamed.

"Hey, ladies," he said. "You two look lovely tonight."

Marley glanced down at her jeans and colorful pullover short-sleeved shirt. She and Bonita Faye were both dressed nicely, but casually, with summer sandals on their feet. Their intention at gatherings like these was not to impress guys, but to dance until they sweated. They jokingly said that at least they'd get a good workout. But now all she wanted to do was grab Sebastian and dance the night away.

"Thank you," Bonita Faye spoke up, her brown eyes eagerly looking for reactions from her and Sebastian, Marley knew. Bonita Faye often teased her that she and Sebastian would make the perfect couple. At least Bonita Faye didn't come right out and accuse her of being in love with Sebastian like Tandi did.

Marley tried to appear nonchalant when she said, "You're not bad yourself." Then, "When did Miguel get here? I haven't seen him in ages."

"Today," Sebastian told her, peering behind him where he'd left Miguel. Now it seemed that the entire Fuentes family were taking turns hugging Miguel.

The music started again and some guy came up and grasped Bonita Faye by the hand, pulling her onto the makeshift dance floor. Marley didn't recognize him. Perhaps he was one of the guys Diego had threatened to invite to the party to try to pry her and Bonita Faye apart since Diego accused them of being joined at the hip.

Bonita Faye went willingly, laughing at

something the guy said to her. And Marley and Sebastian were alone.

He peered down into her upturned face. His expression softened and he continued smiling. In his eyes, she saw something she'd never seen before: Was it longing, desire? In two heartbeats, though, it had been replaced with his usual look of caring and pleasure at being with her. She always felt he was happy to be with her, which she was sure he could read in her own demeanor. Friends were always pleased to see one another, right?

The look of desire and longing must have been her imagination. Wishful thinking. Still hopeful after all these years. How would she react if Sebastian suddenly swept her into his arms and declared his love for her? Would she believe it? Her heart said yes. But her gut, her intuition, told her she wouldn't trust it. His love might be pity in disguise. She could never give herself to him as long as she wondered if he pitied her. Or that there was some residual guilt from the accident that had happened when she was six and he was eight. He still blamed himself, even though she didn't. She didn't blame him at all.

He reached for her hand. "Come on, Miss Wallflower 2022, let's dance."

"How dare you call me a wallflower," she said in mock horror. "There are plenty of men here who're just waiting to dance with me."

"No doubt," Sebastian answered, and firmly pressed her against his chest as the music turned slow and sensual. "I'll just be the first of many. Now, relax, you're as tense as a cat in a room full of ferocious pit bulls."

Marley's emotions were at war with one another. Yes, she wanted his arms around her. However, she didn't trust her body not to betray just how good it felt to be held by him.

She allowed herself to be pulled into his strong embrace, nonetheless, hoping that he wouldn't notice.

It was rare that they got this close to each other. There appeared to be some tacit agreement between them about not touching. She wondered if he was aware that, even though they saw each other quite often, they kept a discreet distance from one another.

Therefore, this was a surprise. One that she wasn't prepared for. She melted inside. She was nervous, yet oddly relaxed. As if she'd finally arrived where she was always meant to be. It was scary. Scary, and exciting.

Then, someone had the bright idea to switch up the music and "Despacito" by Luis Fonsi, featuring Daddy Yankee, began playing. The tone of the dance changed from slow and tame to a competition among the couples to express emotions Marley was very uncomfortable with. She peered up at Sebastian and saw an understanding smile on his face.

"We'll sit this one out," he whispered in her ear. He took her hand and they walked over to a table on the sidelines, where various kinds of drinks were in tubs of ice.

"I think you need to be married a few years before it's legal to dance to that," Sebastian joked as he handed her a can of Diet Coke and grabbed a bottle of water for himself.

Marley laughed. "Agreed. Married and, perhaps, be parents of at least one child."

Sebastian threw back his curly-maned head and laughed. He then regarded her with smoldering eyes. "But, our dance was nice, even though it didn't last long enough."

Marley's face grew hot. What exactly was Sebastian up to?

She pulled the tab on her Coke and drank

some of the refreshingly cold liquid. Was he joking with her? Because if he was she'd teach him that she wasn't to be trifled with like that. Their relationship had been fraught with unspoken attraction for years now. Come on, they had been meeting secretly at their cove for two years. What kind of behavior was that for platonic friends? True, all they did was talk and swim and float their troubles away. It was fun, it was freeing. It was worth more for her than time on a therapist's couch.

Their attraction was always there, though, sitting between them like a barrier neither of them dared cross. She knew it and, apparently, he knew it, too. Had he decided to actually do something about it? If so, she was more than ready.

She waited, breathlessly, to find out.

SEBASTIAN FELT FROZEN in time as he looked into Marley's beautiful golden brown eyes. He'd loved her all his life, and he'd been *in love* with her for nearly five years now. She was the only woman he wanted to wake up next to for the rest of his life. But now, he had to risk losing her in order to win her. There, on Diego and Sandy's deck, he'd finally made the decision to tell Marley how he felt about her.

The impetus for his change of mind had been the argument he'd had with Miguel about two hours ago. They'd been talking about each other's lack of a love life and Miguel had laughed when he'd found out that Sebastian still had a thing for Marley but hadn't said a word to her about it.

"Man, do you realize how much time you've wasted?" Miguel, apparently wise beyond his years now that he'd been brought down a peg or two by life himself, laughed heartily. "Beautiful Marley Syminette. She's the sweetest woman in town, and also the most clueless. I wonder if she's ever asked herself why you spend so much time with her. Yes, your son loves her. She was there for you both when Darla decided married life wasn't for her. But, has she ever noticed how you look at her?"

"How do I look at her?" Sebastian asked, curious how he appeared to someone else.

"As if she is your reason for breathing," Miguel said, and from the expression in his old friend's eyes, Sebastian knew Miguel envied him for that. Envied him, and pitied him just a little for not seizing the moment with Marley.

So, here Sebastian was, peering into the eyes of the woman he loved, hoping what he was about to say wasn't going to tear them apart.

"Marley…we've been friends forever. And I love being your friend, but there is something I need to tell you—"

His sentence was cut off by two whirling dervishes in the form of Selena and Ariana Fuentes, Diego and Sandy's six-year-old twins. They barreled into Marley's midsection and nearly knocked her down, they were so happy to see her.

"Marley, Marley!" they chorused.

Marley, of course, knelt to receive their hugs and kisses, her eyes moist with happy tears. She loved those two hellions. Sebastian took a deep breath and stepped back to avoid being toppled by the energetic girls. The twins' antics had attracted the family golden retriever, who joined in the fun, licking Marley's face while she laughed and returned the affection by hugging him, too.

Sebastian supposed he could have stood there inwardly grumbling about a missed op-

portunity, but instead he set his hopes on later
tonight when they would meet at the cove.
Neither of them had ever failed to show up.

He put on a determined smile in spite of
his disappointment.

A few minutes later, Marley was again
unencumbered, after having redirected the
twins' attention elsewhere. She had a way
with children. She knew what made them tick
and was loving and extremely patient with
them. He, on the other hand, didn't have her
patience, although he did have a special place
in his heart for little ones, especially Bastian.

Bastian had wiped the selfishness right
out of Sebastian after he'd been born. Yes,
he wasn't ashamed to admit that his world
had revolved around himself before he became a father. He'd tried to be a good husband to Darla. In fact, he was certain he never
let her feel neglected or as if he didn't love
her. He was stumped to this day as to why
she'd left him. However, even her own mother
had admitted Darla had always been rest-
less and never satisfied. She'd had her head
in the clouds. She'd loved to sing and had
dreamed of one day making a living with her
voice. Sebastian guessed the musician she'd

run away with had promised to help her get started. He'd heard that nothing had come of it, though. The other man had left her for someone new and more exciting.

Sebastian actually felt bad for Darla. And she'd always be Bastian's mother. She'd given him the greatest gift of all, the gift of fatherhood. He could not bring himself to hate her for abandoning him and Bastian. People made mistakes. He'd certainly made his share over the years.

As he looked at Marley, now engaged in conversation with Bonita Faye, who had extracted herself from the guy she'd gone to dance with and was obviously now telling Marley all about it, Sebastian knew the biggest mistake he'd ever made was letting Marley slip through his fingers.

"He asked me what my sign was," he heard Bonita Faye say to Marley, then the two of them dissolved in gales of laughter. Apparently, asking one's astrological sign was a big no-no these days. He noted that for future reference.

His attention was drawn from the girls when Diego walked up and grabbed him by the arm. "Hey, brother," he said in the friendly way he addressed all of his male friends. "We're getting ready to dance. Are you in? If so, grab Marley. I promised her she wouldn't be without male attention tonight."

Diego disappeared and shortly afterward, Mariachi music began playing. Couples began lining up, and Sebastian glanced around for Marley. Some tall, attractive blond guy who looked like he was a ranch hand in his authentic Western gear had already claimed her.

Foiled again, Sebastian asked one of Diego's sisters to dance with him. A few minutes into it, he realized his mistake when she kept grinning at him and suggestively pursing her full lips in mock kisses. She had to be all of nineteen.

"Listen," he told her. "I'm old enough to be your father and you have three brothers here tonight. Don't start anything."

After that, she maintained a straight face and had the decency to look slightly embarrassed by his reprimand.

OH, LORD, HERE we go, Marley thought as Jim led her onto the dance floor and they took their places on the line. A few minutes later, after several intricate steps, she realized he was a good dancer and she started having fun. Maybe this time line dancing wouldn't be an utter disappointment.

But then the music got faster and Diego and his inner circle of dance fiends began doing steps that most of his guests had not learned. Jim went to join the men and Marley moved off the dance floor. Were they actually improvising, trying to outdo each other?

Her question was answered when one of the younger guys started break-dancing. Everyone formed a circle around him as he did complicated twists and turns, once even ending up on his head. She thought he was going to break his neck! Meanwhile Diego and his pals were shouting from the sidelines, cheering him on.

She heard Sandy yell, "Diego, this is supposed to be a celebration of a happy marriage, not *America's Got Talent*. If you dudes ruin my deck cutting the fool, you're going to build me a bigger, better one. Look at the scuff marks you all have left with those darn cowboy boots."

The other women, who'd all gone over onto Sandy's side of the deck, nodded their heads in agreement, sending belligerent glares at the men.

The break dancer was finally pooped after a few more minutes of death-defying antics and stopped twirling. He ended up on his side on the floor of the deck, apparently awaiting much-deserved applause from the cocky expression on his face. The men applauded. The women booed.

Diego, noticing the thunderous expression on Sandy's face, went over to her, got on bended knee, took her hand in his and said, "Ah, mi amor, lo siento. Please forgive me. No more hijinks, I promise."

Sandy withdrew her hand. "You said there would be no dance competition tonight. Just a quiet celebration."

"I forgot myself," Diego pleaded.

Sandy turned to the ladies. "Should I forgive him?"

"No!" was their resounding answer.

Sandy smiled down at Diego. "I never listened to their advice ten years ago, why should I listen now? I forgive you."

Marley might have been mistaken, but Diego looked confused by that answer. Perhaps someone had advised Sandy not to marry Diego ten years ago. At any rate, it had turned out all right. They were happy and had two little girls to show for it.

After that, the couples went back to dancing together and the evening started winding down.

Marley glanced around for Sebastian and saw him talking to Miguel a few feet away. Bonita Faye was sitting on one of the deck's rails chatting with the astrology guy.

"Hey," a deep voice said in her ear, "I was wondering if you'd like to go somewhere for a quiet drink."

Startled, she looked up into Jim's deep brown eyes. "Sorry," she said, "I'm with someone."

Her gaze automatically went to Sebastian. Jim followed her line of sight and he gave a good-natured nod of his head. "I see," he said, sounding disappointed. "Well, thanks for the dance."

"Thank you," Marley said pleasantly. "It was fun."

He ambled off. Marley stood there wondering why she'd given him the impression she was with Sebastian. The impulse had been so natural, she'd done it before she could catch herself. Maybe it had been that smoldering look Sebastian had given her earlier.

Half an hour later, as she was driving Bonita Faye home, wearing her glasses because she was near-sighted, Bonita Faye laughed suddenly. "Oh, I meant to tell you—Akira phoned me earlier today and asked me to lunch. I said Sunday would be the only day I could do it since I work all week."

Marley was pleased to hear of the invitation. She was glad Akira was acting on his plans to woo Bonita Faye slowly in order to give her time to get used to the notion of dating again.

"Then, you like him?" she asked cautiously.

Bonita Faye was noticeably silent for a few beats. "Well, that isn't the problem. I could tell he liked me when we spoke via FaceTime. I like him, too. But if you have a notion to matchmake us, don't. My grandmother falling in love with a Black man and marrying him was quite rare. Let's just say that staying in Japan would have been a problem for them. Luckily they moved to Hawaii, which was a place that welcomed them. My grandmother has been happy there. My grandmother taught me the importance of tradition to the Japanese."

"But maybe that's not true for Akira. Not all Japanese people think alike. It's the twenty-first century," Marley said.

"I'm just telling you not to get your hopes up. Akira is not a celebrity. He's a good boy. He said his mother is in the process of choosing a wife for him. He would have to be very courageous to go against tradition. Like my grandmother. But why are we talking about this? I haven't even gone on a date with him yet. And who even knows how long he's going to be in town?"

"You're right," Marley said with a disappointed exhale. "I just get excited at the thought of at least one of us getting a happily-ever-after."

Bonita Faye laughed. "Yours is coming," she said confidently. "Me? I've had my big love—Cory. My heart's not ready to accept love again, anyway. His loss left me empty. It would take a very special man to touch me like he did. Personally, I don't know if I have the heart to let someone even try to reach me. It's an impossible task."

"Then the man who reaches you has to be

not only brave but someone who's really up for a challenge," Marley concluded.

"And that man doesn't exist," Bonita Faye said sadly.

"We'll see," Marley countered, then concentrated on her driving. Speaking of bravery: she could use a bit of that herself. Maybe it was time to tell Sebastian just how she felt about him and let the chips fall where they may.

And tonight at the cove would be the perfect opportunity…

CHAPTER SEVEN

THERE WERE SEVERAL reasons why Sebastian had bought the property his house sat on. It was secluded and covered in trees. At ten acres, there was plenty of room for Bastian to romp and play. To his utter delight, the property also abutted the ocean and featured a cove. Which made buying it irresistible.

The cove wasn't huge at a depth of only about eight feet and a width of a thousand feet. But it was plenty big enough for his purposes, which was to swim laps after a long day. Fish and other sea creatures lived in the cove, but he had yet to encounter anything dangerous.

Swimming got the kinks out of his shoulders. The cool temperature of the water, especially on warm, humid days, relaxed him and made him grateful he was a Florida boy and didn't need to build a swimming pool.

The cove's water was aquamarine and crystal clear. The Florida Gulf Coast wasn't also called the Emerald Coast for nothing. What's more, the land surrounding the cove was dotted with palm trees. It was an idyllic spot and he'd selfishly only shared it with Marley, who'd been sworn to secrecy to never reveal the location to anyone. It was their spot. It seemed a fitting place to tell her how he really felt about her.

The moon's light reflected off the water, and the sepia effect was breathtaking. The world was black and white, like one of his favorite old-time movies.

Sebastian floated on his back, gazing up at the sky, his mind drifting but his thoughts never far away from Marley, and where she could possibly be. Earlier, they'd texted and she'd refused his offer to pick her up. His truck was built for off-road, and he often drove it to the cove, which her Corolla was not. Yet she said she preferred to drive herself to his house and hike the rest of the way through the sparse woods until she reached the cove. It wasn't far from his home, and she could find it blindfolded. So, where was she?

He knew he was just anxious because he couldn't wait to talk to her. He'd been thwarted at every turn at Diego and Sandy's anniversary party. Someone had constantly been manipulating her time. It was almost as if Fate or some supernatural force had been keeping them apart. Which was ludicrous, but at this point that's how he felt.

Over to his left, he heard a splash and knew she'd arrived. His hearing had been muffled by the water lapping against his head as he was floating on the water's surface. He eagerly turned onto his stomach and swam toward her. She was doing a breaststroke, her head covered in one of her swim caps—the white one—and she was wearing her white one-piece swimsuit to match. He was familiar with all of her swim togs. They made him think of that actress who was popular in the 1930s for making films that always featured her swimming skills. He couldn't remember her name. He blamed his mother for his even being aware of an actress whose heyday was that long ago. His mother had let him stay up late to watch black-and-white films on Turner Classic Movies.

A few strokes later, he and Marley were within speaking distance. "You're late," he accused lightly, grinning at her.

She flashed a smile and playfully flicked water in his direction. "The older you get, the more you're a stickler for time. And stop looking at me like that. I know you're imagining me as Esther Williams in *Million Dollar Mermaid*."

That's her, Sebastian realized triumphantly, Esther Williams. But he wasn't about to let Marley get away with that crack about him getting older.

"Because I have less of it. Time, I mean," he countered, after which he treaded water. "How are you? I've barely had a moment alone with you lately to say two words to you."

She did the backstroke around him, which allowed her to keep her face out of the water. "I'm a wreck waiting on word from Children and Families. Otherwise, I'm just fine."

"Why are you worried? You're the perfect candidate for becoming an adoptive parent."

"You sound like Bonita Faye. But what neither of you are willing to see is I'm not in perfect health. They have to take into account how I'd fare keeping up with a young child."

"You keep up with a room full of young children five days a week!"

"But I send those children home to their parents every afternoon. They don't come home with me. I don't feed them, bathe them or put them to bed."

"You're being too hard on yourself, as usual," Sebastian said. "Most days your leg doesn't even bother you."

"True, but I do have days when the pain is so bad I have to use a cane and take pain medication. And I imagine it's going to get worse, not better, as I age."

"Don't borrow trouble," Sebastian said. "You're dreaming up every bad scenario. Think positive. You're going to become Chrissie's parent. What's more, you're going to find a man, get married and give her brothers and sisters."

Marley laughed at that. "Quite the imagination you've got there."

"Can we get out of the water for a few minutes?" Sebastian asked her. "I've got something I want to say to you without having to tread water."

They swam to a shallow spot where they stood up and stepped onto the shore, shaking themselves as they came out of the water.

Sebastian's truck was parked a few feet away with the tailgate open. He'd left towels there.

He grabbed one and handed it to Marley, then took the other for himself. They sat on the tailgate and turned toward one another. He could see the curious expression on her lovely face in the moonlight.

"Marley," he began. He stopped and took a deep breath. He was nervous. His pulse was racing and the words he'd practiced did not come easily to his muddled brain.

"Marley, if I could turn back time, I would've realized you were following me that day. If I'd only realized you were behind me, I could have caught you and you wouldn't be in the predicament you find yourself in."

She stiffened. She didn't like talking about that day. He supposed the memory of the excruciating pain she'd suffered as a six-year-old was still vivid. Of course it was. And after she'd fallen out of that oak tree, she'd had to remain on the ground wailing while he ran for help. He couldn't imagine what torture she'd suffered while he'd been gone. He was sure he'd made it to his parents' house in record time and her father and his had raced back with him. His dad had been a medic in the army, and so he'd been able to instantly assess the situation. To Sebastian's eight-year-old eyes, his dad had been the hero that day. His father had fashioned a splint from nearby branches and a torn shirt. Then, Marley's father had gently picked her up. She'd bravely stopped crying by then and was only slightly sniffling.

They'd taken her to the hospital, and poor Marley had undergone an operation due to various fractures in her right leg. Unfortunately, the break hadn't healed neatly, and she'd then had to undergo another operation. Her leg was better after that, but she still periodically had pain. And it was true that when the barometric pressure dropped, people who have old injuries can detect the change in pressure and have swelling in the soft tissue of their joints and experience expanding of fluid in their joints, as well.

Marley jokingly said she was able to predict the weather depending on how much her leg ached.

Now, Sebastian reached for her hand and gently covered it with his own. "I'm so sorry. I wish I'd noticed you climbing that tree behind me."

Marley snatched her hand out of his and jumped to her feet, whirling to face him, a finger pointed at him in anger. "I've told you—I don't want your pity, Sebastian Contreras!"

Calling him by his full name always denoted she was fed up with him. "You were eight years old. What do you think you could have done? You're not Superman. You have no superpowers. When you were eight, you could barely string a sentence together, let alone save a six-year-old obstinate tomboy who always did whatever she wanted, no matter how hard her mother tried to turn her into a sweet little girl."

Sebastian couldn't help it, he laughed. "You're right about that. You were one hard-headed little girl. If your mom told you not to do something, *that* was the thing you had to do."

"Or die trying," Marley agreed. Then, she went silent, maybe because she could have died the day she fell out of that oak tree. "I've learned to listen to good advice," she said quietly. "Even if I still choose not to accept it."

Sebastian felt it was safe to grasp her hand again and pull her back down onto the tailgate. She came willingly, sighing and seeming to let go of her momentary anger. Looking into his eyes, she said, "You know it makes me mad when you try to take the blame for what happened. Can't you let it go? It makes me wonder if you're only my friend because you want to keep me close so you can protect me. You're such a gentleman. You're also a gentle man. I like that about you. But it isn't your job to protect me. I'm a very independent woman. I'm Eula Mae's granddaughter, after all." She said this with a laugh.

Sebastian chuckled, too, and affectionately squeezed her hand.

"That's true," he said. Clearing his throat, he added, "But that's not what I wanted to talk to you about. I'm not smooth like some men. I don't have a line that melts women's hearts. No charm whatsoever."

"I wouldn't say that," Marley offered with a smile.

Feeling slightly more confident, Sebastian pressed on. Gazing deeply into her eyes, he said, "Marley, I love you."

He let that simmer for a few minutes. His throat was so dry, his nerves taut in expectation of her reaction, that he didn't think he could get another word out, anyway.

Marley stared at him with a wondrous expression on her face. She opened her mouth to say something, thought better of it and snapped her lips shut again.

To Sebastian it seemed like an eternity passed before she finally said, "I hate you, Sebastian Contreras, for doing exactly what I just told you makes me crazy. I don't want, or need, your pity! You love me? You love me how? Like a little sister? Like a friend? Like a plus-one?"

She leaped off the tailgate, snatched her cover-up and flip-flops, which she must have left there before coming into the water, clutched them to her chest and started walking in the direction of his house. She was leaving him. Just like that. She obviously didn't believe a word he'd said. He'd been afraid of this. He jumped off the tailgate and followed.

"Marley, why aren't you listening to me? I love you like a woman. Like a woman I want to marry. I want you to be the mother to my son and I want to be Chrissie's dad, once you—or we—adopt her. Then I want to have more babies with you. I'm dreaming big because you make me believe everything is possible. My heart belongs to you, Marley Nesta Syminette. Yes, your mother loved Bob Marley so much, she gave you his last name and his first name. I remember that because I love you with all my heart. I don't pity you. Are you crazy? I pity myself for having waited so long to tell you I love you. I'm jealous of all the time we've wasted! Do you think you could love me back?" Now he was talking too much, when before he couldn't find his voice.

That last sentence stopped her in her tracks, though. She pulled the swim cap from her head and her black, curly, lustrous hair fell about her shoulders. She turned around, dropped everything that she'd been clutching and slowly walked toward him. He held his breath and swore he wouldn't breathe again until she reached him.

When she got to him, he noticed tears in her eyes. "Is that really how you feel?"

He nodded and breathed again. "I swear it is. You don't know how hard it's been to be close to you and not touch you. But I wasn't sure how you would react. What if all you wanted from me was friendship? And I've already had one failed marriage. Maybe I'm not marriage material. I thought I had to protect you from all of that. I thought being your friend was what you needed most. But, still, I fell more in love with you every day."

She reached out and placed her right hand on his chest as she moved in closer. "Sebastian, you're a good man. You're a wonderful father. Just because your marriage failed doesn't mean you were a bad husband. You tried your best. Do I think I can love you? I've loved you for as long as I can remember, and I've been in love with you since I got back home from college. I cried the day you got married," she whispered, and that's all Sebastian needed to hear.

He gently wrapped his arms around her waist and pulled her firmly into his embrace. "I'm going to kiss you now, Marley, and it isn't going to be the kiss of a friend."

She smiled and he wiped that smile right off her face when he lowered his head and slowly kissed her the way he'd always wanted to: with passion strengthened by years of accumulated longing.

They were both breathless when they parted

a couple of minutes later. They gazed into each other's eyes in the moonlight.

"You were right," she said softly. "We've wasted a lot of time." She put her arms around his neck and kissed him. He could barely contain his happiness. Marley loved him. His Marley was in his arms, finally.

He reveled in the moment, breathing in her essence. He pulled back from the kiss.

He inhaled her unique scent, jasmine and spice, he thought. Sweet and sensual. He could live in that scent.

She slowly pushed away from him and regarded him with a smile.

Sebastian brought her hand up and kissed her fingers. "Hop in the truck and I'll drive you to the house."

It took a few minutes to wipe off as much sand from their feet as possible before climbing into the truck. Sebastian couldn't keep his eyes off her the whole time. How graceful she was, her body toned in just the right places. Her legs were beautiful. There were faint scars on her right leg. A couple of them were keloid, little bumpy ridges distinguishing themselves from the rest of her smooth skin. He knew she tried her best to hide those scars. But he loved them as much as he loved the rest of her.

She glanced up from her bent position as she wiped sand from her feet and smiled at him. "What are you looking at?"

"You," he said, grinning. "I'm taking my fill of you and not feeling guilty about it. There were so many times I had to stop myself from staring at you. Then I'd try and stop myself from feeling the way I did about you. Our mothers raised us to treat each other like brother and sister, after all."

"But then something changed over the years for them," Marley reminded him. "Because they, not so subtly, started hinting that we should be together. Just the other night when you were telling us about the Nishimuras, Eula Mae nudged me toward you."

Sebastian laughed. "Oh, yeah, I noticed."

They'd finished wiping themselves down and climbing into the truck's cab. After they'd buckled up, Sebastian started the engine. He glanced over at her. "You know we're not going to be able to mention we love each other to anyone. Not if we want to just enjoy the fact we're both on the same page for a while."

Marley sighed in resignation. "You're absolutely right. You can't imagine the people who've encouraged me to pursue you over the years—my mom, Eula Mae, Tandi, even Bonita Faye. We're never going to be able to simply enjoy each other if we tell anyone."

"On my side there was Miguel. He's always known I was in love with you. So, we're in agreement?" Sebastian asked.

"Yes," Marley said softly. "Now, meeting at the cove isn't our only secret."

WHEN MARLEY GOT home it was almost two in the morning. She parked the Corolla around back and was walking through her small garden when she saw Eula Mae's cat, Ellery, lying on the welcome mat at the door, sleeping. Usually, the sound of her car door closing would have roused the big Maine coon cat, but he must have been exhausted.

She stooped to rub his head a little to wake him up. He lazily opened his eyes and meowed softly, giving her a look she interpreted as questioning. She had a few questions herself.

"Ellery, what are you doing here? Eula Mae locked you out?"

Ellery was a spoiled house cat. He didn't enjoy the elements. Marley couldn't remember him ever sleeping outside before.

He liked a soft bed, a full food dish and his own cat-dominium, which he could climb on and pretend he was an intrepid lion. Or so Marley imagined.

Marley unlocked the back door and stepped across the threshold. Ellery followed her inside. She closed and locked the door, switching on the light in the kitchen almost simultaneously.

Ellery walked farther into the kitchen and stopped in front of the refrigerator. He pointedly looked up at the appliance, then back at Marley.

Marley sighed. "I know Eula Mae gives you water from the fridge, but this isn't Eula Mae's house. You'll drink tap water in my house. I'm not your human."

He yowled in protest and didn't budge from his position in front of the refrigerator.

Marley wanted to take a quick shower and go to bed. There were church services to attend at ten tomorrow morning, and she needed her rest.

"All right," she conceded to the stubborn

cat. "But tomorrow you've got to go back home."

She got a plastic bowl from the cabinet and held it underneath the water dispenser in the refrigerator door, allowing it to fill.

After placing the bowl on the floor, she watched Ellery thirstily lap up the water. He was a fastidious drinker, not wasting a drop.

"Mmm," Marley said as she retrieved her belongings from the kitchen table where she'd put them upon entering the kitchen.

"Good boy. Now, you should treat the rest of my house the same way. You can sleep in here for the night." She pointed to a rug in front of the back door. "That would be a cozy place." She turned and walked away. "I'm going to bed."

As if he'd understood her, Ellery went over to the rug, sniffed it, seemed to find it not too objectionable and settled down on top of it, his head resting on his front paws.

"Good night," Marley said, smiling in spite of herself. She and Ellery rarely interacted. He was her grandmother's cat and Marley hardly gave the feline a second thought. But now his unusual behavior had her wondering what was wrong.

Something else also occurred to her: "Sebastian and I are in love," she said out loud, laughing. "Don't tell anyone. Now, if only Chrissie's adoption would come through, I'd be deliriously happy."

Ellery just gave her an inscrutable look and closed his eyes. Human goings-on didn't interest him. Just supply his water, preferably chilled, when he was thirsty, thank you very much.

CHAPTER EIGHT

THE NEXT MORNING, she found Ellery where she'd left him, on the rug in front of the back door. He stretched languidly when she entered the kitchen.

She stretched herself and yawned, as she walked over to the back door. Ellery got up and watched her.

"Are you ready to go home?" she asked. "I don't have any cat food over here, so you won't get anything to eat. And Lord knows, if you need to do your business, you need to get to steppin', and fast!"

She opened the door and Ellery ran through it. She didn't even look to see in which direction he'd gone. It was time to get ready for church.

A few minutes later, though, as she was pouring herself a freshly brewed cup of coffee, she heard her grandmother calling from next door: "Ellery! Ellery!" Eula Mae had the kind of soprano that in its high registers could make you want to cover your ears. And this was one of those earsplitting instances.

Marley went outside and saw Eula Mae walking around in her garden wearing a bathrobe over her pajamas and a pair of fuzzy slippers. She noticed Marley and said, "Good morning. Have you seen Ellery?"

"Good morning," Marley replied, smiling as though she had a secret, which she did. She decided to divulge one of them. "He slept in my kitchen last night. He left here a few minutes ago. I assumed he'd gone back home."

Eula Mae sniffed derisively. "That cat thinks he rules me. But I'm not going to let him."

Now Marley's curiosity was piqued. "What's that supposed to mean? What happened?"

"Albert put in another appearance last night," Eula Mae said. "And after I'd gotten him out of the house, I tried to get Ellery to come back inside, but he ran away from me. I gave up after a time and went inside myself. When he didn't come meowing at the back door by my bedtime, I locked the door and went to sleep. I expected to find him out here this morning."

"Well, he was at my back door when I got home, so I let him inside, gave him some refrigerated water—you really spoil that cat— and let him sleep on a kitchen rug."

Eula Mae gave a frustrated humph and turned around to go back inside her house. "He'll come home when he gets hungry," she said with finality. "I'm getting ready for church."

Marley turned to go back inside also. "Okay, see you in a few minutes."

Marley drove them to church every Sunday. Eula Mae still drove her old Chevy Impala, but let herself be talked into allowing her family to squire her around town under special circumstances, such as making sure she got to church on Sunday.

About an hour later, Marley stood next to the Corolla wearing her glasses and dressed in a simple, off-white sleeveless dress that cinched her waist and modestly flared at the hips and whose hem fell to just below her knees. She wore two-inch-heeled black pumps with it, and a matching shoulder bag was slung over her left shoulder. Her hair was combed away from her face and the curls cascaded to the middle of her back.

When she saw Eula Mae coming out of her back door, though, she whistled. Her grandmother hadn't given up the tradition of wearing a hat to church. She was wearing a two-toned fitted skirt suit in deep purple and lavender. Matching purple pumps with a kitten heel, leather purse in the same shade and purple gloves completed her outfit. Her chapeau, because you couldn't call the work of art that was sitting on her head a hat, was made of intricately woven straw and colored a deep purple. The crown was almost shaped like a stovepipe hat, like the kind President Lincoln had been fond of wearing; however, it was smaller and there was a velvet band around it just above the brim. Eula Mae's long, silver natural hair had been braided and twisted into a sophisticated style that Marley envied but could never duplicate. She'd tried and failed.

"You look fabulous," she cried.

Eula Mae made a dismissive gesture with her right hand as she hurriedly walked to the car. "Just dressing for the Lord."

When they were in the car and buckled up, Marley asked, "No further sign of Ellery?" She was concerned for the cat. He might be her grandmother's pet, but she'd known him for five years and was used to having him around.

"No," Eula Mae answered, and Marley thought there was sadness in her brown eyes. "It's not like him to skip breakfast. He wakes me up to feed him."

A short drive later and they were pulling into the packed parking lot of Saint Domingo Catholic Church, the largest church in Port Domingo. Father Ortega had left a legacy behind when he'd founded the first house of worship in town over a hundred years ago. There were other denominations now, but Saint Domingo was the oldest church. People from all walks of life attended. Because of the mix of cultures, the church, in Marley's opinion, was very inclusive. Father Rodriguez performed mass and oversaw the partaking of the Eucharist, as all good Catholics observed. However, occasionally, while giving his sermon, she could have sworn his voice had the passion and cadence of a Baptist preacher. He was beloved by the parishioners.

She'd recently read an article somewhere that the numbers of Catholics attending church on a regular basis was dwindling.

However, Saint Domingo Catholic Church wasn't noticeably suffering from a lack of members. When she and Eula Mae walked in this morning, the pews were almost full.

Her mother stood up and waved them over to the middle of the church where the rest of the family was already sitting. Nevaeh had saved seats for her and Eula Mae. Her father was there, as well as Tandi and Torin. Her father always sat on the aisle as if because he was the head of the family, it was his duty to ensure the spiritual safety of his brood as well as its physical safety. Or so Marley liked to think.

The choir, which was composed of at least fifty men and women of all colors, rose and began to sing the entrance song. Every Sunday, Marley felt the absence of Aisha in the choir. Her beautiful soprano was usually heard above the rest of the singers. A tear rolled down Marley's cheek at the memory.

Beside her, Nevaeh nudged her arm and offered her a tissue.

"You okay?" she whispered.

"I'm fine," Marley said. She settled down, closed her eyes and just listened to the beautiful, lilting tones of the hymn. After the song ended, Father Rodriguez, a tall, trim, brown-skinned man in his fifties with wavy brown hair that had gray at the temples, walked up to the podium, greeted the parishioners and commenced Mass.

There was something soothing about the ceremony to Marley: the tone of Father Rodriguez's baritone, the lyrical, singsong rhythm of spoken Latin. It all made her feel closer to God. Which, she supposed, was the point of it all.

Minutes later, after the Holy Eucharist, the choir once again rose, but this time the song was an old spiritual, "Just As I Am." This was how services were conducted at Saint Domingo Catholic Church. While Catholic rituals were definitely observed, a nod was given to the traditions of other doctrines, as well. Those reared in Baptist churches or African Methodist Episcopal churches were treated to songs that brought back childhood memories. Marley was sure Eula Mae, who'd been brought up a Baptist in the Bahamas, but had married a Catholic, was now recalling her youth.

Seeing who was leading the song made Marley's heart beat faster in anticipation. It was Kaye Johnson, her old friend and café owner. Kaye's voice was a beautiful contralto. It was so beautiful, Marley often wondered why Kaye hadn't pursued music instead of the culinary arts. But, she supposed there were lots of people out there who were extremely gifted, but chose simple, sedate lives instead of the spotlight.

Kaye's voice was mesmerizing: "Just as I am, without one plea…"

Soon, many of the parishioners were singing along, standing and swaying to the music. Marley stood, too, and that was when she spotted Sebastian standing with Bastian in his arms several pews ahead of where her family was sitting.

Her happiness quotient rose just at the sight of him. His back was to her, so he probably hadn't noticed her yet.

The fact he was at church did her heart good. It wasn't that he didn't believe in God, but attending church wasn't something he did on a regular basis. He allowed Bastian to go to church with his mother and father every Sunday, though. What had induced him to attend church today?

Later, while she was standing on the massive lawn outside, communing with others in the congregation, she was surprised when Miguel Fuentes, wearing a blue suit and black loafers, strode up to her and touched her on the arm to get her attention.

She turned, smiling warmly. She hadn't had the chance to speak with him last night at the party and was glad to see him.

"Miguel, welcome home," she said.

The tips of his ears went red, a sure sign that he was embarrassed by her greeting.

"I'm going to start feeling as if I haven't been home in years if people keep saying that," he said in a low voice.

Marley screwed up her face, trying to recall the last time she'd seen him. "It's been at least three years since I saw you last."

He looked slightly pained. "You're right, as my mother won't let me forget."

Marley now regretted bringing up the subject. His mother was one of the sweetest women she knew, and the thought of her having to endure being without her eldest son for three years made her want to tear up.

So, she changed the subject. "How is work?"

Again, he gave her a pained expression. Was this also a touchy subject? She would have to ask Sebastian later if Miguel was doing all right.

Luckily, Kaye Johnson walked up to them and said hello. Kaye was wearing a sleeveless pale blue shift—that fit her perfectly—and strappy white sandals. Her look was modest, but very feminine and appealing. Marley could tell by Miguel's appreciative smile that he liked Kaye's choice in clothing, to say nothing of the lovely restaurant owner herself.

As for her, Marley was so happy to be rescued by Kaye that she gave her a hug. "Kaye, your song was beautiful, just beautiful!"

Kaye beamed as she hugged her back. Her reddish-brown skin was flawless, and her abundant black braids with auburn highlights glistened in the afternoon sunshine. She fairly glowed with good health and natural beauty.

"Thanks, girl, I appreciate that, coming from you," Kaye said lightly after Marley let her go. She gave both of them the benefit of her sunny smile.

Marley glanced at Miguel. His eyes were riveted on Kaye. Kaye now regarded him, the smile never leaving her face. "Hello, Dr. Fuentes. I won't say welcome home because,

I confess, I overheard you mentioning to Marley that you were tired of hearing that."

Miguel blushed. "I'm such a grumbler, my mother would say. I should be grateful people missed me."

"Exactly," Kaye said positively. "It would be awful if we simply looked you up and down and said, 'Oh, you're back in town? I didn't even notice you were gone.'"

"Yeah, I prefer the welcome home greeting," Miguel admitted with a laugh. "How are you, Kaye? I heard the café is the spot to eat at in town." Then he must have recalled that Marley's family also ran a restaurant, and hurriedly added, "And your family's restaurant, of course, Marley."

The two women laughed good-naturedly. "There's room for both," Marley said, and she and Kaye gave each other high fives.

"You ought to come by before you head back to Chicago," Kaye invited Miguel. "We're closed today, but we're open from nine a.m. till nine p.m. Monday through Saturday. I'll make you something special."

With that, she looked up as if spying someone across the lawn gesturing to her. Marley followed her line of sight and saw Kaye's mother beckoning her. "Gotta run," said Kaye. She gave Miguel a hasty hug. "Don't be a stranger," she said to him before hurrying off.

When she was gone, it dawned on Marley that Miguel and Kaye had a past. They'd dated in high school. The manner in which Miguel was watching Kaye's retreating back told her that perhaps he still had feelings for the talented singer and chef.

He watched Kaye for so long that Marley had to clear her throat to get his attention. "Hmm, so how long will you be in town?"

Miguel had to focus once he'd turned his gaze back on her. "I'm not really sure. I took a month off from work to clear my head. My doctor says I've been working too hard."

"The festival's coming up in early June. That should be a lot of fun. Do you think you'll still be around for that?"

The annual Seafood/Music Festival was held the first week of June. Marley was on the planning committee. "This year is going to be the best yet. We've got some talented musicians coming. And the competition for best seafood is fierce. Chefs from all over the world will be competing."

"Sounds good," Miguel said, actually appearing interested and not glassy eyed as some men looked when she started talking about the festival. It was the biggest event held in Port Domingo each year. Some of the proceeds went to keeping the day care running smoothly at Saint Domingo Catholic Church. Its members were big supporters of the festival.

"What I wanted to talk to you about was your leg," Miguel finally got around to saying. "How is it doing? Still experiencing pain now and then? Is the pain less or more than the last time we talked?"

For years Miguel had been trying to persuade Marley to come to Chicago so he could run some tests and see if there was anything he could do about her leg. But she had inevitably declined his offer. She'd already had two operations and the second one hadn't done anything to improve upon the first, in her opinion. She was thirty-two. What could Miguel possibly do to end her chronic pain?

"It's about the same," she said of her pain level. "If I thought I could get noticeable results I might take you up on your offer, Miguel. But I'm living with the pain. It's not constant and when I do have it, I know what to do to relieve it."

He shook his head, seeming to understand her viewpoint. But the determined gleam in his eye to do something to help her was still there.

"You're a doctor," she said softly. "I understand it's your duty to alleviate pain. Especially in someone you know. But I'm okay."

He smiled at her. "If you say so." Then, with a mischievous grin, he said, "How are you and my boy Sebastian getting along? Has either one of you been brave enough yet to actually admit you care for the other one?"

Marley put on her best deadpan expression. "Of course we care for each other. Our families have been friends for years. We grew up together. You know that."

Miguel turned away. "Aw, forget it. You two deserve to never be happy. You're both stubborn and blind as bats when it comes to affairs of the heart."

"Wait," Marley called sweetly. "I was just going to invite you to our wedding."

In parting, Miguel waved her off. "Keep your invitation. Don't talk to me until there is something serious going on between you two nuts."

After Miguel departed, Marley spun slowly around, trying to spot Sebastian somewhere among the throng gathered on the lawn.

He must have been searching for her, too, because before she could turn back around, someone grabbed her from behind and gave her a quick, perfunctory hug. A hug entirely respectable enough to be witnessed by the churchgoing crowd.

She knew from the feel of his muscular arms around her that it was him. When she turned around, a glance into his laughing brown eyes made her melt inside.

"What are you doing here?" she asked playfully.

"Well, I thought it was appropriate to come to church and thank God for answering my prayers," he said as he leaned down close to her right ear. "And, in case you didn't know, that would be for us to be together."

Now she was blushing worse than Miguel had been under Kaye's scrutiny. It didn't have a chance to ripen into utter speechlessness and a lack of feeling worthy of such lofty words because her mother and Eula Mae walked up. They started hugging Sebastian and marveling at the fact that he was on church grounds.

"See?" Eula Mae chastised him. "Lightning didn't strike you dead when you came through the door. So, I expect you here again next Sunday." She was tilting her head back so far to look up at him from her little-over-five-foot disadvantage that Marley worried her chapeau would fall off her head. But it held on tight.

Sebastian only laughed more and squeezed Eula Mae tightly. Marley knew he wasn't going to make any promises because, with him, if he said he was going to do something, he did it.

Her mother took her turn hugging Sebastian, too. "Good to see you," Nevaeh said softly. She was the sentimental one and she let her warmth and love speak for her. No recriminations. Just acceptance.

Then they were joined by the rest of their families. Since they were all together, the women started talking about the midday meal, and before Marley knew it, Nevaeh and Isabella had pooled their resources, meaning the meals they'd prepared before coming to church, and they decided it would be a splendid idea if Nevaeh brought over that baked ham and the sweet potato pies she'd cooked and Isabella would provide the arroz con pollo and various fresh vegetables. The men would take care of the wine and soft drinks.

Marley noticed the resigned look that passed between her father, Aloysius, and Uncle Emiliano. They would probably prefer to sit home in comfortable sweats and watch soccer on TV for the rest of their Sunday afternoon. But what their wives said was law, and they might as well go with the flow. She didn't doubt for a minute that they would be able to sneak in some soccer watching wherever they ended up today anyway.

CHAPTER NINE

SEBASTIAN SAT AT the dinner table at his parents' home with only Bastian separating him from Marley. When they'd promised to keep their love a secret, he hadn't realized just how hard a task that would be.

He was enjoying watching her interact with Bastian who, understandably, considered her a surrogate mother. Her face had been the one he'd seen since he was two months old, cooing, smiling, singing nursery rhymes, providing comfort and love. Now, Bastian was so attached to her, Sebastian sometimes wondered if the five-year-old loved her more than him.

He smiled now, as Bastian crooked a finger at Marley as if he had something to whisper in her ear. When she bent down, his son planted a kiss on her cheek, and left a smudge of sweet potato pie behind.

Marley laughed, eyes sparkling. She kissed

him back, then gingerly touched the place where Bastian had left his kiss. She glanced at Sebastian, her golden brown eyes filled with happiness. He leaned over Bastian, who had contentedly returned his attention to his piece of pie, and wiped the sweet potato pie bits off her face with his cloth napkin.

"He made that kiss extra sweet," he joked.

Marley merely smiled at him. She was more reserved than usual today. She was probably as nervous as he was around family. No doubt about it, finding a bit of privacy to celebrate their newfound relationship was going to be difficult. Everyone was there today except for Augustin, whose location he had no clue about. He'd not been at church. Sebastian suspected he was camped out at one of his many female friends' homes.

"Does anyone want any more dessert?" his mother, Isabella, who was the hostess since they were gathered at the Contreras home, asked. She rose, a half-full pie plate in her right hand.

No was the answer all around.

"Then, I'll clear the table," she said briskly. His mother couldn't abide a messy table, or messy anything, really. He believed she had a touch of OCD, she was so disturbed by a less-than-organized room.

"I'll help," Auntie Nevaeh said, rising, too.

"That doesn't seem fair," Marley said, smiling first at his mother, then her own. "I'll do the cleaning up. You two prepared a delicious meal. Go play cards with Eula Mae, or something."

Sebastian grinned at her recommendation. His mother and Auntie Nevaeh and Eula Mae were prodigious bid whist players. Cutthroat. He'd never been able to win a game against them.

He got to his feet, too. "I'll help Marley, if someone will volunteer to keep an eye on Bastian. I have a feeling he's going to be pretty energetic for a while from all the sugar he's eaten. Then he'll find a spot to curl up in and take a nap."

"We'll take him into the den with us," Grandpa Emiliano volunteered, speaking for himself, Uncle Aloysius and Torin.

"That's settled," Marley said, reaching for the pie plate in his mother's hand.

To Sebastian's disappointment, Tandi offered to help clear the table and wash the dishes, as well. However, Marley was quick to say, "Nah, we've got this, sis. Relax. You work in a kitchen five days a week."

Tandi flashed a smile. "Okay." She left the table with the other ladies, who were already headed to the sunroom where his mother kept the family games.

Sebastian eagerly began collecting plates, glasses and utensils, humming as he did so. With luck, he and Marley would have a good hour alone cleaning up this mess and washing dishes.

After everyone else had gone their separate ways, Marley seemed more relaxed. She and Eula Mae had gone home and changed clothes after church services, so now she was casually dressed in jeans, white athletic shoes and a royal blue T-shirt with Zeta Phi Beta on the front. She'd pledged that sorority while at college.

He was free to admire the way she moved as he followed her into the kitchen with his arms full. Once they were alone in the spacious kitchen and Marley was filling the sink with hot water and putting dish detergent in it, he complimented her ingenuity. "That was smooth," he said.

She playfully bumped his hip with hers as

they stood side by side at the white porcelain farmhouse sink. "Never underestimate the powers of a love-starved woman."

"Love-starved?" he queried.

"I haven't been kissed by you in over twelve hours."

He turned and pulled her into his arms. "If you don't mind my tasting like sweet potato pie, I can remedy that right now."

"I'm pretty sure I'm going to taste the same," Marley said, peering into his eyes, her full-lipped mouth looking tastier than dessert.

Once their mouths met, he forgot all about where they were, and what they were doing. Now, with Marley's backside against the farmhouse sink, the kiss deepened.

Finally they came up for air, and Marley had an alarmed expression in her eyes as she stared at him. When she got her breath, she said, "That won't do. We're going to be found out in no time if we lose ourselves when we touch."

Sebastian sighed. It was true. Anyone could have walked in on them while they'd been kissing and they would not have heard them.

He smiled at her. "Sorry, but I've been waiting a long time to kiss you."

She laughed softly. "Tell me about it!"

After that, they made short work of cleaning the kitchen thoroughly. Their pent-up passion compelled them to work hard and once they were finished, his mother's normally spotless kitchen was once again pristine.

He was placing the dish towels on the handle of the double oven, just the way he'd seen his mother do on numerous occasions, when the swinging door entrance to the kitchen opened and Eula Mae strode in. She surveyed the room. "Good job, children. It's a shame that all you were doing in here this whole time was cleaning up, though. Couldn't you young people find anything more interesting to do when you're alone?" She turned back around and headed out. "Young people today. I don't know what's wrong with them!"

Marley and Sebastian burst out laughing. "Hint number one million and one," Marley said, shaking her head at her grandmother's antics.

ON MONDAY MORNING, Marley let Ellery out of the back door. He'd come meowing at her door last night, and she'd made sure his thirst was quenched and he had a safe place to lay his head.

She wondered where he went when he left her house, because when she'd left her house to walk to school, she'd encountered Eula Mae in her garden, not happy and obviously trying to pretend she wasn't looking for the recalcitrant cat. Marley had called good-morning to her. Eula Mae had responded and wished her a good day. That was all. Her stubborn grandmother went back into her house and closed the door. *This is getting weird*, Marley thought.

However, Marley relished the clear, blue day as she walked. She refused to let her grandmother's sour mood spoil her own.

Her right leg felt great. She made the walk in record time, pausing only to chat a moment or two with Akira and Daichi. They were enjoying an early breakfast on the huge porch of Mason's Bed and Breakfast. She knew Julie Mason, the proprietor's daughter and the person who truly ran the bed-and-breakfast, prided herself on providing a first-rate breakfast. She even baked part of the breakfast menu herself. Marley's favorites were her English scones, cinnamon rolls and blueberry muffins.

Akira's smile was broad. "Good morning, Marley. How was your weekend?"

"It was wonderful," she answered. *Truly awesome*, she thought, remembering her time with Sebastian, but she didn't share that with him. "How was yours?"

"It was quiet, but I like it that way," Akira said, glancing in his grandfather's direction.

Daichi made a comical face at Marley. "He likes it quiet because he thinks it's the best thing for his old grandfather. Me? I have a different opinion."

"How are you, Mr. Nishimura?" Marley asked Daichi.

"I am enjoying myself in your lovely hometown," Daichi replied, smiling warmly at her.

"I'm glad to hear it," she called back. "Let me know if there's anything I can do to make it even more enjoyable. Well, I'd better run. Have a good day!"

"You, too," Akira called, waving.

She saw him lean toward his grandfather and say something. Daichi laughed.

Their relationship reminded Marley of hers and Eula Mae's. The grandchild and grand-parent roles were reversed. Akira was treating his grandfather somewhat like a child because he wanted to guard his health and keep Daichi with him as long as possible. Of course, Daichi would rebel against it. Just like Eula Mae had to claim her independence from time to time. Marley understood the desire to hang on to self-rule. In her and Akira's defense, they were simply doing the best they could, and their actions were done out of love for their grandparents.

As she walked, she wondered at how life could often be complicated. For example, she liked Daichi and Akira, but she didn't want Sebastian to sell them the fishery. The fishery was a family business that was integral to Port Domingo. She felt a sense of pride knowing how hard the Contreras family had worked to turn it into the biggest employer in town.

As she walked onto the school grounds, she noticed the staff parking lot was filling up. She spotted Bonita Faye getting out of her Prius.

Bonita Faye looked up after shutting the car's door and smiled at her. "Good morning. How was your weekend?"

Marley's belly did a guilty flip-flop because she would've liked nothing more than to tell Bonita Faye all about her and Sebastian's moment of satori. She loved that word. In Buddhism it meant "sudden enlightenment." To her, it perfectly described what they'd experienced early Saturday morning. She was still ecstatic.

But even though she was blathering on in her head, she needed to appear sane to Bonita Faye, so she said, "Good morning. Oh, you know—same old, same old. And you?"

Bonita Faye's eyes lit up and she swiftly covered the space between them. She was around five inches shorter than Marley, but was quick on her feet. "Akira phoned Sunday night and we talked for two hours. This, after we'd already lunched together earlier that day. He let me talk for more than an hour about losing Cory and he was such a good listener. Men like that are rare."

Marley was smiling knowingly as they climbed the steps leading to the big double doors of the school. "Has he changed your mind about him? That, perhaps, he's not a momma's boy who's waiting for his mother to choose him a bride? Or some such thing you mentioned Saturday night when you told me not to get my hopes up about you two?"

Bonita Faye laughed shortly. "Yes, and no. Yes, I'm beginning to think he might be his own man. And, no, you shouldn't get your hopes up. I'm a long way from letting my guard down. No matter how disarming Akira Nishimura might be."

"So, you think he's disarming."

"He's very charming," Bonita Faye admitted. They were walking down the hall now, the sound of their footsteps echoing off the hardwood floor. The air was redolent with glue, old books and industrial-strength disinfectant. Smells of a school, as far as Marley was concerned, and she loved them.

The two women arrived at Marley's classroom first. Bonita Faye stopped a moment, stood erect in a stance she utilized when she had something important to impart and expected to be listened to. Marley recognized the signs and postponed unlocking her classroom door to pay attention.

Bonita Faye cleared her throat and looked Marley in the eyes.

"Listen, girlfriend, you're probably not going to do anything about this… You haven't heeded my advice in all the years I've known you when it comes to Sebastian. But he couldn't keep his eyes off you Saturday night. I've had the whole weekend to decide whether to open my mouth or if I was just imagining his interest in you. But I'm sure I'm right about this. He was watching you, and I was watching him. It was very entertaining. When you were dancing with the blond cowboy, he wanted to snatch you out of the guy's arms. That's how intently he was watching the two of you."

Bonita Faye expelled a longing-filled sigh as she continued. "Boy, the way he was staring at you reminded me of the way Cory used to look at me. I married him because of those looks."

Marley couldn't have been happier to hear Sebastian had been observing her Saturday night. So, the whole night had been a prelude to what happened between them at the cove later on.

She smiled at Bonita Faye now. And surprised her friend by not pooh-poohing her theory about Sebastian's interest in her.

"Sebastian is interested in me, huh? That's a lot to digest on a Monday morning."

Bonita Faye appeared hopeful. "Does that mean you like him, too?"

Marley laughed. "We're starting to sound no better than prepubescent school kids, but, yeah, I like him, too. But…"

"I know," Bonita Faye interrupted her, "Don't get my hopes up."

Marley nodded. "Exactly."

Bonita Faye spun around, heading farther down the hall to her classroom. "I'll get my hopes up if I want to," she said defiantly.

Marley laughed at her friend's display of irritation with her. "Ditto about you and Akira."

They didn't part without sharing a quick smile, though. Acrimony simply had no place in their friendship.

Marley unlocked the door of her classroom and switched on the lights. The room was one huge space with hardwood floors and, instead of individual desks as the classrooms for older students had, there were workstations in her classroom. Round white tables with four plastic chairs with steel frames. There were six workstations, and the chairs at them were six bright colors: red, yellow, blue, green, purple and orange.

To the right as you walked into the room

was a door leading to her private office. She went in there and stowed her shoulder bag in the bottom drawer.

Coming back out into the main room, she surveyed her kingdom.

Everything was as she'd left it on Friday afternoon. The walls were decorated with both posters and cardboard cutouts of fantasy creatures and real-life people her students admired or simply got a kick out of, such as SpongeBob SquarePants, Dora the Explorer and Tiana from *The Princess and the Frog*. She also thought it was important for her students to recognize important personages from history and the present day. There were several past US presidents, Nelson Mandela, remarkable women like Harriet Tubman and Supreme Court Justices Ruth Bader Ginsburg and Sonia Sotomayor. A corner of the room was devoted to music and storytelling. She kept her first acoustic guitar in it and often sang for her students.

She was changing the quote of the day on the blackboard when her first student arrived.

Bradley Anderson's parents dropped him off at seven every morning because they had to be at work by seven thirty. But this morning he walked in with his head down, dragging his feet and looking generally dejected. He was usually a cheerful child. In fact, he was sometimes so loud Marley had to remind him to use his inside voice in class.

Even his usually enthusiastic, "Good morning, Miss Syminette!" was missing.

She put the chalk down and walked over to him. He was busy putting his backpack in his bin in the corner of the room where the students stashed their belongings. There was also a long wooden bench in that area where students could sit.

He slumped onto the bench after putting his things away. Marley joined him on the bench and smiled at him. "Hi, Bradley. How are you doing today?"

He looked at her, but he didn't say anything.

Blond-haired and blue-eyed, Bradley was wearing a long-sleeved plaid shirt and jeans. He sat with his legs swinging, staring at his white athletic shoes with Velcro fastenings. Marley wondered if his father was also partial to plaid shirts. Bradley had one for every day of the week. Bradley was adorable in them.

"Miss Syminette, my daddy's gone," he finally said, his voice forlorn.

Marley's heart seemed to plummet to her stomach. His father had died? She tried her best not to appear as stricken as she felt, though, as she pulled the little boy into her arms.

"Oh, baby, I'm so sorry," she said.

Bradley began to cry quietly. "I wanted to stay home to look for him, but Mommy said I had to come to school. She said maybe he'll be back when I get home."

Marley didn't know what to think. If his father had died, why would his mother say he might turn up again after school? That didn't make sense.

It occurred to Marley that the school should have been notified if there had been a death in Bradley's family. The school would have then informed her about the turn of events.

Something else had to be going on. She slowly released Bradley and got to her feet. "Bradley," she said in her instructor's voice that her students understood to heed. "You stay right here until I get back. I've got to speak to someone for a moment."

Bradley nodded his head, tears glistening

in his eyes but at least he'd gotten the flow under control. "Yes, ma'am," he said.

She went into her inner office, closed the door and dialed the school's secretary. Patrice Clemons knew everything that was going on at Port Domingo Elementary.

Patrice answered immediately, her twangy Southern accented voice a delight to hear on any occasion. The feisty redhead was sunshine personified.

"Hello, Patty here," she said. "What can I do for you?"

"Patty, Marley. Is something going on with Bradley's family?" She didn't have to give Patrice Bradley's last name. Patrice knew all of her students and their families. She'd been at Port Domingo Elementary since 1988. Nothing got past her.

Marley heard Patrice blow air through her lips in an exasperated manner. "Yes, child, something definitely happened on Saturday night. That poor baby's daddy got himself arrested for drunk and disorderly conduct—for the second time this year. Bradley's momma is fed up with him and I hear she's planning to divorce him after this. I'm sure Bradley's hurt and confused. You're gonna have to give him some extra love today."

Having gotten an explanation for Bradley's behavior, Marley sighed with relief. No death, but possibly a divorce in Bradley's family. To say nothing of the effects Bradley's father's drinking could have on him. Her heart went out to the little guy. "Thanks, Patty. You have a good day."

"You, too, sweetie," Patrice said, and hung up.

When Marley got back out from her inner office to the classroom, Chrissie had arrived and was sitting beside Bradley holding his hand. Chrissie glanced up when Marley approached. "Good morning, Miss Syminette," she said and gave Marley a smile.

"Good morning, Chrissie," Marley said, smiling cautiously as she tried to formulate what her next move should be. Chrissie was such a loving child. She was also sensitive to her classmates' moods. Twice Marley had observed Chrissie calmly breaking up spats between two other children. It appeared that she had done for Bradley what Marley was incapable of doing: shown him that there was someone his own size who understood his predicament and was willing to show sympathy. Chrissie had Bradley grinning again.

Marley went to Bradley and knelt down in front of him. "Bradley, I just spoke to someone who told me your daddy is fine. You don't need to worry about anything. I'm sure he'd want you to enjoy your day at school. Okay?"

Bradley smiled at her. "Really?"

Marley nodded. "Yes, really."

He spontaneously threw his arms around her neck. "Thank you, Miss Syminette."

"You're welcome." Marley straightened up and put on her teacher's mantle. She made her voice more authoritarian. "Now, you and Chrissie need to go get your breakfast before class starts in half an hour." Because the two of them got to school extra early, they had breakfast at school.

Chrissie rose, still clutching his hand, and the two left the classroom. She didn't worry about Chrissie and Bradley finding the cafeteria or coming back on time. There were hall monitors who watched the children like hawks. They made sure everything ran smoothly.

Marley watched the kids go, then went back to the blackboard and made a second attempt to write the day's quote on it. She sighed. It was getting close to the end of the school term and she was going to miss Bradley tremendously. She hoped to be Chrissie's mother soon, so she didn't think of losing her. She would miss all of her other students, though, and at their graduation ceremony she would shed tears at the loss of her class while at the same time she would be anticipating meeting her new students at the beginning of the new school year. It was a cycle filled with emotions, much like life.

CHAPTER TEN

TWO WEEKS LATER, June arrived with warmer temperatures and afternoon showers. Sebastian sat in his office at the fishery on a rainy day going over the latest offer for the business from the Nishimuras. He had hoped that their interest in the fishery would have waned by now. However, their offer had increased by several million dollars.

Initially, he told himself he would never consider selling the family business. It was an institution here in Port Domingo. His father's father, Pedro, had founded the company with only one fishing boat over seventy years ago. Sebastian felt it would be sacrilege to part with the business.

But now, with Marley in his life, he had so much more to consider. Their families could do a lot of good with the money. Bastian could go to any college he wanted. None of the elderly members of their combined families would ever have to worry about medical bills or going to live at a health care facility away from their loved ones. He knew Eula Mae dreaded that prospect and had only welcomed her granddaughter purchasing the house next door to her own—somehow infringing on her privacy—because Marley had promised she would worry less about her and the possibility of her grandmother going to a care facility in the future would be lessened. And now that he and Marley had an understanding, he saw them as a family—Marley, Bastian and himself. More money in the bank would ensure he'd have plenty of time for them.

But, on the other hand, he loved running the fishery. He was proud of what his family had built. It would be extremely hard to give that up. Plus, he was sure Marley was on his parents' side and didn't want him to sell the business. She probably thought their little town would collapse without it.

He contemplated all of these things as he perused the file on his computer that Akira had emailed this morning.

Selling was sounding better and better. However, something in the back of his mind was niggling him. When he'd told Miguel, who was still in Port Domingo on his hiatus from work, about the offer from the Nishimuras, Miguel had excitedly encouraged him to take the offer. It would be a boon not only for the Contreras family but the entire town. What fascinated Miguel even more than practicing medicine was money. He'd recognized Daichi Nishimura's name the instant it had left Sebastian's mouth.

"Do it," he exclaimed. "That man is a financial genius. Everything he touches turns to gold. If he sees potential in Port Domingo and your fishery, you'd better believe something wonderful is going to come of it. What are you waiting for? Go for it!"

Sebastian thought back to that day. His friend had come to him tired and depressed. He'd been in Chicago living the life. A sought-after surgeon. Making money hand over fist. More women, to hear him tell it, than he knew what to do with. And for Miguel, that was saying a lot because he considered himself a ladies' man. Yet, none of that had made him happy.

Sebastian was sure he and Marley were going to be happy no matter what. They didn't need millions of dollars and a mansion and expensive cars, clothes, jewelry. Marley was happiest around family and helping her students to learn and grow as human beings. She loved the simple things like family get-togethers, long walks, swimming in the cove, old movies and good books, church on Sunday and the occasional trip to far-off places you can reminisce about when you get home again. Things he loved, too.

More money would not make them any happier. He felt that in his bones. Therefore, he was in no rush to respond to the Nishimuras' latest offer.

As for Akira and Daichi, they didn't seem to be in any hurry to leave Port Domingo. He'd heard through Marley that Daichi's energy level was still good. She said he and Eula Mae were becoming the best of friends. His remission had lasted longer than he'd dreamed it would. From what Sebastian had heard about Daichi's form of cancer—pancreatic—it was usually extremely aggressive and had quite a low survival rate. But he hoped those statistics were improving. He felt sorry for both Daichi and Akira. Daichi no doubt considered he was living on borrowed time, and Akira was praying for more days

with his grandfather, whom he absolutely
adored. Sebastian could tell that much just
by the way Akira looked at his grandfather.
Sebastian's sympathy for them was the only
thing preventing him from turning their offer
down outright. He wanted Daichi's last days
to be pleasant ones.

The buzzer of his office phone interrupted
his train of thought. His administrative assistant, Mrs. Claire Stewart, a woman who'd
been with the company for over thirty years,
was on the line.

"Yes, Mrs. Stewart?" She was his senior.
Therefore he found it uncomfortable to call
her Claire.

"Mr. Contreras, your ex-wife is here to see
you."

Those words caught him so off guard, for
a moment he couldn't respond. Darla? Here?
Why on earth would she come to see him?

She hadn't bothered to get in touch with
him since she'd left.

No phone calls to inquire about Bastian's
health, his progress, nothing! Now all of a
sudden she just showed up?

He mentally ran through every reason that
she might be back in town that didn't concern

him and Bastian. Was she one of the musical acts performing at the upcoming Seafood/Music Festival? Nah, Marley would have told him if that were the case. Had there been a death in her family he hadn't heard about? Unlikely. News of anyone's death in Port Domingo traveled fast.

He realized he'd kept Mrs. Stewart on the line while he'd had a mini-meltdown, and apologized. "I'm sorry, Mrs. Stewart. All right, please show her in."

A minute later, Mrs. Stewart was opening his office door, the expression on her face strained. No wonder. The whole town knew under what circumstances he and Darla had parted.

"Miss Cramer, here is Mr. Contreras," Mrs. Stewart hastily said. She stood aside for Darla to enter and made her escape as quickly as possible.

Sebastian had risen when the door opened and now was standing behind his desk. His office was comfortably and efficiently decorated. Hardwood floor, large desk with his computer atop it and behind him a credenza on which were a copier/fax machine and below, drawers in which he kept some business files. A large leather couch sat near the window. It was rarely used for anything except an occasional nap. The picture window looked out over the docks. Another door led to a half bath.

When he was done wondering what kind of an impression he was making on his long-absent ex-wife, he turned his attention to appraising her.

Darla hadn't physically changed a bit. Five foot five and very shapely with "curves for days," as she used to like to joke when they were together. Her face was expertly made up. Skin the color of caramel. Eyes dark brown, and almond shaped. Lips juicy and inviting. She knew she was beautiful and had enjoyed reminding him of that fact. It appeared that she hadn't gained an ounce of added weight. She'd always seemed impervious to anything that might mar her beauty. It was her biggest asset, after all. But, to be fair, maybe her priorities had changed.

They stood there like two gunslingers about to have a shootout. Both wary and cautious and plenty nervous. He certainly felt awkward, and, for the life of him, he couldn't come up with what to say.

After a long moment, though, he gave up and just accepted that life sometimes threw you curves and you just had to roll with them or just go right through them.

"Hello, Darla," he finally said, his tone emotionless.

She seemed relieved he'd spoken to her and began swiftly walking toward him as though she wanted to embrace him. But he held up his right hand, stopping her in her tracks. Was that hurt and disappointment in her wide eyes that he didn't want her touching him?

He cleared his throat and gestured to the leather office chair in front of his desk. "Have a seat," he suggested quietly.

She sat on the chair. The hem of the short skirt she was wearing rose as she got comfortable. She crossed her legs and placed her shoulder bag in her lap. Her black hair was long, falling almost to her waist. Some of it fell across her face as she sat down, and she tossed her head back to get it out of her face.

She smiled tentatively. "I know this is a surprise."

"That's an understatement," he said as he sat down behind his desk and leaned forward. "I haven't seen or heard from you, except through your lawyer, since you left. To what do I owe the honor of your presence now?"

"I came to your office because I figured you wouldn't want me coming to the house in case Bastian was there. I'd be hard to explain."

"If you said that because you believe Bastian isn't aware you're his mother, you'd be wrong. Bastian knows who you are. I've shown him photos over the years. Your family is also part of his life. I assumed Miss Evie would have kept you informed."

"Oh, she's told me a lot," was Darla's reply. "I just didn't know how much to believe. Momma has been trying to get me to come back home for years. But I doubted I'd be welcomed."

"What difference does it make whether you would be welcomed or not? Bastian is your son. I would think you'd be curious as to how he's doing. How he's growing up in your absence. Whether he misses a mother figure. Which he may. He has a mind of his own. To me, it appears he has lots of mother figures in his life. But, who knows, maybe he misses you. Did you ever wonder about that?"

He realized that the shock was wearing off

and he was finally getting the chance to say things he'd wanted to say to her for years. He took a deep breath. He didn't want to just let them spill out. He wanted to think about what he needed to say, for Bastian, and for himself.

So he waited while she gazed at him with sorrowful eyes. He wasn't buying it. It was going to take a lot more than a sad face for him to ever trust her again. Or to be able to let down his guard around her.

Tears rolled from the corners of her eyes. He steeled himself. He hated to see a woman cry. It just did something to him. He was raised a gentleman, and not offering comfort to a crying woman was wrong to him. Like not stepping in when someone needed rescuing. He instinctively wanted to save people. His grandfather and his father were volunteer firemen in Port Domingo before his and Augustin's births. Now, he and his brother served. He didn't move in this case, though.

Darla got a tissue out of her shoulder bag and wiped her face. Then she took a deep breath and began speaking. "I know I've stayed away too long. But some people are thickheaded, and it took me a while to realize how much I've missed not seeing Bastian all this time. I went through some tough years after I left. J.J. and I didn't last long."

Sebastian would never forget the musician she'd left him for. J.J. Starr. What kind of name was that? A stage name, more than likely. J.J. had been the lead guitar player in a now defunct rock band Darla had apparently lost her mind over when she'd watched them perform at Port Domingo's annual seafood and music festival five years ago. Sebastian had no idea how unhappy she'd been in their marriage, how terrified she was about taking the responsibility for a new life: their son, Bastian, who'd only been two months old then.

Sebastian had been a first-time father, too, and yes, he'd been afraid of making mistakes, but he'd also been thrilled to have Bastian. Darla and Bastian were his world and he'd been determined to be a good husband and father. Yet, he must have slipped up somehow because Darla had been desperate for a way out. J.J. Starr had offered her that escape from her responsibilities and she'd taken it. A hastily written letter to him was all she'd left behind.

He still remembered every word of it:

Sorry, Sebastian, but I'm not cut out to be a wife or a mother. I thought I could fake it, but I'm not that good of an actress. I hope you'll one day realize you're better off without me. You and Bastian.

He wasn't going to lie: she'd broken him. He blamed himself for her abandoning him and Bastian. Maybe he'd been working too hard and not paying enough attention to her. Maybe he wasn't as demonstrative as she'd wanted him to be. He'd naively believed that you went into a marriage without hiding who you really were. You showed the real you to your partner. But after Darla left him, the fact that he never really knew her hit him hard.

How could he have worn his heart on his sleeve like that, and let her trample all over it? He'd felt like a fool. Over the years, though, he'd matured and came to understand that Darla's choices shouldn't affect his happiness or Bastian's. He'd stopped hating the mention of Darla's name. He'd chalked up her behavior to just another instance of just how fallible all humans were. He had Marley to thank for that. She'd shown him what unconditional love was. That, no matter what, you stood by the people you loved. During bad times, especially. She'd never given up on him. And she'd loved Bastian like he was her own.

"I haven't been with him in over three years," Darla was saying. He was sure he'd missed some of what she was telling him while he'd been thinking about the past.

"I've done some backup singing. I toured with his band for a while, but I was mostly doing the job of a roadie, and that's glorifying my role. I was desperate to sing, Sebastian. You knew that. I always loved to sing. Unfortunately, so do quite a few other people. People who have real talent. I stopped singing after J.J. and I broke up. He left me flat broke. I worked at fast-food restaurants until it dawned on me that I could be doing something else with my life. So, I went back to school. I was in Portland, Oregon, by then. The state has a good unemployment program where they'll pay for your training if you display a real desire to work hard and better yourself. I became a licensed practical nurse. That was a year ago. I'm doing all right for myself. Really standing on my own two feet."

"Good for you," Sebastian said, and meant it. He didn't want to think of Bastian's mother suffering.

Darla smiled. "Now, to the reason why I'm here."

Sebastian held his breath. *Please don't let her want joint custody of Bastian*, he thought. That's the only reason he could come up with that explained her sudden appearance.

"I want to get to know Bastian. I'm not proud of what I did. And over the years I figured I wasn't worthy of seeing him, being a part of his life. But now, I'm convinced I can bring something positive to the table." Her eyes were pleading with him as she spoke. "Please, Sebastian, let me see him."

Sebastian had suspected that's what she wanted, yet he still hadn't been prepared for the visceral reaction he would have when the actual words left her mouth. At that moment, he quite easily could have done something he regretted.

Instead, his tone deadly serious and louder than he intended but it was as controlled as he could be at that point, he said, "There is no way in hell you're going near my son. I have full custody of him. A right you eagerly gave me when you wanted your freedom. You *got* your freedom. It doesn't concern me that now you're feeling confident about yourself and you think you can be a fit mother for Bastian." As he was speaking, he was slowly rising.

He saw a glimmer of fear in Darla's eyes, which stopped him cold. He took a deep breath and slowly released it.

She rose, too, clutching her shoulder bag to her chest as if that would serve as some kind of barrier between them. Some safeguard against assault, not that he'd ever hurt her. True, he was as angry as he'd ever been in his life, but he'd never put his hand on a woman in anger in his entire life and he wasn't going to start now.

"Get out," he ordered her.

Darla was, at her core, a fighter. She stood her ground, even if she was doing it on shaky legs. He kind of admired that. But he was standing his ground, too. She had a lot of nerve to show up like this without even a phone call to warn him.

He moved around the desk. She backed up a little, her eyes panicked.

"Now, think about it, Sebastian," Darla said loudly. "All I want is a visit with Bastian. There doesn't have to be any drama, any acrimony. I'm not trying to get custody of him.

All I want to do is see him," she repeated, her tone so reasonable it just made him angrier.

He stood there with his arms akimbo. He stared at her hard. "Please leave," he said again. "I can't talk to you right now. I'm trying my best to control my anger."

He stomped his right foot loudly on the hardwood floor and a startled Darla sprinted for the door. At that moment, the door flew open and Marley was suddenly standing there. Mrs. Stewart was behind Marley up on her tiptoes trying to see inside, but Marley blocked her view since she was much taller than Mrs. Stewart. The wide-eyed expression on Mrs. Stewart's face made Sebastian regain more of his senses.

Distressed by Darla's presence in his office, Mrs. Stewart had obviously phoned Marley to get down to his office because all hell was about to break loose. And Marley had come running.

Marley closed the door with Mrs. Stewart still craning her neck to try to get a glimpse inside the office. Marley thrust Darla behind her and said, "Please go, Darla, while you can." The look she gave Darla was so fierce, if she had been the mythical Medusa, Darla would have instantly turned to stone.

Darla didn't have to be warned twice. She left, but with one last show of defiance, she slammed the door behind her.

Sebastian, having run out of steam, sat down on the corner of the desk and concentrated on breathing. Marley walked up to him. He opened his arms and she went inside his embrace where she just held on to him as tightly as she could.

MARLEY CLOSED HER eyes as she held Sebastian in her arms. She had never seen him so emotional before. His muscles were like coiled springs, he was so tense. He'd been trembling when she first put her arms around him, but the tremors had subsided. His breathing was now once again calm and even. She didn't know what to say to further soothe him, though, so she remained silent.

After a few minutes of his burying his face in her neck, she heard him say, "I guess I'm not a saint, after all. That's what Augustin calls me. The golden child. Our parents' favorite. The one that can do no wrong. I do believe my brother thinks I'm a sap because I've always been a good son."

"Little brothers can be a pain in the butt," Marley whispered. "It's just his insecurity talking."

They straightened and looked into each other's eyes. He smiled half-heartedly. She smiled back. "You have a loyal assistant in Mrs. Stewart. She said she knew something wasn't right the moment Darla strolled into the building. She was breathless when she phoned me. 'Darla Cramer is in Mr. Contreras's office,' she said. 'You'd better get over here before I have to call the police.'"

He pulled her back into his embrace. "And here you are."

She grinned. "Of course. I didn't want my man in prison for murder. They put you in the electric chair in Florida for that, you know."

"I had heard about that," he said, laughing now.

"Well, it's true," she assured him. Then, she got serious and said, "Let me guess—Darla wants to share custody of Bastian."

"She said she only wanted to see him." Sebastian sighed. "But we both know that would just be a prelude to what she's really after. We didn't get into any details because when she said she wanted to visit Bastian, I saw red. All the scenarios I imagined about meeting her again just went out the window. I was so sure I could remain calm and talk rationally about it, but I turned into the Incredible Hulk."

"Baby," Marley soothed, "don't be so hard on yourself. None of us are perfect. We don't know how we're going to react until we're in the situation. You had a lot of pent-up emotions about your marriage to get off your chest. It's not as if you've spent the last five years in a therapist's office, working through them. Plus, she launched a surprise attack. I don't know what possessed her to come right to your office without phoning first to give you a heads-up. A choice, even, about whether or not you wanted to see her. Something's up with her and I intend to get to the bottom of it. It's suspicious that she's back in town after the offer from the Nishimuras."

"There hasn't been a general announcement about it," Sebastian pointed out. "No one knows except our families. Oh, and I told Miguel about it. I haven't mentioned the offer to the employees because I don't want them to worry about their jobs. I can't imagine how Darla would have found out."

"I haven't even told Bonita Faye," Marley said. "And I agree with you about our families. They wouldn't spill the beans. Not on purpose, anyway."

She thought hard for a moment.

"Darla has lots of family in town, and I heard from Eula Mae that Miss Evie's always trying to entice her to come back home. Maybe that's why she's here, and it has nothing to do with the Nishimuras."

"Darla said her mother didn't have any influence on her coming home to get to know Bastian. She said she took everything her mother said with a grain of salt. And even though her mom was always trying to get her to return, she didn't think she'd be welcome."

Marley sighed. "Do you believe her? That she's just here for Bastian? You know her better than I do."

"It's obvious that I don't know her at all," Sebastian disagreed. "Frankly, I'm not sure what to believe."

Marley hugged him. "You've got a tough decision to make."

He shuddered at the prospect. "I have to do what I think is best for Bastian."

She kissed his forehead. "Yes, you do. And I'm sure you're going to make the right decision."

He took her chin between his forefinger and thumb and gently kissed her lips. Afterward, he said, "I hope I'm able to live up to your high opinion of me."

"You always have," Marley told him.

CHAPTER ELEVEN

"OKAY, YOU CAN get up now," Marley said to Chrissie. The little girl was standing on a step stool so she'd be tall enough to bend over the kitchen sink while Marley washed and conditioned her long, curly hair. Chrissie rose to her full height, and Marley began towel-drying her locks. Once Marley had the dripping under control, she placed the towel about Chrissie's shoulders and helped her down from the step stool.

Marley had been washing and styling Chrissie's hair almost as long as she'd been in her class. The Koontzes, the couple who were fostering Chrissie, had never taken in an African American child before. When Chrissie started coming to school day after day with her hair looking dry and tangled, Marley had no choice, she had to have a long talk with Cheryl Koontz about hair care for African American children. To her surprise when she offered to do Chrissie's hair, Cheryl had thanked her profusely. She recognized she was ill-equipped to handle Chrissie's hair. It was of a texture she wasn't familiar with.

Every other Saturday, Cheryl would drop Chrissie off at Marley's house so Chrissie could get her hair done. When Marley was finished, she'd drive Chrissie home. Their time together served more than one purpose. Chrissie's beautiful hair was taken care of and she and Marley also got to spend quality time together. On some occasions, Bastian came over and he and Chrissie enjoyed a playdate before Marley took her back home.

After Marley had started the adoption process, she'd asked Mrs. O'Neal, her caseworker, if it was okay to tell Chrissie that she wanted to adopt her. Mrs. O'Neal explained that if Chrissie were an older child, maybe. It depended on the emotional maturity of the child. However, because Chrissie was only five years old, she wouldn't understand what was going on.

And she didn't want to traumatize a five-year-old should Marley's attempt to adopt her fell through. Therefore, Marley hadn't mentioned the adoption to Chrissie. Marley was simply being her friend outside of the classroom.

The two of them went into the living room and Chrissie sat on the floor in front of Marley on one of the decorative pillows from the sofa, while Marley sat above her on the sofa. Marley finished towel-drying her hair and began oiling her scalp. Chrissie seemed to enjoy the whole process from shampooing to conditioning to sitting patiently while Marley oiled her scalp with hair and scalp conditioner.

After Marley had finished oiling Chrissie's scalp and massaging the conditioner through the rest of Chrissie's hair, she began sectioning her hair. It was at that point that she heard a knock at her back door.

Well, it can't be Ellery, Marley thought, *he doesn't knock.*

The cat had been her guest for more than two weeks now. He still refused to go home to Eula Mae. But, in a sense, he returned home every night to his mistress by camping out at her granddaughter's house next door.

"Hold on, baby girl," Marley said to Chrissie as she rose.

When she got to the kitchen, she peered

through the peephole at her grandmother's face. Eula Mae didn't look happy.

Pulling the door open, Marley cried, "Eula Mae. What's wrong?"

Eula Mae stepped inside. Marley closed the door and regarded her with interest. Her grandmother's face was flushed and her hair, which she had in one long braid down her back, was in disarray. There were even pieces of leaves in it. Marley reached over and began brushing the leaves out of her hair. "What have you been doing?"

Eula Mae took a deep breath. "I've been trying to catch that darn snake. And I almost had him. But when I tried to grab him while he was under the garden bench, I missed and fell into a pile of leaves I'd raked up and forgotten to put in a bag. My mind isn't what it used to be. I've been so aggravated by Ellery refusing to come home."

Marley was upset, too, by the time Eula Mae finished talking. "You could have broken a hip or something. Why didn't you call me if you wanted to catch it? Next time you get it in your head to do something that crazy, please reconsider."

Eula Mae took a deep breath and gazed

at her granddaughter with a remorseful expression. "I'm sorry, but you know how determined I am when I make up my mind to do something."

"I *do* know, and that's what frightens me," Marley said. "You think you're Superwoman, but in actuality, you have to be more careful. And why're you worried about Ellery? He's over here every night."

"I just found out today where he goes when he leaves your house in the morning."

"Oh?" Marley said, intrigued. The war between her grandmother and that resourceful Maine coon cat was very entertaining. She was beginning to wonder if either of the stubborn combatants was going to give in. Apparently, her grandmother had decided it was time for Albert, the green snake, to go. She missed her Ellery.

"Evie Cramer's house!" Eula Mae announced, her tone accusatory and, if Marley wasn't mistaken, a little bitter. "Those traitors," Eula Mae continued. "I can understand his behavior. He's just a cat, and that woman will buy him choice salmon every day for a few cuddles. But I don't understand why she'd feed him for over two weeks and not say why she was doing it. Is she that lonely? She ought to get her own cat! I'm so mad at her, I may never speak to her again."

"Now, Eula Mae, don't be like that. Miss Evie was doing you a favor, making sure Ellery got a good meal every day."

She gave her grandmother a hug. "Don't worry about the snake. I'll call animal control. They have people who'll come out and set a trap for Albert. They won't hurt him. They'll set him loose in the woods miles away. Hopefully, he won't find his way back. Though who knows, he might be as stubborn as Ellery."

Eula Mae laughed. "I hope not."

Marley released her and Eula Mae smiled up at her. "I noticed Cheryl dropping Chrissie off earlier. How is she?"

"Why don't you come and see," Marley said cheerfully. "I was just getting ready to braid her hair."

"Then I'm just in time," Eula Mae said. "I'm the one who taught you how to braid, after all."

Marley realized that she and Chrissie were about to be regaled by Eula Mae on how she'd learned the art of braiding hair from her own grandmother, an African woman from Mali.

In the living room, Chrissie glanced up as Marley and Eula Mae entered. She grinned at Eula Mae, whom she adored.

"Miss Eula Mae!" she cried excitedly.

Eula Mae went and hugged Chrissie. "I'm here to tell you about the country of Mali in West Africa while Marley braids your hair. It's where my grandmother Fatoumata was from. Can you say her name?"

Chrissie said the name slowly but perfectly. "Fa-tou-ma-ta." She seemed to enjoy the sound of the name.

"You've got it," Eula Mae said gleefully.

Marley believed Chrissie was so taken with Eula Mae because she didn't have a grandmother. *But once I adopt her,* Marley thought, *she'll have three grandmothers: Eula Mae, my mom and Auntie Isabella, after Sebastian and I are married.*

She sighed a little at the thought of Sebastian. After the incident with Darla in his office, she'd been worried about him.

She sat back down on the sofa and Chrissie resumed her position on the pillow in front of her. Eula Mae sat across from them in an armchair.

"You know I used to be a teacher, right?" Eula Mae asked Chrissie.

"Yes, ma'am," Chrissie said, nodding.

"Just answer her with your voice," Marley said softly. "Try not to nod while I'm doing your hair."

"Okay," Chrissie said. She turned and smiled up at Marley, after which she sat still.

A few minutes later, Chrissie was so enthralled with Eula Mae's voice and her story that she didn't wriggle for the next hour and a half while Marley braided her long hair into an intricate style.

"A long time ago in Timbuktu, a city in Mali, there were a bunch of learned people who recorded the history of Mali onto scrolls. The scholars put these scrolls in a library that still exists today. You don't have to try to remember its name, but I remember because I'm an old lady and I remember a lot of things. It's called the Ahmed Baba Institute of Higher Islamic Studies and Research. And it contains over twenty thousand manuscripts about Mali's history. And know what else? It was all written by hand. They didn't have computers to type things on back then."

Eula Mae eyed Marley. "The children are familiar with computers even at five, aren't they?"

"Yes, they are," Marley said. "But we limit computer use so they'll learn to think for themselves before the enticement of electronics catches hold."

"Oh, I'm glad," Eula Mae said.

"Tim-buk-tu," Chrissie said.

Marley and Eula Mae laughed. "She's a fast learner," Eula Mae said.

Marley bent and gave Chrissie a hug. "That, she is," she said proudly.

"Now, Chrissie," Eula Mae said, "let me tell you about how nimble my grandma Fatoumata's fingers were. She taught me how to braid hair when I was around nine years old…"

"DADDY, HELP!" BASTIAN screamed as he held on tightly to his fishing pole. Sebastian, standing next to him on the pier near the fishery in town, snapped to attention. He'd been daydreaming because the day was bright and sunny, and there was a nice breeze off the ocean. But now he quickly came back to reality and grabbed his son's pole, but didn't take it from him. He'd guide him through this.

Bastian loved fishing from the pier. Sebastian regarded it as a way to introduce his son to fishing without taking him out in a boat. For safety's sake, he made sure Bastian wore a life jacket even while fishing from the pier.

"It's big," Bastian said excitedly.

Sebastian could feel the weight of the fish. He guessed it was a good-sized yellowtail snapper. He'd noticed other fishers around them pulling snappers out of the water, too.

"We're going to slowly move backward," he instructed Bastian.

Bastian gritted his teeth and the two of them moved backward in tandem. Sebastian, of course, bore the brunt of the weight as they lifted the yellowtail snapper up out of the water. It was wiggling mightily.

Sebastian reached out with a gloved hand and took hold of the fishing line, pulling the fish toward him and his son. Up and over the pier's railing, and they had him. Sebastian let the fish down and it flopped onto the wooden planks of the pier. It was easily a three-pounder.

Bastian, free of the burden of holding onto the pole, jumped up and down in glee. "He's so big! Can we take a photo, Daddy?"

Sebastian put the cane pole down on the pier, too, reached into his back jeans' pocket, retrieved his cell phone and snapped a couple of photos of the yellowtail snapper.

Afterward, he said, "All right, then, let me get the hook out and put him in our cooler."

Bastian suddenly gazed sadly at the fish flopping on the pier. "Put him back, Daddy. Please?"

Sebastian didn't hesitate. He bent and gently withdrew the hook from the snapper's mouth. A glance told him the fish was unharmed. He got a good grasp on the fish by its tail, held it above the water and dropped it into the ocean.

Bastian came to the railing and called, "Bye, sorry!"

Sebastian knelt, turned his son around to face him and said, "Every time we come here, you always throw the fish back. And I understand, truly I do. But you do realize what our family does for a living, right?"

Bastian nodded. "We're fishermen."

Sebastian smiled. "God put fish in the

ocean so we could put food on our tables. But we humans have a responsibility to take care of the fish and the ocean, too. So, I'm glad you felt sorry for the daddy fish and sent him home to his kids. You have years before you'll have to think about not throwing the fish you catch back into the sea."

He wasn't sure if Bastian was grasping what he was trying to say, only that it was what he'd been taught when he was Bastian's age. Sebastian hadn't been able to bear killing and taking any of his catches home, either, when his father had brought him fishing.

"Now, let's get our poles and load up. We'll go for a burger and a milkshake."

Bastian started grinning when he heard the word *milkshake*. It was his favorite treat. Sebastian felt a pang of guilt as he and Bastian began collecting their poles and tackle box and cooler.

Ten minutes later he and his son were sitting across from one another in a booth at Kaye's Café. As they were walking in, friends called hello. His son was more popular than he was. He had the waitress, Tish, cooing over him and two young women who were obviously mothers of children who were in

Bastian's class greeted him by name with enthusiasm and promises of making sure to tell whomever it was Bastian went to school with hello from him.

School was out for the summer. These were the halcyon days that memories were made of when Sebastian was a kid. He was trying to make the same sort of fond memories with Bastian.

Tish delivered their orders and Sebastian allowed Bastian a few minutes to enjoy his food before saying, "Son, um, I have something important to talk with you about."

Bastian was pulling hard on the straw, which was stuck in his vanilla milkshake. But now his eyes flew to his dad's face.

"Bastian, a few days ago, your birth mother, Darla, came to see me. I know you've been shown pictures of her over the years and I, and your grandmother Miss Evie, have told you stories about her. So you know who she is."

Bastian was nodding and drinking his milkshake. Sebastian hoped he wouldn't get brain freeze, he was sucking so hard.

"The thing is, Bastian, your mother wants to see you. But before I say yes to her, I wanted to ask how you feel about it. Take your time and think about it. Do you want to see her?"

He had agonized over the decision himself. Was it wise to not fight Darla's return to Bastian's life? What if she performed another disappearing act? Ultimately, he figured it would be a good idea to go straight to the source.

"Yes!" was Bastian's immediate answer. His face lit up. "Now Chrissie and I won't be the only ones who don't have a real mom. Me and Chrissie can share."

His mention of Chrissie, whom Bastian loved, made Sebastian realize what a good heart his son had.

"My birthday is soon. Can my mom come to my party?" Bastian looked so happy, Sebastian was slightly ashamed of his overwhelming sense that this was all going to end badly.

He didn't really think Darla had changed. However, Miss Evie had paid him a visit a few days ago, begging him to give Darla a chance. It was the plea of a mother for her child's life, it seemed. To Sebastian, it was evident that Darla's desire to get to know her son was proof to Miss Evie that Darla was finally beginning to appreciate the blessing that being a mother could be. A blessing and an honor, Miss Evie had passionately cried when she'd ended her fifteen-minute speech on her daughter's behalf.

The number of people on the side of Sebastian allowing Bastian to visit with his mother had grown to three by the time he'd made up his mind to ask Bastian. His parents had only to say, "She's his blood," to convince him they also thought it was the right thing to do.

Marley had decided to remain neutral on the subject. He was certain she'd done that because she didn't want to affect his decision on the matter. She knew her opinion meant a great deal to him. She'd been there, after all, when Bastian had been colicky, was cutting his first teeth, started crawling, then pushed himself to his feet and started tentatively taking steps, his chubby legs not holding him up too well at the time. Before long, though, he was running. To Sebastian, Marley was more of a mother to Bastian than Darla was. However, he couldn't go to his grave with the knowledge that he'd denied his son the right to a relationship with his birth mother. Therefore, he was going to phone Darla and give her a date and time during which she could visit Bastian.

"Okay, buddy, I'll arrange it so you can meet her," Sebastian finally said. "And if she's still here by your birthday, she can most definitely come to your party."

Bastian cheered, then turned his attention to his milkshake.

While Sebastian sat across from him and brooded about the situation. He was certain of only one thing. It was his confidence in his relationship with Marley that was making him more malleable when it came to trying to cooperate with Darla. He knew the sudden appearance of his ex-wife was not going to affect him and Marley. And if everything went sideways and Darla didn't live up to her end of the bargain, the two of them would be there for Bastian as they always had been.

CHAPTER TWELVE

MARLEY GOT TO the main venue of the Port Domingo Seafood/Music Festival in the city park, which was near the pier, bright and early Saturday morning. She and Julie Mason, the other organizer, met up under the tent of the information booth. From there they greeted early arriving vendors who were there setting up their tables and putting their wares on display for, hopefully, eager festivalgoers to peruse and buy.

Marley and Julie's job was to make sure things ran smoothly throughout the day. They would give the vendors directions where they could set up. Musical performers were reminded of their schedules, and to try their best to begin their sets on time and end them on schedule. Julie was going to man the information booth today and Marley was going to be there dispensing information tomorrow,

Sunday. Volunteers would relieve them half-way through the day.

The two of them stood now, both dressed appropriately for what would be a ninety-degree day. Marley was in a flowy, white muslin midi-dress and flat-heeled sandals, looking serene and confident. She had sat for hours while Eula Mae had braided her hair. She'd come prepared to withstand the heat. Julie, a brunette with brown eyes, was wearing a tan linen sleeveless pantsuit, sandals and a straw hat, looking monochromatic. Marley could tell the heat was already bothering her because she kept pulling off her hat at intervals and fanning herself with it.

"Hey, Marley, Julie." Tucker Richards, a guitarist in his early thirties, walked up to the booth, a broad smile on his attractive face. They returned his greeting.

Tucker was with a country band, and he was wearing well-worn jeans, cowboy boots, a black T-shirt and a black Stetson. After removing his hat, revealing thick, black, wavy hair, he addressed his concerns to Marley, "I noticed we're on at two this afternoon. My bass player is having car trouble. Is it possible for us to switch with another performer who's on later?"

"How much later?" Marley asked.

He winced, his green eyes squinting. "Six?"

"I'll see what I can do," Marley said. "But I can't promise results. I've got your cell phone number. I'll call you as soon as I find out if someone can switch with you."

He smiled warmly, and his tanned face got a little red. "Sorry, Marley."

"These things happen," Marley said, her tone understanding.

"Y'all have a good day," he said with a lingering glance in Julie's direction. Tucker put his hat back on and left.

"Same to you," Marley said with a smile.

After Tucker was out of earshot, Julie said, "And so it begins."

"Yes, indeed," Marley agreed, preparing to leave since it was Julie's day to be stationed at the information booth. "I wish you as few frustrations today as humanly possible."

"You, too," Julie said, laughing.

As Marley walked around the area, she felt confident that they were, indeed, going to have a good day.

The festival didn't officially begin until eleven o'clock, a good three hours from now, but the vendors were going to need that time to get things set up.

For the festivalgoers it was a great opportunity to get outdoors and enjoy good food, wine, beer and live music.

Marley had been in charge of booking the musicians, and she was happy with her choices of a talented selection of regional performers, vocalists who performed alone and with bands. She'd grown up knowing a lot of musicians because at one time her mother had harbored hopes that Marley would be a professional singer, too.

Marley started learning the guitar at age seven. She'd loved the instrument and sang and played for anyone who would listen. She had talent. As her voice matured, people said she sounded like a cross between Lauryn Hill and Tracy Chapman, but she didn't think she did. Her voice was deep and soulful with plenty of teenage angst thrown in for good measure back then. In high school she was in a local band that played at nearby pubs and festivals. She was the lead singer. But by the time she was a senior in high school, she realized that she wanted to become a teacher like her grandmother, not a professional musician. Now, she still played for family and friends, but she'd chosen not to pursue a career as a singer. Although she truly loved to perform and could be coerced into singing a song or two on special occasions.

She was nearing one of the pavilions where the bands were scheduled to perform. She tilted her head up, observing the blue sky and the cumulus clouds. July was smack in the middle of hurricane season. Weather reports hadn't mentioned any storms headed their way, though. For the past few days they had been enjoying very good weather. There might be a shower in the afternoon, but it would probably be very brief. The temperature had been in the high eighties up to the low nineties, but with the breezes coming off the Gulf of Mexico, the temperature was pleasant if you dressed appropriately and stayed hydrated, as most people who frequented the festival did.

There were wooden benches throughout the park and she sat down on one of them to get her cell phone out. She started going down her list of today's performers. Maybe the performer who was scheduled for six could switch with Tucker's band and perform at two instead. The bench was in a quiet, rather secluded spot because it was underneath one of the town's oldest oak trees. Its branches were leaf- and moss-laden, and its appearance reminded her of those spooky black-and-white movies in which monsters like the Creature from the Black Lagoon lurked in swamps. Those scenes had always been filmed underneath a tree like this.

She gazed up through its branches, the sunlight streaming through them while she waited for someone to answer the phone.

"Marley," said a sleepy female voice. "Is something wrong? Has the festival been canceled?" There was panic in the tone, and Marley understood why. This was Harry Nunez's first big gig. The twenty-year-old had been busking on the streets of Miami for a couple of years. She earned enough to pay the bills, but now she wanted to do something that would take her off the streets. And even though Port Domingo's festival was small by some folks' standards, there were actually reputable people from the music industry who made it their business to attend each year. This could be Harry's big chance.

"Harriet," Marley said calmly. Harry was her professional name. "It's nothing like that. I'm calling to see if you'd be okay switching performance times with another band. They were supposed to go on today at two, but their bass player is having transportation problems. You're supposed to perform at six. Would you be willing to perform at two instead?"

She heard Harry release a relieved breath. "Sure, then I don't have to stew in my juices for quite as long. I'm so nervous!"

"No need to be," Marley said with a laugh. "Girl, you've got chops. Just come and do your thing."

Harry chortled. "It's just me and my guitar, but I'll be there by one."

"I'll meet you there," Marley told her. "I can't wait to hear your new songs." Marley admired artists who not only sang but wrote their own material.

The two rang off, then Marley sat back on the bench. *One problem solved*, she thought, relieved. Then, she went down her phone's contact list and touched the screen, dialing Tucker's number.

The phone rang and rang, but Tucker didn't answer. She set the phone on her thigh and decided she'd try him again in about ten minutes. In the meanwhile she was just going to enjoy this beautiful day.

WHEN SEBASTIAN PULLED the pickup truck to the curb at Miss Evie's house Saturday morning, there were knots of anxiety forming in his stomach. Bastian, sitting beside him, was animated, though. His son's expression reminded him of how Bastian had looked when they'd driven to Disney World and Bastian had spotted the road signs advertising the amusement park.

On one hand, he was glad his son was happily anticipating meeting his mother. On the other, Sebastian had no faith that Darla would actually do what she'd promised: get acquainted with Bastian without causing chaos in his young life. But, he prayed he would be proved wrong.

Miss Evie must have seen them pull up because she had come onto the porch, wiping her hands on a dish towel. She must have been so excited to see them that she hadn't taken the time to dry her hands and leave the towel in the kitchen. Sebastian's heart broke just a little. Miss Evie had gone through emotional turmoil due to Darla's choices, too. She'd lived through the questions and rumors. In a small town it was impossible to avoid rumors. And the ones about Darla had been particularly vicious. Sebastian had been hurt by her abandonment, true, but he still didn't believe anyone should be talked about like Darla had been talked about. The gossipers had said she'd used him and dropped him as soon as a better prospect came along. J.J. Starr had been a successful musician at the time, making much more money than Sebastian, but was it fair for people to throw stones as if they were saints themselves?

Now he tried to think more positively as he got out of the pickup, went around to the passenger side and opened Bastian's door. Bastian energetically hopped out of the pickup. Miss Evie saw that her grandson was in a good mood from his cheery actions and wasted no time crossing the lawn and sweeping him up in her arms.

Sebastian stood aside and waited, Bastian's bag in his right hand. He glanced at the house. No sign of Darla. Was she afraid to face him?

But, no, there she was coming out of the house. She stopped on the porch and looked toward them, her eyes wary. Sebastian wondered what she had to be afraid of. He'd agreed to bring Bastian over here for the weekend. He tried to convince himself it was just another weekend that Bastian would spend with his grandmother, but he'd never been good at fooling himself.

This was serious. This could change his life, Bastian's and the whole family dynamic. Darla was back. He had to accept it, but he didn't have to like it.

Miss Evie, probably sensing her daughter's reticence and his own semi-belligerent feelings, turned on the enthusiasm. "I'm so happy you're here, Sebastian. Give me a hug!"

It was hard to remain in a rotten mood when your ex-mother-in-law was the possessor of the world's greatest hugs. For a little woman, she also had a good grip. As he bent down to hug her, she whispered, "Thank you! She's so sure you hate her after what happened at the fishery that she's walking on eggshells, worrying she's going to say or do the wrong thing and spoil this truce."

Then, they straightened up and she looked

him dead in the eyes. "Don't worry, I'm watching her like a hawk. I've got trust issues myself. If I sense she's going to try something stupid, I'll be on her like white on rice!"

Meaning, Sebastian assumed, that if Darla tried to kidnap Bastian, her mother would do everything in her power to stop her. This admission sobered Sebastian. Darla's vanishing act had obviously caused Miss Evie trauma more serious than just worrying that her daughter might have ruined her life by blowing off the rest of them.

Making sure his tone was calm, he said, "Don't let this raise your blood pressure, Miss Evie. I'm sure everything is going to be fine."

He said that for her benefit. No use putting more stress on this kind lady. After that, they all walked up onto the big porch. Still remembering to control the emotions in his voice, he said, "Good morning, Darla."

"Good morning, Sebastian," Darla said with forced brightness.

Her gaze was on Bastian, though, who was standing between him and Miss Evie, whose hand he was holding. Darla knelt in front of Bastian, and Sebastian noticed that her hands were trembling.

Bastian looked her in the eyes and smiled. "Good morning, Mommy."

Darla reached out for him, pulled him into her arms and sat back on her legs, hugging him and weeping. Sebastian wasn't sure what he'd expected, but it definitely hadn't been this show of emotions. It was as if Bastian were Darla's lifeline. "Good morning, baby," she said through her tears.

Bastian, sweet boy that he was, hugged her back and cooed, "Don't cry, Mommy. Don't cry."

Darla cried harder.

Uncomfortable with her display of emotions, Sebastian didn't know what to do. Offer comfort? As he stood there wondering what his next move should be, he glanced at Miss Evie, hoping she'd intervene and get her daughter up off her knees. But Bastian, like all children, got right down to brass tacks and asked his long-lost mother:

"Did you bring me anything?"

That question struck the adults as hilarious and they started laughing. Darla got to her feet, took Bastian by the hand and led him into the house. "I sure did. Let me show you what I brought you."

Miss Evie heaved a sigh, looked up at Sebastian and said, "Out of the mouths of babes." She quickly hugged him again. "Thank God for children. But don't worry none, I feel all right now. I think this is going to work out."

Sebastian wasn't as positive as she was, but he said, "I guess I'll be going, then."

And he left.

When he got back to the pickup and started the engine, he wondered how he was going to pull off behaving normally around others the whole weekend when his mind was so unsettled. Then, he thought of Marley. Today and tomorrow were going to be big days for her, what with the festival going on in town. He would pop over there and see what he could do to support her.

MARLEY HAD FINALLY got hold of Tucker and told him Harry had agreed to switch times with him and his band. She was about to put her cell phone in her shoulder bag when it rang with Sebastian's ringtone: "My Guy" by Mary Wells.

Suddenly, she was smiling. She felt like a teenager who'd fallen in love for the first time. She couldn't answer the phone fast enough. However, she didn't want to sound like a breathless lovesick idiot, so she took a calming breath beforehand.

"Hey there," she said softly, holding the phone up to her left ear.

"I was wondering if there was anything I can do to help you out today," Sebastian said.

Marley's soaring spirits suddenly fell flat. The truth was, they already had enough volunteers to work in the background, making sure everything ran smoothly at the festival this year.

Her mind worked furiously, however, trying to come up with some kind of excuse to have Sebastian by her side. She could never get enough of his company. She was on a love high she hadn't experienced before.

She could think of no legitimate reason for Sebastian to come here and spend the day following her around, though, so she truthfully said, "I wish. But the fact is, we've got enough people behind the scenes."

"Too bad," a deep voice said in her right ear. "I was looking forward to seeing your sweet face before tonight when you'll be onstage singing your heart out."

Marley sprang to her feet. There he was,

grinning at her. She ran behind the bench and pounced on him, wrapping her arms around his neck. Sebastian was laughing, his rich baritone a delight to her ears. While she clung to him, he stuck his cell phone in his back pocket and then pulled her more firmly into his arms.

He breathed her in. She loved it when he did that. It made her feel as if her essence was one of the things he loved about her. She knew she couldn't get enough of the way he smelled: like he was fresh out of the shower. He wasn't the type who wore a lot of cologne. Just his natural scent was enticing. She breathed him in, too.

He was admiring her in her summer dress. He was wearing jeans and a black short-sleeve T-shirt with the Harley-Davidson insignia on it. He was wearing his motorcycle boots. She hadn't heard the Harley, so she assumed he'd driven the pickup over here.

His deep brown eyes were taking her in, the expression in them totally possessive. Before now she'd thought of that word as negative, denoting ownership. What modern woman wanted to be owned by a man?

But Sebastian would never want to own

her. She was free to be who she was, as far as
he was concerned. She was positive of that.

His possessiveness was protective. It was
loving and kind. To be possessed by him
meant she was his forever, and he was hers
forever. In that way, they possessed each other.

They circled one another without speaking, eyes devouring, senses on alert, for a
good three minutes, she was sure. That wasn't
unusual. Since they'd confessed their love
for one another they often simply relished
the time they got to spend together, without
speaking. They'd said enough over the years.
Those sessions in the cove had left no stone
unturned. She knew him. He knew her. All
else was the cherry on top. Their interest in
this game they were playing, not letting their
friends and family know they were in love,
was coming to an end.

She sensed that both of them were getting
nearer to the time when they would abandon
the ruse that they were still just friends.

Besides, it was getting harder and harder
to hide their love from everyone else. The
game could be delicious, though. As it was
right now when he pulled her into his arms
and kissed her right out in the open.

She lost her train of thought when his mouth descended on hers. He tasted so good. His arms around her made her spirit feel light. She was giddy. And every nerve ending in her body came alive with joy. She wound up on her toes, trying to get closer. She only realized she'd risen after he released her and she came to her senses.

She got off her toes and straightened the hem of her dress, which had hitched its way up a few inches while they were in a clinch. "That's the best 'good morning' I've had in ages," she quipped, smiling at him.

Sebastian grinned. "I aim to please." Then he sobered and said, "I just dropped Bastian off at Miss Evie's house. I'm nervous about it."

She took him by the hand and pulled him over to the bench. They sat down facing one another. She clasped his hand. "You want to talk about it? I have a lot of free time. I'm only here because I'm such a worrywart that I have to see for myself that the vendors get set up right. Julie is handling any crises they might have, though. I'm available to the performers via cell phone. So far, only one of them has had a problem. I really don't have to be here until I perform tonight. No wait, I promised a young artist from Miami that I'd meet her here at one. Other than that, tomorrow is when I'll be handling crises."

He nodded, acknowledging that he understood her situation. "No, babe, I don't want to talk about it because I'll wind up getting angry all over again. I'm just going to have to wait and see how Darla behaves. Has she changed? I don't know. But I'm sure she'll show her true colors before long."

Marley had no doubt he was right. She hoped Darla had changed for the better. She didn't want Bastian to be disappointed or for Sebastian to feel as though he'd been duped once again. His faith in humans had been tested when she'd tossed him away. His pride, too.

As for her opinion on the situation, she was happy that Darla seemed to have come to the conclusion that she wanted to be a mother to Bastian. Every child deserved to be loved by his mother. However, she was afraid that if Darla abandoned Bastian again, he might not be the optimistic, happy child he was now. He was a well-rounded little boy and she wanted him to stay that way. And she wasn't jealous

of Darla or worried that she could come between her and Sebastian. She believed that
their love for each other was strong enough
to withstand any assault. What was love without faith?

"All right," she agreed. "Oh, I didn't tell
you that Ellery went home. A day after the
snake was captured and driven away. Eula
Mae was so happy, she actually gave him
fresh fish last night."

"That cat has champagne tastes and caviar
dreams," Sebastian laughed, quoting Robin
Leach's catchphrase from *Lifestyles of the
Rich and Famous*.

"And knows how to play hardball," Marley added.

CHAPTER THIRTEEN

MARLEY AND SEBASTIAN spent the morning together, having breakfast at his house and just chilling. They parted at noon when he got a call from Miguel. Miguel was leaving tomorrow. He said he'd prolong his visit so that he could come to Marley's performance tonight. Marley suspected Kaye Johnson had something to do with his still being in Port Domingo when he'd been due back in Chicago over a week ago. But she kept her opinion to herself. She happily kissed Sebastian goodbye so he could spend a little extra time with his best bud.

An hour later, she was at the festival again, as she'd promised Harry she would be. Harriet "Harry" Nunez had auditioned for Marley via a video someone had shot of her performing on a street in Miami. Marley had thought Harry was very talented then, but she was even better live.

Marley was standing in the crowd of about three hundred people, which was a good turn-out for two in the afternoon. If Harry was as nervous as she'd said earlier, she didn't show it. Her set was beautifully done, with not a hitch in her guitar playing or her voice. Her original songs were heartwarming and mem-orable, the tunes getting into your head and finding a home.

Harry wore a tie-dyed T-shirt and jeans, and she was barefoot. Hispanic, she had dark brown skin and a mass of wavy chestnut hair. She was tiny, maybe five-three and very slen-der. Her acoustic guitar was almost as big as she was.

But her size belied her big, rich voice. And her storytelling skills were admirable. She reminded Marley of one of her favorite sing-ers, Brandi Carlile.

"Oh, she's different," Zenia Thomas said appreciatively.

Marley smiled at Zenia. "Totally brilliant. Please say you're interested in talking with her after her set."

Zenia nodded her head, her huge red afro flowing in the afternoon breeze. She was an African American in her early thirties with warm mocha skin. She earned her living as a scout, or an A&R, which stood for Artists & Repertoire. Her specialty was matching artists with recording companies. She'd been coming to the festival for the last four years. She'd recruited a couple of artists as a result of dropping by this regional gathering.

"Good," Marley breathed, happy for Harry. To get the notice of a person like Zenia would be to Harry's advantage. There were so many con artists in the music business, but Zenia was legitimate and actually cared for the artists she represented.

They listened to the rest of Harry's set and when the applause had died down enough for Harry to distinguish Marley's voice from the cacophony, she called out to the singer: "Harry, get down here. There's someone I'd like you to meet."

After Harry joined them and she'd made the introductions, Marley gave Harry a quick hug and left them alone.

As she was navigating her way through the crowd, she spied her parents walking hand in hand a few yards away in the vendor area. Her dad was a tall, trim man who'd played soccer in his youth in the Bahamas. He had smooth dark brown skin, golden-colored eyes, which was where she'd gotten her eye color, and a tight cap of curly salt-and-pepper hair, which he kept cut short. He was wearing white cotton, knee-length shorts, a green golf shirt and white athletic shoes. A white Kangol cap sat atop his head. He wore a cap year-round.

Her mom was about five inches shorter than her dad, medium reddish-brown skin, ten years younger, and she wore her thick natural hair in braids, which she had redone quite often, making sure that her stylist didn't do them too tightly. She was not going to go bald at the hands of a tyrant stylist. Today she was wearing a cute sleeveless cotton shift in pale blue, the hem of which just covered her knees, and a pair of white Chucks, her favorite tennis shoes. Marley started walking in their direction.

She thought it was sweet that her parents still held hands after thirty-six years of marriage. But then, romance knew no age. Her father was semiretired. He'd been a carpenter all his life. There was nothing he couldn't build: houses, furniture. When she was around seven he built his children a tree

house. It was the Frank Lloyd Wright of tree
houses. It had two floors and was so sturdily
built their mother didn't go apoplectic when
she climbed up into it, even after her accident
a year earlier. She believed her father had
built the tree house because he didn't want
the accident to leave a lasting fear of climbing trees in her. A version of falling off the
horse and getting right back on it. She loved
her dad.

Her mother didn't have a trade, per se.
Up until she was in her late thirties, she was
strictly a wife and mother, but one day she'd
gotten it in her head that she wanted to open
a seafood restaurant. She'd collected volumes
of recipes handed down from her own mother.
Eula Mae, her husband's mother, also knew a
little something about making seafood delicious from years of experience cooking Bahamian seafood dishes. So her mother and Eula
Mae had put their heads together, wrote a
plan and presented it to their husbands. Marley's grandfather, Albert, who had also been
a carpenter, had still been alive then. Eula
Mae had just retired from teaching, so contributing to the running of a restaurant had
been her way of keeping busy. She believed

people who retired and just sat on their cans died faster than those who stayed busy. She wasn't going out like that.

When they pitched their idea, Port Domingo hadn't had a seafood restaurant. Fact was, there wasn't a really good one in the whole of Escambia County, according to Eula Mae. No one thought to verify that fact, they just took her word for it.

Marley's father and grandfather looked over their wives' plans and saw that the idea was solid. They drew up the building plans for the restaurant and within nine months, the restaurant was open. No one could have predicted how successful it would be, but theirs was the most frequented seafood restaurant in the county according to a news segment on a local TV station that reported on restaurants in the area. They certainly had a loyal clientele. Marley had grown up working in the restaurant, and still helped out whenever she could.

Her parents stopped at a booth whose vendor sold crystal jewelry in myriad colors. There were earrings, bracelets and necklaces made from amethyst, citrine, tourmaline, garnet and moonstone. At least, those were the stones Marley could recognize by sight.

Her parents' backs were to her, so they didn't see her approach them. "Buying jewelry for your girlfriend, Dad?" she joked.

Her parents couldn't be startled. She'd learned that as a little girl when she'd tried to sneak up on them a number of times. If they were surprised back then, they never let on.

Which was how they reacted today. Her mother calmly placed the necklace she'd been looking at back on the table and turned to her. "Imagine running into you here," she said dryly.

Her dad smiled at her. "Hello, sweetheart." He glanced around them. "Everything's looking good. And, I might be wrong, but it seems like more people are here this year. Or maybe I'm just annoyed at how long it took us to park."

Their house was outside town. Unlike where she and Eula Mae lived, which was within walking distance of the town center.

Marley chose not to acknowledge his complaint. There was nothing she could do about it. So, she smiled, and said, "Well, I'm glad you made it. I haven't been over to the restaurant's booth yet. I'm sure Tandi and her crew are doing great. Has it been a problem for her not to have Torin helping out this year?" She missed her brother since he'd gone to make the air force his life's career a few weeks back. It felt like longer. He texted frequently, though, so she knew he didn't regret his decision.

"Oh, no," her mother answered. Which she did whenever there was a question about the restaurant. "She's got dependable people helping her. We were just there, and the booth is doing a brisk business."

Festivalgoers drifted around the area, eating, drinking and taking in a few minutes of music. Sometimes they did all three at once, Marley observed with satisfaction.

She was about to tell her parents goodbye when she was interrupted by a little boy walking up to her and hugging her around the waist. Out of the corner of her eye, she saw her parents moving along.

It was Bradley, from her kindergarten class. "Miss Syminette, I miss you." He turned his adorable face up to her and smiled at her. She couldn't stop the flutter of her heart. She loved the little guy.

He was accompanied by his parents. She recognized both of them from parents' night. "Bradley, I've missed you, too," she exclaimed, hugging him back.

His mother, Jeannie, looked slightly embarrassed, but also quite tired. Marley had seen that look before. It meant his mother had missed her, too. Parents derived respite when their little ones were at school. During the summer break, however, they pulled double duty keeping up with the kiddies.

"It's good to run into you, Marley," said Jeannie, her tone not energetic, but the expression in her brown eyes sincere.

Marley smiled warmly at Jeannie. "Hi, Jeannie, Matt." Matt was grinning. He was a grown-up version of towheaded Bradley.

He was big, blond and blue-eyed. After hearing about his recent trouble with the law, she was glad to see them here as a family.

"Marley," Matt acknowledged her. He grabbed Bradley by the arm and pried him off Marley. Marley fondly ruffled Bradley's hair. "I hope you're enjoying your summer, Bradley. And don't forget to go to the library and check out some books to keep up with your reading." After a year in her class, her students knew their ABCs and certain sight words. Books were important even if they were essentially picture books. She encouraged them to consider books as enjoyable as games on electronic devices, which she knew some of them frequently played. Encountering Bradley made her miss that she used to see him and Chrissie on a daily basis. But, her Saturdays with Chrissie hadn't ceased during the summer. She was still doing her hair every two weeks and getting to spend time with her.

She waved goodbye to Bradley as she walked away. Her musical set didn't start until eight tonight. She was going home to rest a while, maybe rehearse her songs a little and check on Eula Mae. She hadn't been home in over six hours and hadn't seen Eula Mae before she'd left the house this morning. She liked to do a wellness check on her grandmother a couple of times a day, at least.

When she got home, she discovered Eula Mae was doing fine. In fact, she was having a garden party. Marley had parked the Corolla out back and was surprised to see the patio table set up in Eula Mae's backyard and her grandmother entertaining Akira and Daichi.

As she was watching her grandmother sitting at the table gabbing with the two men, Bonita Faye strolled out of the back door carrying a sushi tray laden with several different kinds of the Japanese dish. Ellery followed, looking regal since he was once again king of the house. Plus, where there was fresh fish, there also was Ellery.

Her first emotion upon seeing Bonita Faye with sushi in her hands was jealousy. She had never eaten sushi until she met Bonita Faye, who'd been taught how to make it by her grandmother who was from Kyoto, Japan. If Bonita Faye opened a sushi restaurant she would rack up, her sushi was so good. Marley, who had grown up on seafood, had never eaten raw fish in her life, but now she was hooked.

"What is this?" Marley cried, walking swiftly over to her grandmother's garden and confronting the conspirators. She glared at Bonita Faye accusingly. "You made sushi and didn't invite me?"

Bonita Faye laughed, and said, "I was going to call you but everything happened so fast."

"Let me tell it," Eula Mae said. Her grand-mother loved a juicy story.

Remembering her manners, Marley said, "Hi, Akira, Mr. Nishimura."

The two men smiled and greeted her back. All eyes were on Eula Mae, though, who had gotten to her feet as if she were about to give a speech. "It's like this," she told Marley. "Daichi said he missed sushi made by his favorite sushi chef in Tokyo. And I said Bo-nita Faye makes the best sushi in Florida."

Her grandmother had a gift for exagger-ation, but as far as Marley was concerned, that wasn't a huge exaggeration. Bonita Faye had learned from a master chef, and she'd learned well.

"And I said she must be kidding," Daichi spoke up. "I've never known a woman who could make sushi better than a man."

"And I called him a male chauvinist. I left out the pig part," Eula Mae said. "Then, I phoned Bonita Faye and told her we had to show him he was wrong. I got so fired up that I offered to pay for the ingredients."

Her grandmother was tight with money. She must have been really angry.

"As it happened," Bonita Faye put in as she

carefully set the tray with the sushi on it in the center of the table, "I was skyping with my grandmother in Hawaii at the time. She overheard our phone conversation and said, 'Show him.' I knew she was angry, too. My nerves can't take two angry grandmothers, so I went shopping. We agreed to meet over here, and I've just finished preparing the first batch."

Marley had watched Bonita Faye make sushi on numerous occasions. It was like watching an artist at work. Her skill with a knife was remarkable. Bonita Faye said the key to good sushi was the rice, the shari. The rice was seasoned with vinegar and other seasonings like sugar and salt. She said if your rice wasn't just the right consistency—sticky but not dry—the rest of the ingredients were wasted. Other ingredients included thinly sliced fresh fish, often raw, and fresh vegetables. Then you had to have steady hands and the knife skills of a ninja. Also, not all sushi was made with raw fish. When using shrimp, Bonita Faye cooked it first.

"Enough talking," Eula Mae said. "It's time to see who's right and who will be eating crow along with his sushi!"

Bonita Faye was more composed. She smiled down at Daichi, who grinned up at her from his seat at the table. "Today, I honor my grandmother by offering you a chance to try sushi made by a woman."

Daichi reached for a piece of sushi that had been made with salmon. It looked delicious and Marley's mouth watered in sympathy. Daichi was in for a treat.

That he used his hand and not chopsticks didn't surprise Marley. Bonita Faye had told her that in Japan, you ate sushi with your hands. In spite of all the depictions in movies and on TV that showed people eating it with chopsticks.

Everyone waited breathlessly while Daichi chewed, his face not showing any emotions. Then he slowly closed his eyes, took a deep breath and said, "Where's the crow, Eula Mae? I admit it. This is better than my chef's sushi."

Her grandmother clapped her hands in excitement. Bonita Faye had a beatific smile on her face, like some Renaissance angel. Akira reached over and took Bonita Faye's hand in his, bent and kissed it. "I'm honored to kiss the hand of the sushi chef who made my grandfather retract his chauvinistic comments."

Marley just laughed, moved closer to the table, picked up one of the small plates provided for the guests and started filling it.

"Hallelujah, now move aside, sushi lover coming through."

They then all sat down together and devoured the treat Bonita Faye had so lovingly made for them. Marley knew Bonita Faye was proud that she'd defended her grandmother's honor. As for her, she had been rewarded for coming home to check on her grandmother with the best sushi in the state of Florida.

CHAPTER FOURTEEN

WHAT A NIGHT! Sebastian couldn't believe his luck. He'd thought Marley was going to drive to the festival this evening with Eula Mae in tow. However, she'd called and told him Eula Mae would be coming to her performance with Bonita Faye, Akira and Daichi. She'd intimated that it was a double date. He chalked it up to wishful thinking on her part due to her matchmaking obsession. He was just grateful he was going to have his girl to himself tonight.

He pulled up to her curb in his pickup promptly at seven thirty as she'd suggested. He grabbed the fresh bouquet of red roses from off the front seat and got out. He didn't care one wit about nosy neighbors spotting him stepping under the portico of Marley's house looking like a suitor. From what he was hearing from "concerned" friends and family, people had suspected he and Marley had a thing going on for some time now. Had Marley heard? Yes, more than likely. But, as long as she was having fun with their clandestine meetings and stolen kisses at every opportunity, he was willing to play his part. However, not for too long. In his opinion, marriage was the ultimate goal. Marriage and sisters and brothers for Bastian. Starting with Chrissie, whom he adored and wanted to give a good home along with Marley.

He rang the bell and waited impatiently. He glanced down at his polished black cowboy boots. He was wearing black jeans with those boots, a pristine white cotton long-sleeved Western-style shirt and a black bolo tie. Where did he get his sartorial splendor? From his best friend, Miguel. This was considered dressing up on a Saturday night when they were two young men trying to capture the attention of the ladies. He was half Afro-Cuban on his father's side and Catalan on his mother's Spanish side of the family, yet he'd picked up this habit. It worked for him.

He was smiling and shaking his head at his weirdness when Marley pulled the door open, a big grin on her face. His breath caught. From her feet, which were encased in sexy black high-heeled sandals, to her braids, she exuded confidence and excitement. It looked good on her. She was wearing a sleeveless red dress that accentuated her…well, everything. The bodice nicely outlined her bosom, the waist accented her midsection and the skirt flounced outward, so her bottom was nicely camouflaged, which was perfect because he didn't want other guys staring at it, anyway. But her legs, gosh. She tended to hide the scars on her right leg, but if only she knew what a distraction those legs were to the opposite sex.

The hem of her dress fell just above her well-shaped knees, and the length and muscular yet feminine lines of her legs were perfectly mesmerizing.

"Come in," she said. The inviting look in her eyes was already doing things to him. Which was another reason he was getting tired of pretending they were still only friends. He had to speak with her about giving up the ruse. He was ready for marriage.

He stepped inside with the roses thrust behind him.

Once he was inside, Marley was careful to shut the door before she wrapped her arms around him and kissed him. She must have wondered why he wasn't wrapping his arms around her. But they enjoyed that kiss. He felt it deep, deep in his heart. Her kisses always affected him like that.

"Mmm," she murmured when they parted. She glanced down. "What are you doing with your hands behind your back? I knew there was something peculiar about that kiss."

He presented her with the roses, which still had dew on their petals from the florist shop's cooler. Her golden brown eyes lit up and she flashed her white teeth, her full red lips widening in the prettiest grin. God, she was beautiful.

"Thank you!" She inhaled the fragrance of the roses and pressed the bouquet to her chest. He worried she'd stick herself on the thorns.

"Don't impale yourself, sweetheart," he said.

But she wasn't listening because she'd already turned away, walking swiftly toward the kitchen where, he assumed, she'd find a vase and put the flowers in water.

On his own in the foyer, he strode into the living room, where he noticed she had propped her guitar in its case against the wall.

He picked it up by its strap and put it on his shoulder.

In a couple of minutes, she had returned to the living room. She walked up to him and briefly kissed his mouth. "Thank you," she said again. "They're beautiful."

"No, you're beautiful," he disavowed. "They pale in comparison to your beauty."

She gazed at him, misty-eyed. Then she spontaneously kissed his cheek and said, "I've got a surprise for you tonight and don't ask me what it is because I might chicken out and you won't get it. Now, no questions because I might start crying and I can't sing when I've been crying."

He laughed as he pulled the door open, then gestured for her to precede him. "Liar. You could sing, no matter what. The show must go on. You could sing through a hurricane."

"Let's not get crazy," she exclaimed. They hurried out to the waiting pickup and into what promised to be an eventful night.

"LADIES AND GENTLEMEN, one of the organizers of this event, our own hometown girl, Marley Syminette!"

Marley's vision was a bit obscured by the bright lights, but from the sound of the applause there were thousands of festivalgoers in the audience.

Father Rodriguez, in his clerical best—white collar and all—was serving as master of ceremonies. He insisted on contributing every year. Some proceeds, after all, went to the day care center at the church. She could tell he was thoroughly enjoying himself from the enthusiasm with which he approached his role tonight.

Marley walked up to the microphone strumming a melodic tune on her guitar as she always did. She behaved as if she was already in the middle of a song and only stopped strumming when she addressed her audience. "Good evening, everybody. I hope you're enjoying yourselves so far this year."

More applause, this time even louder. Shouts rose from the crowd. "You're looking good, Marley!"

"Red's your color!"

"Sing the song you sang at our wedding!" She recognized Sandy Fuentes's voice right away. *No, Sandy, there will be no Selena songs tonight, even though I love her, too.*

She strummed the guitar some more, then launched into the opening notes of "Redemption Song" by Bob Marley, her mom's favorite.

"This is a song written by the man I was named after. You all know him. I got kidded about it enough in school."

Laughter from the crowd.

She played the intro, the tune familiar and nostalgic to so many people who loved Bob Marley. Then she opened her mouth and began to sing, "Old pirates yes they rob I. Sold I to the merchant ships…"

Emotion gave her tone a deep, soulful vibrato. She'd sung this often in the past but never the same way twice. She was mindful of what the song was about, the suffering of people who still clung to hope for a brighter future. Tonight, the song held more meaning for her since she held out so much hope for a bright future for her and Sebastian. So each word hung in the air as if it had a life of its own. The audience went silent and for the next few minutes she was transported to that place a good song could take her, to a paradise where for as long as the song lasted you had no troubles at all and everything was light and love. That's what Bob Marley's songs did for her.

The audience showed their appreciation by applauding, yelling indistinguishable words of praise, or derision, she couldn't be sure, and in many cases, by raising their cell phones in the air with the screens lit up.

She did make out one voice in the crowd— her mother's—shouting, "That was beautiful, baby!"

After her mother's outburst, the crowd moaned "Aw…" as one. So much for performing in front of your friends and neighbors. She laughed and then said, "I'll always be her baby, no matter how old I get."

Laughter from the audience. She waited for it to die down a bit and then said, "My next song is an original I wrote for someone special. It's called 'He Said His Heart Belongs to Me.'"

She played the beginning, which was a lilting melody with a soulful downbeat. By the time she got to the hook, she hoped she would be able to contain her tears.

"You and I had a history long before I fell out of an oak tree. For years we danced around each other. Seemingly just friends.

*Afraid to upset the status quo. I fell deeper
and deeper in love with you. Did you know?*

"*Did you know you broke my heart when
you got married? I buried my feelings deep.
You destroyed all the dreams I carried. Turning my future from bright to bleak.*

"*My heart has always been full of love
for you. But you never found out. You never
knew. And I couldn't make you see. It was
better to be with you than without you. Now
you say your heart belongs to me?*

"*You trembled when you said it. Because
you weren't sure I felt the same. I won't take
the blame.*

"*All I can say is, it's about time I get to hold
you. It's about time I felt your kiss. It's about
time I told you you're secretly my bliss.*"

Her voice took on an angry quality during
the chorus. She was feeling all of the pain
and frustration of being in love with someone
who didn't even notice. In spite of that tinge
of righteous anger, though, the song had an
upbeat quality to it that she believed the audience was enjoying because when she went
into the refrain, "It's about time I get to hold
you…" they were singing with her.

Squint as she might, she was unable to find

the one face in the crowd she wanted to see at this moment. He had to know she was singing about them.

SEBASTIAN WAS STANDING at the front of the stage with Miguel and Kaye Johnson. He was frozen in shock, yet elated all at once. His face split into a rictus of a grin so wide he knew his cheeks were going to be sore tomorrow. So, that was the surprise she'd promised him. He wanted to shout, "That's the woman I love up there!" But he didn't want to embarrass her. He was also mortified that he'd broken her heart when he'd married Darla. She sounded mad at him. If he'd only known... No, no use thinking about what-ifs. The fact was, this was his and Marley's time. It wasn't odd for one person to fall in love before the other. He'd loved Marley for as long as he could remember, but as a little sister. He'd fallen in love with her after Darla left. One night, when they'd been sitting up with Bastian because he had a fever and they were both too worried about him to leave his side, Sebastian had looked over at her sweet face and realized he adored her. And not like a brother. He adored her with every fiber of his being. He wanted to hold her. He wanted to protect her. He wanted to spend the rest of his life with her. However, there was the whole stigma of Marley being like a sister to him.

Their mothers were best friends, like sisters themselves. How would they take it if he'd wanted to date Marley? In recent years his mother and hers along with Eula Mae had started throwing hints around that he and Marley ought to be a couple. However, back then Marley, to be fair to him, hadn't given him any indication she wanted more from him than friendship.

Plus, there was the fact that he'd failed at one marriage already. Marley was vulnerable. What if his revealing he loved her caused her yet more hurt and disillusionment with men? That one guy she'd dated had done a number on her self-esteem for a while, but she'd fought and gotten it back.

So, he'd felt stuck. Stuck in limbo. But in a pleasant limbo because like she'd said in that song a minute ago, it was better to be with her, no matter the circumstances, than to be without her. Now, though, if she let him try, he would make sure that her heart was never broken again.

He saw her wipe away a few tears, but then, trouper that she was, she said, "No more sad songs. Let's end this with something that'll get you dancing! 'One' by U2, the version with Mary J. Blige."

She hummed deep in her throat, a bottom growl that reminded Sebastian of the delta blues. Then she began to sing, "Is it getting better. Or do you feel the same?"

By the time she got to the chorus, the audience was dancing. Marley's version of the song was soulful, but it was also a rock anthem. He didn't know how she did it. She had only her guitar, no band, yet she commanded the stage because her voice itself was the greatest instrument up there. She had everyone smiling and waving their lighted cell phones in the air. By the time she finished, she was sweating, and her voice was as growly as ever. He'd heard her sing many times over the years, and he was one of her biggest fans. But tonight, there was a different quality to her performance. She'd left everything on that stage. Maybe he'd felt there was magic in the air because she'd taken the bull by the horns and announced that she loved him to the world. Her new song made that perfectly clear. There was no doubt friends and family who were here had gotten the message. She had rocked.

Now he knew why people followed musical artists around the world, just wanting to be near them. He would follow her anywhere.

WHEN MARLEY GOT off the stage, which the largest pavilion in the park was doubling as tonight, she went round back where there were fewer festivalgoers. She took her time coming down from the high that performing was for her. She felt good about the set, and the people hanging around the back confirmed it by offering congratulations and praise. She thanked them and kept walking, her guitar in its case again and the strap thrown across her right shoulder.

The first friend she encountered when she got around to the front of the pavilion was Zenia Thomas. Zenia went up to her and grabbed her by the arms. "Girl, what are you doing teaching kiddies when you've got a voice like that? That original song was beautiful, just beautiful. Who's the lucky guy?"

Marley breathed a sigh of relief that Zenia had never met Sebastian. She, therefore, didn't answer the other woman's question. Zenia didn't give her time to reply, anyway, she was so bent on getting out what she wanted to say. Zenia was in A&R mode as she gazed up at her intensely. "When are you going to let me represent you? You're better than a lot of professionals opening at arenas, let alone small venues like this. Can't I reason with you, once and for all?"

Marley smiled patiently at Zenia. "I have everything I want right here in Port Domingo."

Zenia gave a disgusted huff, let go of Marley and put her hands on her hips. "If everybody I tried to recruit was like you, I'd starve to death. Happy people. Lord, save us!" But she was laughing toward the end and gave Marley a quick hug before she departed, probably to scope out another musical act. There were two other pavilions in the park where musicians were warming up to start their sets.

"Thanks for coming, Zenia," Marley called.

Zenia chuckled. "I love you, girl. I just don't understand you."

Marley turned and kept walking. There was nothing left to be said. To her, her life was nearly perfect. Sebastian loved her. The only thing that would make her even happier would be if Mrs. O'Neal phoned and said the adoption of Chrissie had come through.

Her mind didn't have time to go off traveling on that train of thought, though, because Sebastian was coming toward her, smiling widely, with his arms already open wide.

She leaned the guitar in its case against one of the pavilion's outer supports. An instant later, she was engulfed in his arms, her nose pressed to his chest.

They started talking at the same time:

"I wasn't sure how you'd react..." she began.

"I loved it," he said.

He laughed and kissed her forehead. "You go first. But I have to quickly warn you that family and friends are waiting to leap on you as soon as you turn the corner. Now, what were you going to say?"

She relaxed in his arms. "The night you told me you loved me, I started writing that song. I've been working on it ever since. I finished it about a week ago, but I was going to play it for you in private. But, tonight as I was dressing I decided it was time to sing it. Sorry I sounded so angry."

He hugged her tighter. "Never be sorry for expressing your truth. I'm a big boy, I can take it. I'm sorry for inadvertently hurting you when I married Darla."

"Don't apologize for that. You loved Darla. Part of me just wanted your happiness. The other was dying inside because it wasn't me you were marrying."

"I get that," he said softly in her ear. "On my wedding day, you cried more than my own mother. I thought you were expressing your happiness for me."

"I was," she maintained. "Happy for you. Sad for me."

He bent and kissed her gently on the mouth. For a moment, she forgot about how difficult it had been for them to get to this moment. They were here, and that was enough.

When they parted, he gazed into her eyes. "The secret's out. There will be no stopping our mothers and Eula Mae from planning our wedding. To which I say, the sooner the better. How do you feel about that?"

She laughed. "I agree. But I think we should have a talk with Bastian before we get engaged. He's already trying to adapt to having his mom back in his life. We should sit down with him and explain the situation. He knows me as just Marley, a mainstay in his life. But when we marry, I'll be living with him. His dad's wife. He's never had a woman living in his house before."

"Valid points," Sebastian agreed. "We tell him first. Then you and I will have a wedding this town will never forget."

"Oh?" she said coyly, planting a kiss on his clean-shaven chin. "I can't wait."

Then they were kissing again, this time more lingeringly.

After all, they had a lot of years to make up for.

They didn't come up for air until someone loudly cleared her throat behind them. Marley's keen ears recognized that particular sound. She'd been hearing it ever since she was old enough to do something that displeased her grandmother.

She and Sebastian abruptly parted, and if she was reading his expression right, he was about to burst into laughter. She gave him a warning look. This wasn't the time for hilarity. She was trying her best to keep a straight face herself, though, because tiny Eula Mae was approaching them with her umbrella—

she never went to outdoor events without it—drawn like a sword. From the stern expression on her face, she meant business.

"How is it this has been going on under my nose and I knew nothing about it?" Eula Mae demanded.

Marley briefly glanced around them. Where was the rest of their friends and family? Sebastian had said they were all waiting to pounce on her and Sebastian out front.

Sebastian still had his arms around her. "Eula Mae," he said, "or should I call you Grandmother? We were going to let you know when we informed everyone else. We just wanted a little time to ourselves before doing it. You understand."

Eula Mae harrumphed. "Do you think I was born yesterday? Of course I understand. It's just that I always pick up clues better than everyone else and you two got this one by me. I must be getting old."

Sebastian went and put his other arm around her and the three of them began walking around the pavilion toward the spot where he'd presumably left the others. "You, getting old? You're the sharpest person in this town. You almost caught us that day in the kitchen. Remember?"

Eula Mae brightened. "I knew there was something going on. If I'd shown up just a minute earlier, I bet I would've caught you in a cinch like I did just now." Marley smiled. Her grandmother was competitive to the bone. She was obviously happy for her and Sebastian. It just bothered her that she hadn't figured out they had a secret before everyone else found out.

Marley was so caught up in what was finally transpiring, the big reveal that they were a couple, that she almost forgot her guitar. "Wait, my guitar!" she exclaimed and turned back around to grab it. Then, the three of them went to join the rest of their friends and family.

Sebastian had been right. All of their loved ones were gathered—and having a lively discussion, too. Miguel, holding Kaye Johnson's hand, was the first to see them approaching.

"Here they are," he announced, grinning. He went to greet them, pulling Kaye with him. He released Kaye's hand long enough to give Sebastian a manly hug, and to kiss Marley's cheek. "You two are sly," he accused them. "Very sly. But I knew it. Just like everybody here. You couldn't fool us."

The "everybody" Miguel had referred to was their family: Marley's parents; her sister with her date, Marcus Allen, a fireman from Pensacola; Sebastian's parents and Augustin, who looked flummoxed, or maybe just peeved. She could never tell with Augustin. Their friends included Sandy and Diego Fuentes, and Bonita Faye, who had tears in her eyes, bless her. Eula Mae walked over to Akira and Daichi. Akira smiled warmly while Daichi wagged a finger at them as though she and Sebastian were kids who'd been caught being naughty. They were all dear to her. The expressions on their faces were a mixture of surprise and pleasure at hearing the news. She doubted if anyone would admit to being surprised, though.

She walked up to her parents and they hugged her in tandem. Tandi stepped in to make it a group hug. Tandi whispered while they were all hugging, "I read too many romance novels, huh?"

Marley laughed. "You can never read too many romance novels."

"And I'll inherit Eula Mae," Tandi proposed brightly. "I can move into your place. Think she'd be okay with that?"

"She'll complain at first, like she did with me, but she'll love having you nearby."

Tandi kissed her cheek. "I'm happy for you, sis."

Her mother said, "We're all happy. Izzy, your grandmother and I have been praying for this day. When's the wedding?"

Marley glanced in Sebastian's direction. He was surrounded by his parents and brother, too, probably listening to a very similar speech from Auntie Isabella.

She hugged her family tighter and said, "There's plenty of time for that. Let's just enjoy the moment. I wish Torin were here to celebrate with us. I love you guys!"

"Oh, we love you, too, honey," her dad said. She couldn't believe what she was seeing: her dad had tears in his eyes. She glanced at her mom and Tandi. By silent agreement the three of them decided to pretend they hadn't noticed his departure from the norm.

SEBASTIAN TOOK THE opportunity to pull Akira and Daichi aside after he'd been able to extricate himself from his mother's arms. "I'm so glad you could come tonight. First of all, I wanted to ask after your health, Daichi."

Daichi smiled and said, "I've been very fortunate. My T cells are working overtime."

"What Grandfather means is he's fortunate to have an abundance of immune cells, called T cells, which can help him survive longer than we anticipated," Akira explained, excitedly.

Sebastian couldn't have been happier. He spontaneously hugged Daichi, then hugged Akira. After they'd parted, he said, "That's great news. I'm officially inviting you to our wedding."

"We wouldn't miss it," Daichi said, smiling widely.

"Even if I've decided that we are definitely not selling the fishery?" Sebastian asked, wincing slightly in anticipation of a disappointed look from Daichi.

But Daichi just laughed. "Honestly, Sebastian, we've witnessed how invested you are in the fishery and Port Domingo. We didn't believe you would sell. But, we are not disappointed. We discovered a beautiful town and have made friends that we will keep for a lifetime. No matter how long that life will be."

Sebastian gave a sigh of relief. "I'm so pleased you understand. And you are always welcome here. We admire you as much as you've grown to admire our way of life."

Akira laughed softly. "And like most of the town has probably told you, I sensed you and Marley had something special the moment I saw you two together the night of the party at your place."

"You, too?" Sebastian laughed.

"It was so obvious you couldn't keep your eyes off her," Akira answered. He glanced in Bonita Faye's direction. "I totally get that."

CHAPTER FIFTEEN

THE NEXT DAY Marley paid dearly for singing Sebastian's song. She was manning the information booth at the festival, wearing a sleeveless T-shirt and her favorite jeans with summer sandals. Most people simply wanted to pick up a printed flier with information about the festival in it. However, one well-meaning acquaintance after another stopped by the information booth to tell her they'd known all along that she and Sebastian were meant to be together.

Most notably, Mrs. Gayle Brown, the former landlord of Chrissie's mom, Aisha. Marley hadn't spoken with Mrs. Brown since Aisha's funeral. Mrs. Brown suffered from a nervous condition and kept to herself quite a lot.

So when she stopped by the booth on Sunday morning shortly after the day had started at eleven, Marley was surprised to see her.

"Mrs. Brown, I'm so glad you're out and about," she exclaimed, smiling.

Gayle Brown, in her mid-sixties, was short and stout with pale skin the color of mocha. Her medium-length curly hair had been red in her younger days and was now silver. Her eyes were a curious shade of green. Not emerald or like grass but yellowish green. Marley had never seen eyes that shade before.

Today, Mrs. Brown was wearing white knee-length shorts, white lattice lace sandals and a dashiki that would have made Eula Mae jealous, it was so colorful.

She seemed delighted to run into Marley, too. "Marley," she enthused. "I heard about you and Sebastian and all I can say is, I knew it! I can remember when you broke your leg and you started back to school after it had healed. You were such a brave little thing. You insisted on walking to school like the other kids. This was when I lived nearer to the elementary school. You would walk to school by yourself and I'd see Sebastian following you at a distance, keeping an eye on you. He was such a conscientious boy. There was something special between you two even then. It might have been my imagination, thinking how protective he appeared, but now that you two are together, I don't believe it was."

"Really?" Marley asked wonderingly. She loved hearing old stories from her childhood from the perspective of those who'd watched her grow up. That was a bonus of living in a small town. Older folks knew you from way back when. "Thanks for telling me about that, Mrs. Brown." Then, she leaned closer and whispered, "By the way, you're looking sharp in your dashiki."

Mrs. Brown giggled and preened. "Oh, I'm loosening up a little. My doctor put me on a new medication for my nerves, and let me tell you, I haven't felt this good in years. I've got more energy, my spirits are up. I've been cleaning my house like a whirlwind." She paused suddenly as if she'd just remembered something. "Oh, yeah. You were friends with Aisha James, weren't you?"

Marley was glad there had been a lull in the number of people stopping by the booth for information because this conversation was getting interesting. "Yes, ma'am," she said softly. Remembering Aisha made her want to tear up.

Mrs. Brown said with a conspiratorial tone in her voice, "I was cleaning the room she used to live in yesterday and found a diary underneath a loose floorboard in the closet. It had Aisha's name on it. I was spooked, child. So spooked I shut it as soon as I saw her name. I felt like I had to get it out of my house as soon as possible."

She reached into her huge shoulder bag and pulled out the aforementioned diary. "That child didn't have any relatives that I'm aware of."

"She has a daughter in foster care," Marley reminded her. "Remember, she gave birth to her while she was living in your house."

"Yes, I remember, but how old could the child be now? Four or five? And I have no idea where she is."

"As a matter of fact, I know exactly where she is," Marley said. "I'm her kindergarten teacher and she's living with foster parents, right here in Port Domingo."

It was understandable that Mrs. Brown hadn't known where Chrissie had ended up after Aisha had died. Marley still felt a bit annoyed with the lady, though, as she thrust the diary at her. Some people were so superstitious. It wasn't as if Aisha's ghost was attached to it and would run amok in her house if she didn't get rid of the diary as soon as possible. Although, she reminded herself as she took the diary, it was kind of Mrs. Brown to come looking for someone to give the diary to instead of burning it.

Once the book was in her hand, she smiled at Mrs. Brown and said, "Don't worry, I'll make sure that this gets into the proper hands."

"I'm sure you will, honey," Mrs. Brown said, and then reached over and grabbed one of the fliers off the table. "Now, let me see what kind of trouble I can get into."

Marley laughed shortly. "Enjoy yourself!"

She watched Mrs. Brown walk away, then looked down at the tan leather-bound diary with a lion's head embossed on its front cover. *Aisha, you would be so proud of Chrissie*, she thought. *She's a wonderful little girl, and I love her.*

She wanted to open the diary then and there and start reading it. There was no question in her mind about privacy issues. Aisha was gone. What if there was some information in it that would help Chrissie in the fu-

ture? She was going to be Chrissie's mother.
If anyone should be privy to what was in the
diary, it was her. However, she wasn't going
to be relieved by a volunteer for at least four
more hours. She bent and stowed the diary
in her shoulder bag that was in a box beneath
the table and returned to welcoming festivalgoers.

ON HIS WAY out of town, Miguel dropped by
Sebastian's house to say goodbye. They were
standing outside on the circular drive a little after eleven that morning, Miguel leaning
against the Porsche.

"You're actually going to drive back to
Chicago?" Sebastian joked. "You could leave
this car with me and take a flight back. I'd
take good care of it."

Miguel laughed. "I thought of leaving it
with Diego, but I knew he'd be breaking
speed limits around here and Sandy would
have a fit. So I decided the couple of days
that it'll take me to drive home to Chicago
will give me a chance to think."

"About what?" Sebastian asked, though he
had already guessed. Miguel was in a conun-
drum. On the one hand, he loved the power

and prestige his job gained him in Chicago. On the other, he'd enjoyed his stay in his hometown more than he'd probably admit to. Especially seeing Kaye Johnson again. Kaye of the beauteous face, fabulous singing voice and awesome cooking skills.

He patiently waited to see if his guess was right. In the meantime, Miguel's face was scrunched up as if thinking was squeezing his brain between the bones of his skull. That meant he didn't want to confess how he was really feeling.

Miguel sighed heavily. "Okay, the thing is, I like to tease you about living in a Podunk town, but I love this town, too. I love the people in it and the lifestyle. Those emotions are at odds with what my life's like right now, though. Dude, I have to make a choice. Do I want wealth and a whole lot of hassles trying to hang on to it? Or do I want true love, a bucolic setting and yeah, I said it, peace? We were poor when I was a kid, but because of the hard work of my parents, my brothers and sisters and I are doing well. Mami and Papi don't have to worry about anything anymore."

Sebastian laughed. "Do you mean there's

a real possibility that my best friend and I might one day live in the same town?"

Miguel laughed, too. "I'm thinking hard on it."

"Then I guess Kaye is willing to take you back."

Miguel laughed even harder. "Man, don't go there. But since you already have, yes, she's forgiven me for breaking her heart in high school when my head got out of proportion and I dumped her for that cheerleader. I regret that to this day. Kaye says I was an idiot, but maybe I've grown out of my idiocy. She's some woman. Smart, beautiful and she loves her family and this town. I always knew she would settle here after her stay in France. She says France was nice, but there's no place like home."

"Kaye's great," Sebastian agreed. "Just don't hurt her again because there'd be hell to pay. She's got a whole group of girlfriends who'd track you down and put a hurting on you. Among them is Marley."

Miguel feigned a tremble. "I've been forewarned," he said, his hand on the car's door handle. He opened the door and Sebastian stepped away.

Getting inside and closing the door, Miguel said, "I assume I'm the best man in your wedding."

"You assume correctly," Sebastian told him.

Miguel turned the key in the ignition. "Get married in the fall or winter, please. I'd love to get out of Chicago then."

"If you can wait that long to see Kaye again," Sebastian said knowingly.

"There's that," Miguel admitted. "So long, buddy."

"Safe trip," Sebastian called as Miguel eased the sports car down the drive.

MARLEY LEFT THE festival grounds as soon as someone came to relieve her. She went straight home, changed into a comfortable shorts set, popped a can of Diet Coke open and curled up on the sofa in the living room. A mix of old-school rhythm and blues played in the background with various artists like Aretha Franklin, Stevie Wonder, Gladys Knight, Otis Redding and Al Green. Their music always made Marley relax. Why she felt she needed to be in a relaxed frame of mind to read Aisha's diary, she had no idea. The feeling persisted nonetheless.

She opened the diary and read the first entry:

Property of Aisha James.
January 1, 2016.
To Baby: I don't know whether you're a boy or a girl yet. I told the doctor I wanted to be surprised.

The next entry was dated January 7, 2016:

I love you. That's the most important part of this diary. I love you. You are in my tummy now and I'm huge with you. I'm all of eighteen. I've been on my own since the state of Florida told me I was responsible for myself. Your grandparents were drug addicts. I never touch the stuff because of that. They unfortunately overdosed when I was seven. I was a foster kid from then on. I've been in so many foster homes, you can't imagine. Or maybe by the time you read this, you'll be able to imagine it. I'm sure you'll be smart enough. I'm not a dummy, and your father was smart, too.

About your dad. He was a good guy. He didn't abandon us or anything. Fact is, he doesn't even know you exist. It was like this: we dated in high school and we fell in love. But when I got pregnant with you, I just took off because I didn't want to be a hindrance to him. He was primed to go to college on a football scholarship. After that, I'm sure the world will be his. He's that good. Me? I'm nobody and I come from nobody. But the thing is: you ARE somebody, Baby. You can be whatever you want to be. I'm going to work hard to make sure your world is safe and you grow up to be whatever you want to be. I'm not afraid of hard work. I'm going to make sure we have a good life, you and I.

The next entry was dated January 23, 2016. Apparently Aisha wasn't a daily writer.

I recently moved to a small town called Port Domingo. I thought it was time I stopped drifting around from place to place and settled down to build you a nest. People are friendly enough here. The lady I'm renting a room from is kind of peculiar. Real nervous. So I'm hiding this under a floorboard in the closet just in case she snoops in my room when I'm out. My business is mine to keep.

As it happens, Port Domingo is not far from where your dad lives in Pensacola. Subconsciously maybe I chose Port Domingo because it's not far from Pensacola. I'm not good at analyzing myself. I should just tell you his name: it's Khalid Jackson. He comes from a good family. His mom, Miss Belle, was always kind to me even though I'm sure she thought I was no good for her son since I didn't come with a pedigree. Family means something to people. I don't care if they're rich or poor, they want to hear where you came from. What was I going to say: All I know is that my parents were druggies who offed themselves? That's not something that's going to go over big when you're meeting someone's mom.

Maybe my leaving like I did was the wrong thing to do. I took a risk keep-

ing you to myself. Maybe he would've been happy you were on the way. I've had so much rejection in my life I just couldn't take it if he believed I was trying to trap him or something. I've seen it happen with other high school athletes. But I would never get pregnant just to keep a man. I'd rather live on my own for the rest of my life than do something like that.

I want you to know that even though I didn't plan you, you are wanted. I've loved you ever since I found out I was having you. And another thing: Khalid and I weren't just two horny teenagers. We were in love. You were born of love, Baby. You are loved. I never knew if I was loved or not. But you can be sure of one thing: you are loved!

After Marley read the last entry, she had to put the diary down next to her on the sofa and grab several tissues from the box on the coffee table. Aisha had been so alone in the world. What's more she'd felt unworthy of being loved and cared for. It was fear of rejection that had sent her out into the world, pregnant and destitute.

Marley wiped the tears away and blew her nose. She was crying not just out of sympathy for Aisha. She was crying because she was now armed with information about Chrissie's father. Information that might lead to Chrissie being united with him.

I hate to sound selfish, but what about me?

She didn't believe in coincidences. Mrs. Brown's appearance at the festival today was a sign that she'd been entrusted to do the right thing with Aisha's diary. She was very tempted to do the wrong thing, though. She wanted to be Chrissie's mother. She couldn't imagine her life without that little girl in it. Bastian loved Chrissie. Sebastian was fond of her, too. Eula Mae doted on her. They would all be heartbroken that Chrissie very well might never be a part of the family.

She was actually entertaining the notion of simply forgetting she'd ever gotten hold of Aisha's diary. Mrs. Brown had said she'd closed it as soon as she'd recognized Aisha's name, so she wasn't aware of what was in it. It was Marley's secret. She could burn it, reduce it to ashes. No one would ever know.

She got up and turned the music off. Rhythm and blues wasn't going to help her solve this problem. She needed to talk to someone she trusted. Someone who would be on her side no matter what, but who would also strongly suggest she do the right thing. There was no getting around it: keeping information from the state when they were searching for any relation who might want to give Chrissie a home was the wrong thing to do. She simply wasn't ready to give her up yet. She needed time. Why was life so unfair?!

Her doorbell rang. It was around four in the afternoon. She thought of ignoring it. She didn't want to see anyone right now. She would be very bad company.

She kept pacing the room and ignoring the doorbell. Whoever was out there was being very persistent. Soon knocking commenced and she angrily marched to the door and swung it open without peeking outside.

Sebastian stood on her doorstep in well-worn jeans, a white, short-sleeved polo shirt and black athletic shoes. His breathing was labored as if he'd been running, and his forehead was beaded with sweat. She hadn't seen him this stressed and disheveled before. Something was wrong.

He stepped inside and started looking around her place. "Bastian isn't here, is he?"

Dumbfounded, Marley went to him and grabbed him by both upper arms to make him meet her eyes. "Isn't he with Darla and Miss Evie for the weekend?"

"They have no idea what happened to him," he answered. He couldn't keep still. She could tell how frustrated he was by how tense his muscles felt. "Darla said he was playing in the backyard. The fenced backyard. She said she took her eyes off him for a few minutes. Not long at all. But when she looked again, he was gone. The police are there right now, but I've been driving around town going to places he's familiar with. Seeing if I can find him."

She let go of Sebastian and began pacing herself. She was relieved to hear Darla wasn't missing, too. That meant it wasn't a kidnap situation they were dealing with.

She thought hard.

"There are woods behind Miss Evie's house. I overheard her say once that she fenced in the yard to keep animals or criminals out. Is there some way Bastian could have gotten over the fence? Because I know she didn't put a gate in the fence. That would be like inviting burglars into your backyard."

Sebastian shook his head in the negative. "That fence is at least five feet high. Bastian couldn't manage that."

Marley, however, knew the resourcefulness of five-year-olds. "Maybe, maybe not," she said doubtfully. "If he couldn't get over it, he may have found a way through it if there was a kid-sized break in it. We need to search the woods behind her house."

She hurried to her bedroom to grab her shoulder bag and put on jeans and a pair of sturdy shoes. She was following Sebastian to his pickup shortly afterward.

"Why didn't you call me as soon as you heard he was missing?" she asked worriedly.

"Forgive me, but I was in panic mode," Sebastian said as he climbed behind the wheel.

Marley buckled up. "We're going to find him. If he climbed that fence, there was something on the other side that enticed him to do it."

"You mean if someone didn't take him," Sebastian said. "There are bad people in the world, Marley."

Marley firmly shook her head. "No, he either climbed the fence, or he walked around to the front of the house when no one was watching and left that way."

She said a silent prayer for Bastian's safety. *Oh, please don't let anything happen to him! Watch over him!*

A few minutes ago, she was considering breaking the law to hang on to one child, and now she was praying for another's safety.

About five minutes later, they pulled up to Miss Evie's house. Two police cruisers were parked in front. Miss Evie and Darla and other family members were standing on the lawn talking to the officers. Neighbors who'd heard what had happened were lingering in their yards observing it all.

Marley and Sebastian jogged over to join the family and the police officers. "Any sign of Bastian yet?" Sebastian asked, directing his question to the chief.

Marley noticed Darla was in her mother's arms, crying silently. Miss Evie, the backbone of the family, was trying her best to soothe her. But she seemed in need of soothing, too.

Chief of Police David Harrison broke off from the others and pulled her and Sebastian aside. The chief was in his midthirties, tall and husky, with curly brown hair and brown eyes. He'd been a marine before coming back to his hometown and becoming a police officer, eventually being elected chief of police.

"We did find a piece of material stuck on the fence. And on the other side the grass was pressed down in one spot. So we figure Bastian climbed over the fence and dropped down. I've got two men searching the woods in that spot right now, and volunteers are being recruited as we speak. We'll comb those woods until we find him, Sebastian."

"Thanks, Dave," Sebastian said, "but I can't wait on the volunteers. I've got to do something now, or I'll go crazy."

He looked at Marley and she gave him a nod in the affirmative. Then they made their way into the backyard and climbed the fence. Both were physically fit and Marley's leg gave her no trouble. Once they were on the ground on the other side, they began searching the area. The grass was about a foot high. Marley worried about snakes. Bastian had never encountered a snake before. He would be terrified.

"Bastian!" Sebastian yelled. "Bastian, if you can hear me, answer me!"

To the north of them, Marley spotted one of the deputies the chief had mentioned sending into the woods to search for Bastian. He was about thirty yards away and it appeared he was walking in circles. She gazed around for the other deputy and spotted him farther north. Were they searching in the same direction?

She pointed that out to Sebastian, and said, "Looks like they've got that direction covered. Let's go in another direction."

"Makes sense," Sebastian agreed. They waded their way through the high grass, fallen leaves and thick pine trees. She and Sebastian had hiked in these woods, but they hadn't brought Bastian along, which seemed neglectful in a sense now. If he'd been familiar with the woods, he might not be feeling lost right now. She tossed those negative thoughts away. Bastian was a brave boy. Not much scared him. He was somewhere safe, and she wasn't going to believe otherwise.

They had been walking for a good twenty minutes before they spied the Benson farm ahead. The Benson family maintained one of the few fully functioning farms in the area. They raised cows, chickens and goats, and grew crops, as well.

As they neared the cow pasture that they would have to cross to get to the farmhouse, they spotted Claude Benson walking out of the barn in his usual work attire of jeans, work boots and a long-sleeved shirt. Summer, winter, it didn't matter, he always wore a long-sleeved shirt. He was a tall, spare African American in his late fifties. He had a scruffy salt-and-pepper beard and he was bald. He saw them coming, started grinning and waved them forward.

She and Sebastian picked up their pace. Soon, they were in the farmyard. Claude strode up to them, still grinning. "You wouldn't be looking for a little fellow about yay high, would you?" He indicated with his right hand just how high off the ground that fellow he was referring to might be.

Marley had never seen Sebastian look so relieved. She was about to faint with relief, herself.

"Bastian's here!" Sebastian cried.

Claude nodded and pointed to the barn. "I just found him cuddled up with one of the puppies. I was headed to the house now to phone you. Follow me."

Marley assumed he didn't carry a cell phone on, or near, his person like so many others did. There were still some holdouts who weren't fond of the devices.

The three of them went into the barn. Sebastian rushed forward and grabbed Bastian up in his arms, hugging him to his chest. "Boy, why did you climb your grandma's fence and come over here?"

Bastian appeared confused by the question. Claude cleared his throat and said, "I think I can answer that one."

He pointed to the puppy Bastian had been holding when they'd walked into the barn. The puppy, who appeared to be about six weeks old, was frolicking with his siblings. Their mother was nearby keeping a watchful eye over them. "That dog's a troublemaker. Knew it two weeks after he was born. While his brother and sisters were busy at their mother's teats, he'd be trying to find something to get into. He's a wanderer by nature. I figure he wandered down to the fence you're referring to, Bastian saw him and climbed over the fence to follow the pup back here.

I'd say they're both rascals, wouldn't you?" he ended with a chuckle.

Marley had moved a few feet away to update the police. The phone at the police station rang only once before the police officer at the call desk answered. Marley told her who she was and the situation, and the woman promptly said, "Chief Harrison will be right there."

Marley relayed the message to Sebastian. Sebastian, with Bastian still in his arms, Marley and Claude walked out of the barn to await the chief's arrival.

While they were waiting, Claude said, "You know, I haven't found a home yet for the troublemaker. You wouldn't be interested, would you?"

Bastian's eyes lit up with excitement. "Oh, please, Daddy, please, can we take him home? I love him already."

Sebastian met his son's eyes but didn't answer at once. Marley knew he was a softy when it came to animals. And they didn't have a pet. Bastian was old enough to start being responsible for one.

Sebastian glanced in her direction as if asking for her opinion. She gave Bastian a stern look. "A puppy's a big responsibility, Bastian. Are you willing to feed him, take him for walks and clean up after him?"

"Are you, son?" Sebastian asked Bastian.

Bastian put his hand over his heart, which he did whenever he was about to swear to something. "I promise I'll take care of him."

Sebastian smiled at Claude. "Then, yes, we'd be honored to take the troublemaker off your hands."

He then asked Bastian, "What do you say to Mr. Benson?"

Bastian beamed at Claude. "Thank you, Mr. Benson. Thank you so much!"

Claude smiled. "My pleasure, Bastian. I'm sure you two are going to be great friends."

Chief Harrison pulled up in his patrol car and got out to assess the situation. He shook Claude's hand. "You're the hero of the hour."

Claude shrugged off the accolades. "I just walked into my barn and found the two rascals playing like old buddies."

Before they took their leave, Sebastian and Claude set up a time during which he and Bastian could come pick up the puppy.

Bastian looked a little sad that he wasn't going to be able to take the puppy home today.

CHAPTER SIXTEEN

SEBASTIAN, MARLEY AND Bastian were given a ride to Miss Evie's house in the back of Chief Harrison's patrol car. When they got there, Darla, her mother and brothers and sisters, along with neighbors, were still conversing on the lawn. Chief Harrison had left one patrol car there with two officers when he'd driven over to the Bensons' farm.

Cheers arose as Sebastian, Bastian and Marley got out of the patrol car. Everyone rushed over to welcome Bastian back. Sebastian watched as Darla burst into fresh tears at the sight of Bastian.

She was the first to get to him and pull him into her arms. "Bastian, Bastian, you're okay. I was so worried about you." She repeatedly kissed his cheeks. Then, she patted him down as though she were looking for injuries. "You're not hurt anywhere, are you?"

Bastian, who Sebastian was sure was thinking about his next meal by now, was surprisingly patient with his mom. It was past his dinnertime. Plus, his jaunt through the woods had probably expended quite a bit of energy.

"I'm okay, Mommy," he told her, smiling. "Need to go to the bathroom."

Darla glanced nervously up at Sebastian. "Is it okay with you if I take him?" she asked, her tone pleading.

Sebastian wondered why she even had to ask. Then it occurred to him: Darla probably thought he was furious with her for letting Bastian slip off.

"Of course," he said mildly. "I'd like to speak with you when you get back, though."

Darla, still anxious, gently took Bastian's hand and the two of them went into the house.

Sebastian turned to Miss Evie, who appeared much less stressed now. "He was at the Bensons' farm," he told her.

She smiled warmly. "One of the officers updated us. It must have been not long after Marley phoned the police station and told them you had found him safe and sound."

"Oh, good," Sebastian said, pleased that he didn't have to fill them in. "Excuse me."

He walked over to the chief and shook his hand. "Thanks for everything, Dave."

The chief smiled. "I'm just glad Bastian's safe. I don't have any kids of my own, but I imagine you were about to burst a blood vessel."

Sebastian laughed. "That about describes it." Dave was perhaps a year older than he was. They'd been on the football team in high school and Dave had been a tough, reliable teammate and he'd grown into a tough, reliable peace officer.

"Well, we'll be going. I have enough information for my report. No need to come down to the police station."

"All right, good. Thanks again," Sebastian responded.

The chief turned to leave and gestured to his men that they were heading out. They promptly followed his lead and in a matter of seconds, the two police cruisers were leaving Miss Evie's property and slowly driving through the neighborhood.

The small crowd dispersed, relatives going into Miss Evie's house and neighbors returning to their own homes.

Miss Evie said to Sebastian, "I'm sure Bastian's hungry. I'm going to go whip him up something good to eat. Won't you join us? Or are you going to take him home?"

She peered up at him sadly, as if dreading his answer.

"No, thank you, Miss Evie. We won't come inside. And, what's wrong with you and Darla?" Sebastian asked, frustrated. "I'm not some judgmental idiot who doesn't know you can lose track of a small child through no fault of your own. I'm a dad, remember? Bastian is a handful. He's put me through hell trying to keep up with him over the years. No, Miss Evie, I'm not taking him home. I'm going to enjoy the rest of my weekend and you and Darla can watch Bastian like a hawk."

Miss Evie started laughing so hard her other grown children who'd gone into the house came back outside to see what was up.

She waved them off and called, "Don't worry, I haven't lost my mind…yet!"

After they had turned around and gone back into the house, Miss Evie said to Sebastian, "I heard you say you wanted to talk with Darla. I'll send her out and feed Bastian while you two talk."

She then smiled at Marley. "Marley, thank you for being here for us today. You're a sweetheart."

Marley returned her smile and said, "I love him, too."

Miss Evie went to the house. Sebastian and Marley walked over and leaned against the pickup at the curb while they waited for Darla to come outside. He wanted to pull Marley into his arms, but thought better of it. They hadn't had the chance to have a talk with Bastian about their being a couple yet, and public displays of affection might confuse him. Sebastian didn't care about the adults' reaction, though.

His gaze appreciatively took her in. Her skin was glowing. He refused to think of it as perspiration. His goddess glowed; she didn't sweat. He recalled when they were climbing the fence in Miss Evie's backyard to go after Bastian. In that instant, he'd wanted to ask her to stay behind. He didn't want her to risk getting hurt climbing over the fence. But since he knew she would have taken his head off if he'd even suggested it, he'd kept quiet. He was fond of his head. She'd gotten over that fence with no problem at all. He had been a fool to ever doubt her strength and resilience. He should have told her he loved her years ago. There had been no need to protect her.

That was the thing about Marley. She wasn't daunted by challenges. Had never been. Even as a six-year-old, she'd been tough. After she'd healed enough to walk on her own and return to school, her parents had wanted to drive her every day. She'd thrown a fit. She'd realized that special treatment from her parents would've made her stand out, and standing out in elementary school was a sure way of getting picked on by some kids. She'd still been teased because of her limp, but she'd handled it with finesse.

She was standing next to him now, pretending she hadn't noticed he was staring at her. She observed her nails, the backs of her hands, gazed a moment at the sky, which was cloudy. They were going to get some rain this evening. She was probably hoping that the rain would hold off until after 6:00 p.m. because the festivalgoers should be gone, or leaving, by then.

Five minutes or so had passed since they'd spoken. They were content with taking a breather from conversation. Only the sound of Darla coming out of the house and onto the front porch prompted her to speak.

"I'll sit in the car with the air on and the radio playing," she said, and opened her hand for him to relinquish his keys.

"There's nothing I have to say to her that you can't hear," he assured her.

She smiled. "I know, but I prefer to give you your privacy."

He handed her his keys.

She got into the car and started the engine. She let the windows down to allow the hot air to escape, then let them back up after turning on the air-conditioning.

Darla was standing before him by then with a curious but not-so-frightened expression on her face. Her mother must have relayed what he'd said earlier about not taking Bastian back home with him.

He'd forgotten how tiny Darla was. He towered over her. Her eyes were puffy from a crying bout. He had a tendency to want to protect anyone who seemed downtrodden. Was she the one to feel sorry for in this situation? Had life beaten her down to the extent that she had put all her hopes in this working out? He didn't like being put in the position of the bad guy, but apparently, that's who he was. He had no reason to trust her. She'd burned him once. Was he supposed to let down his guard and potentially get seared again?

"Momma said Bastian's staying," were Darla's first words. "Thank you for that."

He had been prepared to read her the riot act. To ask her what she thought being a parent entailed. Did she have some fairy-tale notion of parenting? Reading bedtime stories and going to the amusement park, watching Disney movies together? Well, she'd had a rude awakening today. Did he need to hammer home her need to wake up and embrace the reality of parenthood?

He sighed. He was mentally and physically tired and wanted to leave with Marley. Bastian was fine and he didn't believe either Darla or Miss Evie were going to trust him out of their sight anytime soon.

So he smiled at Darla and said, "Welcome to parenthood. Today was just a taste of what you're in for."

Darla actually laughed, probably out of relief that he wasn't going to lay into her with accusations and the fact that she'd been looking after Bastian a mere day before he'd gone off on an adventure.

"Are you serious?" she asked after she'd gotten control of herself, peering up at him with skepticism evident in her eyes. "I was ready to fall on my knees and beg you for another chance."

Sebastian put his hand on the passenger side door. Marley was behind the wheel of the pickup and, by all appearances, going to drive them home.

"No begging required. I'll see you tomorrow afternoon when I get home from work." They'd agreed that Bastian would stay with her instead of going to his parents' house. His parents usually took care of Bastian after school when he was working and during the summer break.

"Okay," Darla said. She stepped back while he opened the pickup and got inside. "See you then."

Inside the truck, Marley was bobbing her head to the radio with her eyes closed and her hands on the steering wheel. She had already buckled her seat belt and put on her glasses. She turned and looked at him when he got in.

"We're rolling?" she asked.

"Yes, your house?" he asked. Who knew? She might want to go to his house. They were young and the evening was just beginning.

"Sounds good. There's something I need to talk to you about and the visual aid is at my place."

"'Visual aid'?" he wondered aloud.

"You'll see," she said cryptically.

She put the pickup in gear, and smoothly pulled away from the curb. He put his seat belt on and settled in. Searching for a lost child was exhausting.

After a minute or so he summoned up the energy to chuckle and say, "Why don't you go ahead and admit that when it comes to wearing your glasses, you're too vain to wear them all day like most people do."

She wrinkled her nose at him as if his statement had smelled offensive. "You can't make a blanket statement like that. I don't believe most people wear their glasses 24/7. I only wear them when I need to see distances clearly. That's why I only use them when I'm driving."

"And watching TV, or when you're at the movies," he corrected her.

She laughed. "Maybe I am a little vain."

"Have no fear," he said, giving her a smoldering once-over. "You're hot with or without them."

"Of course I am," she returned confidently.

MARLEY PARKED THE truck in the driveway of her Southern-style bungalow. She'd bought the house for a great price after her grandfather had passed away to be closer to Eula Mae. She and her dad, along with some help from Sebastian and Torin, had refurbished it. The previous owners had been an elderly couple who'd been friends with her grandparents for many years. They'd decided to move into an assisted living facility together because of their declining health.

She and Sebastian sat for a minute or two before reaching for their door handles. His stomach growled. They looked at one another and chuckled. "I haven't eaten since breakfast," he said.

"Then come inside and let me feed you," she replied. She stepped out onto the driveway. She waited for him to get out and then locked the pickup.

She met him as he was making his way to the portico and gave him back his keys.

She loved her house, which was painted a pale blue and trimmed in white. It was cheerful and the perfect style and fit for a town so close to the ocean. *That pitiful portico, though*, she thought, once again regretting the house didn't have a porch in the front. The portico had two columns joined by a tiny roof that was attached to the house. The area was only about six feet in length and about three feet wide. It was too small, in her opinion, to call a porch. On a good day it might protect you from the rain. Eula Mae had a front porch, and it was grand and sweeping. Big enough for an old-fashioned swing on a chain and several chairs in which she could sit and watch the world go by. You couldn't get a straight-backed chair on Marley's portico. She much preferred the back of her house, where she had a small garden and her dad had built a plank walkway that connected her house to her grandmother's.

She unlocked the door of the house and they went inside. The interior was cool, open concept, airy and inviting. She locked the door behind them and tossed her shoulder bag onto the sofa on her way to the kitchen. Sebastian had other ideas, though. He grabbed her about the waist and pulled her into his arms. "I'm not so hungry that you need to hurry into the kitchen and start rustling up some vittles," he joked.

She smiled and said, "I see you've been watching Westerns with Uncle Emiliano again."

"What can I say? He's addicted." He lowered his head and kissed her mouth ever so gently. "The only thing I'm addicted to is you."

She relaxed and kissed him, letting her negative thoughts drift away for a few moments. She was in no hurry to have the conversation she needed to have with him. That's why she'd jumped at the chance to prepare him something to eat. Avoidance wasn't healthy but right now she was willing to be its slave. How would he react when she told him what she had been thinking of doing?

They held each other and kissed until they'd comforted each other after the stress of the afternoon.

She pulled away from him and continued walking to the kitchen. "We shouldn't do too much more of that until we're married."

She went to the sink and began washing

her hands. Sebastian came up beside her and washed his hands, too. Finished, they grabbed paper towels from the dispenser on the countertop and dried their hands, facing one another.

"I have to tell you, we should get married soon. I'm not getting any younger, and if you want the prime real estate you should jump on it while it's for sale."

She guffawed and tossed her paper towel into the trash receptacle under the sink. He did the same. "You're not even thirty-five yet. The real estate should be prime for some time to come."

She went to the refrigerator and opened it. "I've got chicken breasts marinating. Think I'll grill them on the stove and we can have a salad, too."

"I'll grill the chicken," Sebastian volunteered.

"Good, then I'll make the salad," Marley decided. "Excuse my tiny kitchen but since there's only one sink, I should make the salad first. Can't risk getting raw chicken juices on the greens."

"Your mom taught you well," Sebastian said. "Plus, I'll have the luxury of watching you use your grilling skills that you've honed over the years, Grill Master," she teased. She wasn't about to let him live down that bragging he'd done at the get-together he'd hosted in honor of Akira and Daichi a few weeks back.

Sebastian laughed. "I'll have you know, Daichi told me my barbecued ribs are among the best he's ever had."

"What a sweet guy," Marley countered as she bent and started taking fresh greens and assorted other vegetables from the refrigerator's crisper. "Lying like that so he wouldn't hurt your feelings."

Her arms piled with vegetables, she returned to the counter and set them down. "Speaking of Daichi, have you heard what his next project is going to be? Eula Mae mentioned it to me this morning before my parents picked her up for church."

Sebastian was sitting on one of the high stools at the midsized island. He'd grabbed a bottle of water from the refrigerator. After taking a sip, he said, "Yes, Akira told me.

After noting the crowds at the festival, Daichi said that what Port Domingo needed was more accommodations. Akira said his grandfather was complaining that their quiet inn had become crowded. Daichi liked it with fewer humans under foot. Now, every room is filled, and someone is beating him to Julie's delicious blueberry muffins every morning."

Marley couldn't help laughing. "You know, when I first noticed Akira and Daichi sitting on the porch of the inn every morning on my walk to school, I never thought I'd become so fond of them."

"Yeah, I like them a lot, too," Sebastian agreed.

Marley was at the sink rinsing two kinds of lettuce to go into the salad. Then she tore the lettuce into pieces and put it in the salad spinner.

She was hypersensitive to his nearness. He might appear to be having a rather ordinary conversation with her right now. But his gaze swept lazily over her, making her blush. She had to get used to being watched this way, she supposed.

He must have noticed her discomfort because he smiled at her and got up from the island. "Think I'll go phone Miss Evie just to remind them that I'm an overprotective father. Got to keep them on their toes."

"Good idea," she said with a short laugh. She was happy to have a few minutes alone to gather her thoughts. She still didn't know how she was going to tell about him Aisha's diary and admit that she wished she'd never seen it without breaking down. Her spirit was crushed at the possibility that she might lose the chance to become Chrissie's mother.

CHAPTER SEVENTEEN

BY THE TIME they'd finished dinner and washed up the dishes, Sebastian was certain whatever it was Marley wanted to talk with him about must be supremely important. He loved her. But when you love someone, you take the bad with the good. His sweetie was a procrastinator when there was something she would prefer to just sweep under the rug and forget about. She eventually got around to facing the problem head-on. However, she would drag her feet until he wanted to pick her up, hold her upside down and shake her like kids do their piggy banks when they're trying to get every cent out of it.

They were sitting close on the sofa in the living room now, his arm about her shoulders, with the lights turned low and some vacuous comedy on TV. She was laughing at unfunny jokes. That told him how desperately she was avoiding talking to him. Marley adored a good comedy. She complained vociferously about bad ones.

He cleared his throat. "Just go on and say it. Don't worry about how you're going to say it. Just let it out."

She jerked as if he'd startled her back to the here and now. Maybe she'd been happy to exist inside a sitcom for a few minutes. But he had to know what was making her so weird.

She stared into his eyes for a good solid minute before saying, "I think it's best if you read the first two pages of this." She reached for a leather-bound book sitting on the coffee table. He'd noticed it earlier and wondered if it were a journal. It had no title, just a lion embossed on its tan-colored leather cover.

He took the book from her and straightened up. He held it in both hands for a moment, feeling the texture of the soft leather. Then he opened it to the first page. He read silently. Property of Aisha James, it read. At the sight of Aisha James's name his heartbeat sped up. Chrissie's mother had left behind a diary? And Marley had it?

He continued to read. The revelations inside blew him away. Poor Aisha, running away because she felt no one could really love her. And refusing to allow herself to be accused of latching onto a football star just for a taste of the good life. But look how her choice had affected Chrissie. Chrissie was in foster care, just like her mother had been. Aisha could have possibly broken that cycle if she'd just had more faith in herself.

He glanced over at Marley after reading who Chrissie's father was. "I recognize that name. He's a local boy from Pensacola. He was drafted by the Miami Dolphins less than two years ago, if I'm not mistaken."

He paused. "How did you come into possession of this?"

Marley had moved over on the sofa, giving him a little extra room when he'd started reading. Now she was sitting with one leg underneath her. "Today at the festival, Mrs. Gayle Brown, the woman Aisha rented a room from, walked up to the booth and told me she'd found it cleaning her house. I was shocked when she offered it to me. She said the diary spooked her and she wanted it out of her property.

"I didn't expect to learn the identity of Chrissie's father. I read it because I figured

I should since, hopefully, I was going to be Chrissie's parent soon."

She stopped talking. Her face crumpled and, suddenly, she was weeping. "Now, all my hopes are gone. I can't pretend I didn't read what's in Aisha's diary. She loved Chrissie's father and I'm sure she'd want Chrissie to be with him if at all possible. So, I thought I'd show it to you before handing it over to Mrs. O'Neal."

By the time she'd finished her last sentence, Sebastian had put the diary back on the coffee table and pulled her into his arms. She was sobbing on his shoulder, her body shaking and, he was sure, her heart breaking. He knew how much Chrissie meant to her. He was amazed she'd been able to keep this in all afternoon while they'd been searching for Bastian. All through dinner. His girl was a world-class procrastinator. And he loved her completely.

He would not utter platitudes about how she would be able to handle this, that the diary had been put into her hands for a reason. She didn't want to hear that.

What he said was, "All hope of being

Chrissie's mom isn't gone. Maybe Khalid Jackson doesn't want to be a father."

"Even if he doesn't," was her reply, "Aisha mentioned his mother. Belle was her name, I think. Believe me, no woman in her right mind can look at Chrissie and not want her as a granddaughter. She's a great kid."

Sebastian couldn't very well deny that. Chrissie was the sweetest little girl he'd ever known. Not counting Marley. His son was besotted with her. Bastian had once told him that he was going to marry Chrissie. He smiled when he recalled how Bastian had said he was willing to share his newly returned mother with Chrissie so that she wouldn't be motherless.

So he just held Marley and let her cry. He felt a little like crying himself. All he'd ever wanted was for Marley to be happy. He knew how much she was looking forward to taking care of Chrissie and ensuring she had a loving family. He had been anticipating the four of them as a family, too. He, Marley, Bastian and Chrissie. Then, one day adding a few others to the Contreras family.

He bent and kissed her forehead. "We don't know what's going to come of this. We just have to wait and see what Mrs. O'Neal will do with the information. Be strong. We'll get through this."

Marley still quietly wept. But her body had stopped trembling. "Am I cursed?" she moaned softly, gazing up at him with sad eyes.

Sebastian looked her straight in the eyes. "Of course you're not cursed. Why would you even say such a thing?"

"I broke my leg at six. I had to fight to hang on to a modicum of dignity when my limp made me a target of bullies. But I came out on top and I'm okay. Then, I fell in love with you, but you fell in love with someone else. It was torture being around you, but I couldn't leave. And I've considered leaving town so many times. Then I figured even if I never got married, at least I could be a mom. Now, that's going to fall through. I adore you, Sebastian, and you're probably thinking I shouldn't take this so hard because you and I love each other. We're still young enough to have several children if we want them. But my heart was set on being Chrissie's mother. I can't simply snap back from that. I may never stop regretting what might have been."

She took a deep breath, her eyes still locked with his. "I thought about burning the diary. I did. I was going to commit a crime to hang on to her. But I came to my senses when we were out looking for Bastian. What right do I have to deny Chrissie the opportunity to know her father? None at all!"

He took both her hands in his and squeezed them. "You're strong. You're going to get through this. And even if Chrissie goes to another family, that doesn't mean we have to lose touch with her. She may still be in our lives. I was looking forward to being her dad, too, babe."

Her face brightened when he said that. She smiled through her tears. "You're a great dad."

They sat back on the sofa, hugging one another, and were silent. He fervently wished he could take away her pain.

After a while, he quietly said, "How can you think you're cursed? You were born into the best family imaginable. You're loved by so many people besides your family. To your students you're a rock star. Girl, you're blessed, not cursed."

She was watching him with such tenderness, all he wanted to do at that moment was to kiss her and keep on kissing her until the end of time. "Don't worry," she told him. "I don't really believe that. I was just feeling sorry for myself."

"Well, stop it," he told her firmly. "You are loved and cherished. No matter what happens in your life you've got an army of people behind you who support you. Never forget that."

"I won't," she promised with a smile that lit up her eyes and warmed his heart.

SEBASTIAN MADE CERTAIN he checked the weather forecast before allowing the company's fishermen to go to sea. His captains were trained to get regular reports while at sea, and if there was a troublesome storm brewing in the Gulf of Mexico, its movement was painstakingly tracked. Therefore, when the weather service predicted there was a storm that had the potential to turn into a hurricane in the next forty-eight hours, he told his fishermen they could spend one day fishing in that area, not two. They were to head back home within twenty-four hours with whatever they had caught.

Augustin was the captain assigned to the

boat, but he had phoned Sebastian and said he had a stomach virus. So Sebastian was now here at the docks when it was still dark out because they were usually more successful catching blue crabs when the sun wasn't up yet. Five crew members were already there ready to go.

They were a motley crew. Sue Lyon, the only woman; Bill Estefan; Gary Watson; Liam McDonald; and Kurt Falco. All of them were outfitted in sturdy pants, long-sleeved shirts, work boots with rubber soles and the customary slickers to help keep them as dry as possible. Their clothing was made to be water resistant, but also protect them from the Florida sun when it did come out.

Since Sebastian was piloting the boat, he wore clothing he would normally wear when prepared to get his hands dirty. Jeans, a thick, long-sleeved cotton shirt and his steel-toed work boots with rubber soles. Because he wasn't scheduled to do any wet work, he wasn't wearing a slicker; there were extras on the boat should the need arise.

The wind was brisk this morning, and the air smelled of the sea. As he climbed on-board the boat, he got slapped on the back by the crew, which was how they welcomed him. It had been a while since he'd captained their boat. He'd taken the Nishimuras out on a trawler. This boat was a crabber. In Florida, blue crab season was all year-round, but there were larger amounts of the crustaceans during the warm months. The rule was you had to throw back any females with eggs during blue crab season. The employees were trained to spot them and toss them back into the ocean.

"Hey, Sebastian, congratulations on your engagement to Miss Syminette. You've got yourself a good woman," Sue Lyon jokingly said after patting him on the back.

"We're not engaged yet," Sebastian said with a laugh. "And you can call her Marley."

Sue, a tall, large woman in her midthirties with short curly blond hair and twinkling blue eyes, shook her head. "I have two kids who were in her class and that's the only name she goes by in my house! Heck, once you're married, we might start calling *you* Mr. Syminette."

Everyone laughed at that, including Sebastian. But after their humor died down, he was all business. "Okay, let's get this tub moving so we can get home as soon as possible. Storm's brewing and I don't want to be out there when it hits."

The crew hustled. They didn't want to be out there, either. All of them had a healthy respect for the sea. Soon, they were under way.

It was still dark when they got to the designated area where they would be crabbing today. The crew worked in harmony baiting the huge wire traps and lowering them into the water.

The blue crabs were in such profusion in that spot that they were pulling up the traps full of the crustaceans almost as fast as they could lower them.

While the crew was on deck, Sebastian was on the bridge, which was above the deck. From the bridge he had an unobstructed view of the entire vessel. He saw that the crew was having a good day, and welcomed it. However, there was a funny smell he kept detecting from the engine.

The engine was at rest now. They'd dropped anchor perhaps five hours ago. Yet he distinctly smelled the scent of burnt rubber somewhere in the vicinity of the engine. He'd had an affinity for engines since he was a teen. He listened closely to them. He recognized their normal sounds and rhythms. He even prided himself on knowing how an engine smelled when it was operating at its full capacity. There was more to the smell of this engine than motor oil or the scent that friction caused. It was the job of the captain of a boat to check his boat's engines on a regular basis. A good captain could diagnose a problem and should be able to fix it, as well.

He wondered if Augustin's dissatisfaction with his life was causing him to be less vigilant about his duties on the job. Like him, Augustin had been taught by their father how to perform every task on a boat from cleaning it to repairing it. Lack of engine maintenance was the leading cause of fishers getting stranded, or worse. He had to have a serious talk with his baby brother.

Because he didn't want any mishaps on his watch, Sebastian went to have a look at the boat's engine.

The engine in this boat was diesel and built to last. With proper maintenance, it would last a lifetime, but parts wore out. Sebastian found the problem right away. A belt was worn thin. It should have been replaced a while ago.

He only hoped that Augustin kept replacement parts onboard.

He went to check the storage area adjacent to the engine room.

The place wasn't exactly organized, with items in a jumbled mess, but, yes, he found a replacement belt. Luckily this engine was made so that replacing parts wasn't a hassle.

It didn't take long to put in the new belt. After that task was done, he went back to the bridge and listened to the weather report.

The weather service was warning that winds reaching seventy-five miles per hour could be expected in the Gulf of Mexico. The report gave the coordinates. The location wasn't far from where he and the crew were now. So, he made the call to conclude the day's outing a good two hours before they were supposed to head back to port.

He hurried down the few steps to the deck and yelled in the direction of the working crew, "Pull all traps. Storm's getting worse. We're heading home now."

The crew acted immediately. Sebastian went back to the bridge and fired up the engines. There was a slight lingering scent of burning rubber but he knew the smell would dissipate soon. The good thing was, the engines sounded like they should sound. He and his crew wouldn't be stuck on the ocean in the middle of hurricane-strength winds and waves so huge they could capsize them.

When they got back to Port Domingo, he saw Marley waiting for him at the docks. It was drizzling and she was standing under the awning of the boathouse dressed entirely in white. He'd texted her as soon as he'd gotten a signal and told her he was coming home. In the future he wanted all his returns from the sea to be like this. Marley waiting with a smile like sunshine on her face. If he could have that, he'd die a happy man. He was certain, at this moment, that he could never sell the business to the Nishimuras. This was the life he loved.

Marley had been busy all day, despite being on summer vacation. She was one of the lucky teachers who didn't have to work during the break from school. She knew coworkers who had a regular summer job lined up each year. She helped out in her family's restaurant during the summer months when they needed her. However, this year Tandi, who was now manager, hadn't phoned her to ask for help.

She didn't need the extra income from a summer job because her mother provided all of her children with quarterly dividends from the restaurant. She'd begun doing that with each of them on their eighteenth birthdays. She'd requested only one thing from them in exchange for her generosity: they had to use the money wisely.

Marley simply banked her income and thought of it as her rainy-day money. Or the cushion she could fall back on if she should ever lose her teaching job. At any rate, the money gave her the luxury of freedom to choose how she spent her summer vacation. Practically every year she would choose a room in her house that needed refreshing and spent her time looking for ideas on HGTV, visiting secondhand furniture stores that carried quality items, if a bit worn. Her dad had taught her how to bring a piece of furniture back to life. The key was starting with a well-made piece of furniture constructed from quality wood. Most of the wood pieces in her house, from her coffee table in the living room, to the dining table and the headboard of her queen-size bed, had been restored by her.

This summer, she was working on the sunroom, which opened onto the back patio. French doors led to the patio from the sunroom. The paint was beginning to chip on them and she was going to repaint them.

Today, she was busy sanding the old paint off with an electric sander, her eyes covered by clear goggles and her nose and the bottom of her face masked so she wouldn't breathe in any paint chips. She couldn't be certain whoever had painted them years ago had been careful not to use lead paint.

When she finished one side of the door, she took a break and went inside to get something to drink. She'd left her cell phone on the kitchen counter and it dinged while she was pouring herself some lemonade. The text was from Sebastian.

Almost home, it read. Should be docking in maybe half an hour. Want to have that talk with Bastian tonight? We could steam some crabs at my place.

Sure, she texted back. Meet you there at six?

Great. That'll give me time to shower. Love you!

Love you, she replied and put the cell phone back on the counter. She drank the lemonade down, set the glass in the sink and went to take a shower.

A few minutes later, she was toweling dry when her phone once again started chiming. She wrapped a large bath towel around her and hurried to the kitchen.

This time it was her caseworker, Barbara O'Neal, with whom she'd had a lengthy conversation this morning. She remembered Mrs. O'Neal got to the office early so she had phoned her shortly after 9:00 a.m. Marley had told her everything she'd learned about Chrissie's father. Mrs. O'Neal had been pleased with the news. She'd insisted on coming to pick up the diary and promised to try to locate Chrissie's father as soon as possible.

Marley now nervously stared at the phone ringing on the kitchen counter. Could the caseworker have gotten results already? And did Marley want to hear what they were? She reached for the phone, deciding she'd done enough procrastinating to last her a lifetime. Better to find out what Mrs. O'Neal had to say than be a coward and avoid speaking with her.

"Hello, Mrs. O'Neal."

"Marley," Mrs. O'Neal said with breathless excitement. "I found them. Well, his mother, Belle Jackson. She remembers Aisha. She says she wondered what happened to her. Her son lives in Miami, but she's going to contact him as soon as possible. She believes he'll be happy about being a father. She says he was really torn up when Aisha disappeared."

Mrs. O'Neal took a deep breath. "Also, she wants to meet you, the woman who loved her granddaughter enough to want to be her mother. And also who'd loved her enough to do the right thing when Chrissie had the chance to know her family."

Mrs. O'Neal paused, as if waiting for Marley to say something. Marley had hoped she'd have more time to get used to losing Chrissie. After a few weeks of Mrs. O'Neal searching for Chrissie's relatives, she would have been reconciled to having been only Chrissie's friend and teacher. But this was so sudden, it felt like someone was lopping off her right arm without anesthesia.

Weakly, she collapsed to the kitchen floor and sat with her back against the cabinetry of the island, her legs splayed out before her.

"Um, can I call you back?" she managed to say to Mrs. O'Neal. She hung up the phone.

She glanced up at the clock on the wall. It was 5:10 p.m. Sebastian would be pulling into port in about fifteen minutes. She had to see him.

So, ten minutes later, she was standing on the dock under the awning of the boathouse. Sebastian's boat was slowly coming into port. It had started to rain five minutes after she'd gotten there. She was wearing a flowy, white summer dress that reached her ankles and a pair of white tennis shoes. Her hair was held back by a white headband. She hadn't felt like putting on makeup, so she hadn't. But she was clean from the shower, and when she spotted the boat, she plastered on the best smile she could muster. She hoped it hid how heartbroken she was. How disappointed that her wish that absolutely nothing would come of her providing Mrs. O'Neal with information about Chrissie's birth father had not come true. Somehow she'd thought that her willingness to do the right thing would turn out in her favor, and she would still be granted the privilege of becoming Chrissie's mother. But that hadn't happened. Instead, this was the end. There was no more hope. Chrissie was going to her blood relatives.

It's for the best, she tried to tell herself. *Somehow, no matter how hard I wish things had turned out my way, this is for the best. I shouldn't be so selfish, wishing I could hold on to a child who never belonged to me in the first place. I have to cope with this loss. But right now I just want to scream in frustration!*

She could imagine Father Rodriguez saying something about not being given more than you can handle. Yet, this felt like something beyond her ability to withstand.

She must have been lost in her thoughts because it seemed that only a minute ago, she'd been watching Sebastian's boat approaching the docks, and now he was standing in front of her wearing a yellow rain slicker and grinning as if she were the most beautiful sight in the world.

He set a white five-gallon bucket down on the wooden planks of the dock and walked up to her, his smile gone and his face was a mask of concern. "What's wrong?" he asked.

She tried to speak but the words were caught in her throat. She made a concerted effort, but it was as if her brain had become disconnected and no synapses were firing. Then, everything went black.

"SOUNDS LIKE SHE had a psychogenic blackout," Dr. Vincent Hall diagnosed in the emergency room. This was after Sebastian had told him that Marley had been under a lot of stress lately.

"It can happen to the best of us," Dr. Hall, who had silver hair and a kind demeanor, continued. He smiled warmly at both of them. "There's no chance she could be pregnant, is there?"

"None at all," Marley assured him. She looked almost like herself to Sebastian now. Earlier, as she was crumpled in the seat of his pickup, buckled up for safety, her skin had been kind of grayish and her lips were pale. Usually her lips were a healthy rosy-brown tone that suited her brown skin so well. He'd never been so worried about her in his life. Not since the day she'd fallen out of the oak tree.

The doctor cleared his throat and took Marley's pulse. "Yes, that's much better."

He then checked her eyes using a penlight, even though he'd done that earlier, too.

"Hmm," he murmured. "You have lovely eyes, young lady."

This comment got a short laugh out of Marley. "Thanks, Doctor. Am I going to live?"

"Probably well into your nineties," he said with a chuckle of his own. "But, whatever caused you to black out should be dealt with. That's how stress is. Get it behind you. Confront it, go through it. Pray about it. Talk about it with your young man. Whatever it takes. But don't let it build up because, and I'm sure you've heard this before, stress kills."

"Yes, I've heard that before," Marley said.

"She's going to deal with it," Sebastian promised the doctor. "Because I'm not going to leave her side until she does."

This made the doctor nod wisely as if he agreed with Sebastian's determination. "Good." He patted Marley's shoulder and said, "You can go, but I suggest you go to your primary physician and get a thorough checkup soon. And don't stay alone tonight just in case it happens again. Which, I suspect it won't. But better safe than sorry." And he winked at Sebastian before taking his leave.

Alone in the examination room, Sebastian pulled Marley into his arms. "I phoned Darla while they were examining you and told her that Bastian's spending another night with her. I'm taking you to my house now because I need to take a shower. Afterward, I'll take you home and I'm spending the night."

Marley opened her mouth to protest, and he just held her tighter. "Just nod your agreement."

So she nodded and said, "Could we get something to eat? I'm starving."

He laughed shortly. "That's a good sign. I hope you don't have your heart set on eating blue crabs tonight because I left them in the bucket on the docks. Hopefully, one of the guys grabbed it and took it home with him." He hated to think of good blue crabs going to waste.

Marley sighed regretfully. "Too bad. I love blue crabs."

"I know. That's why I was bringing some home to you."

"You do know me, Sebastian Contreras."

CHAPTER EIGHTEEN

A lot has happened in three hours, Marley mused when she read the time on the clock in Sebastian's pickup: 8:30 p.m. His boat had come in at around five thirty. They were now on their way back to Port Domingo from Pensacola, where he'd taken her to the hospital. The sun had gone down, and it was still raining lightly. She and Sebastian had ridden in silence since leaving the hospital.

"Do you want to explain what happened?" he asked, his tone gentle.

Marley calmly recapped for him what Barbara O'Neal had told her about locating Khalid Jackson's mother, Belle, and Belle's desire to meet Marley. "My mind goes a bit blank after that, but I remember all I wanted to do was see you, so I went to wait for you at the docks."

He took in a deep breath and released it. "I can understand why your brain needed to check out for a little while. I never imagined Mrs. O'Neal would locate anyone that quickly."

"I should have known things would end up this way," Marley said.

She'd had time to think while she'd lain on an examining table and then been poked and prodded by Dr. Hall at the hospital. At least an hour had gone by before he'd given her his advice about not ignoring stress and sent her home.

"Several things had to happen before Aisha's diary got into my hands. Mrs. Brown's doctor changed her medication. She started feeling so well, she got a shot of energy that made her want to thoroughly clean her house. Then, when she found Aisha's diary, something spooked her and she desperately wanted to get rid of it. She thought of the festival because she suspected she would find me there. She mentioned she'd heard about you and me. In fact, the first thing out of her mouth was, *I knew it!* Several other people had come up to me with similar words that day. But, she wouldn't have heard anything about you and me getting together if I hadn't sung your song. That song got tongues to wagging."

"So, you're saying someone, or something, must have orchestrated it all," Sebastian surmised from her speech.

"Yes, I am," Marley admitted. "I should have accepted that I was going to lose Chrissie. Instead I stubbornly held on to hope when it's impossible to fight divine intervention."

"Divine intervention," Sebastian repeated as if he couldn't quite wrap his mind around the concept.

Marley couldn't blame him. She was having a hard time accepting it, too. "In my heart I feel my place in Chrissie's life was to help watch over her until she was united with her family. Me, the state, Chrissie's foster parents, the Koontzes. We all played our parts. We were her village. Now, I have to let Chrissie go and try to help her make as smooth a transition as possible from foster child to daughter and granddaughter. You do remember Aisha wrote in her diary that her parents had died of drug overdoses. She never mentioned any other relatives. I suppose that's why she'd grown up in the system. After she died, Chrissie became a foster child. But, now, the cycle's broken. Chrissie gets to be with her father."

Sebastian must have been still stuck on divine intervention because he said, "Does that help you?"

"Yes, otherwise I'll never get over losing Chrissie. This way, I'll at least have the comfort of knowing she's going to be all right now. That this was meant to be. This has made me realize I need to accept that I can't be everything to everyone. I wasn't the only one who could help. All I needed to do was know when to step aside."

Sebastian nodded his head as if agreeing with her reasoning. She was sure he simply wanted her to have peace of mind. He was always looking out for her best interests. "All right, then," he said quietly. "I can get with that. Especially if it means you're not going to scare the hell out of me anytime soon. Girl, I thought you were dying on me. Sue and a couple of the guys ran over and helped me carry you to the pickup. They were saying maybe we should call 911, but I said I could get you to the hospital faster than an ambulance. I didn't realize this pickup could move so fast. All the time, my heart was about to burst with worry over you. I saw you were breathing, but you looked like you were dead." He took a deep breath. "Don't ever do that to me again."

Marley laughed with relief. "I'll try my best not to. I'm sorry I scared you, but I'm fine now."

He glanced at her, then turned his attention back to the road. He was smiling now, too, though, so she realized that performance had been only to demonstrate how terrified he'd been then. He wasn't feeling those emotions anymore. Sometimes he could be such a ham. "You're my rock, you know," he told her. "The world tilts on its axis when you start acting un-Marley-like. I'm thrown off balance. Can't find my footing."

"I love you, too," she assured him, reaching out to squeeze his thigh, the muscles of which were rock hard. She removed her hand and laughed with him.

He reached down and momentarily squeezed her hand upon his thigh, then returned both hands to the steering wheel. "You said you were hungry. Want to phone Kaye's and ask them to prepare two take-out dinners for us?"

"Good idea," she said and immediately started tapping the numbers out on her cell phone.

"And then, maybe you ought to phone your parents," Sebastian said. "No doubt news of your fainting at the docks is going to make the grapevine before long. You don't want your mother to hear about it from someone other than you."

Marley glanced at him with admiration. That was her Sebastian. Always looking out for her.

SEBASTIAN SMILED AT Marley's reclining figure on the sofa in her living room. He got up slowly so as not to wake her, pulled the afghan off the back of the sofa and spread it over her. It had been a long night. After picking up dinner from Kaye's, he'd driven them to his house first, and they'd devoured their meals. Then he'd showered and dressed and they'd driven to her house, where they'd talked for three hours until she was talked out. She was at peace now about Chrissie, or so she seemed to be.

But he knew the pain of losing the little girl would be with her forever because when Marley loved, she loved completely. He only hoped someway, somehow, Chrissie would remain in their lives. It wasn't such a stretch to hope for that. After all, from what Marley had said, Chrissie's grandmother lived in nearby Pensacola. Surely her father, who was a professional football player, would leave his daughter in his mother's care while he pursued his career.

Sebastian bent and planted a light kiss on Marley's forehead, then moved over to the recliner. He planned to sleep in it tonight. He wasn't going to leave her alone.

He found another afghan on the back of the recliner and covered himself with it, settling into the comfortable chair with his feet up. In a matter of minutes, he was snoring softly.

The next morning when he woke, Marley was still sleeping. He consulted his watch. It was only six. Last night he'd sent around a general text to employees advising them that due to the hurricane, no boats were going out today. The storm would only cause severe thunderstorms in the vicinity of Port Domingo, but the seas were too turbulent to risk a crew's safety. His employees deserved a couple of days off from work.

He got up and stretched. A few minutes later, he walked through the kitchen to the back door, opened it and stepped out onto the covered patio. Now was as good a time as any to phone his brother to check on him. Hopefully, he'd gotten over his stomach virus.

Augustin sounded groggy when he answered. "I thought you said no boats were going out today."

"Just checking to see if you're feeling better today," Sebastian casually said.

Augustin groaned as if he were sitting up in bed. "Uh, yeah, I'm a lot better."

Sebastian knew that hedging tone. His brother was one of the worst liars. "Were you sick, or nursing a hangover yesterday?"

"What difference does it make? Either way I was not at my best. You don't want me out there when I'm not my best."

"True, but I also need to talk to you about how you've neglected to keep your boat in ship shape. The engine should have been looked at some time ago. We could have been stranded yesterday."

"Oh, you mean that belt? I was going to get around to it. It wasn't that bad."

Sebastian saw red. "I could smell the rubber burning. Augustin, your crew's lives depend on you. Haven't you learned anything over the years?"

"I've learned that my brother is uptight, and thinks he knows what's best for everyone. Why don't you just fire me and get it over with? You've been wanting to for years."

"No, what I've been wanting is for you to step up and be the man I know you can be instead of someone who thinks partying all night on Sunday is fine when you have to get up at five on Monday."

Augustin sighed. "I'm never going to be you, big brother. And now, I guess you have it all. Congrats to you and Marley. I knew she was into you. I could see it in her eyes when she looked at you. But I never would have guessed that you felt the same way about her. I figured you were too much of the perfect son to have a crush on your play-sister. Guess I was wrong."

"You're feeling bad about yourself and trying to take it out on me, but leave Marley out of this. It's not a crush. It's love. One day, if you're lucky, you'll understand what I mean."

"You got all the luck in this family," Augustin grumbled.

"As long as you keep believing that, you'll never be happy, Augustin. One more thing— you're fired. You can officially blame me for your leaving the business and not have to worry about disappointing Mom and Dad by quitting yourself. I know that's the only reason you were hanging on. Just hoping I'd have the guts to fire you. So, you got your wish."

Augustin laughed. "You finally figured me out." He sounded kind of sad when he added, "Don't expect me to come to your wedding after this."

Then he hung up.

Sebastian put his phone in the front pocket of his jean shirt and peered up at the morning sky, which was mottled with fat rain clouds. A rumble of thunder sounded in the east, where the sun had recently risen.

How was he going to tell his parents he'd just fired his brother? But life had presented him with thornier problems and he'd survived them, so he'd get through it.

He loved Augustin. However, Augustin didn't make it easy to love him. Perhaps their six-year age difference was too great a chasm to cross. Augustin was hurting, but Sebastian wasn't sure how to help him.

While he was standing on Marley's patio, Eula Mae strode out of her back door, Ellery running around her as if he was in a hurry to get outside. Eula Mae looked over at Sebastian. She did a double take, which struck Sebastian as hilarious, and removed her glasses, then put them back on.

"Good morning, Eula Mae," Sebastian said, smiling at her.

Eula Mae chuckled. "Good morning, grandson-in-law," she said pointedly.

Sebastian laughed harder. "We're not married yet."

"Might as well be," she said deadpan. "Is Marley up yet?"

"No, she's still sleeping."

"You had your coffee?"

"No, I didn't want to brew any. It'd wake her."

"Then come on over here, I've made a pot."

Sebastian began walking across the wooden walkway between Marley's house and her grandmother's that he'd helped to build two years ago. "Now, don't get any ideas, Eula Mae. I slept on the recliner in her living room last night. She'd had a shock and I didn't want to leave her alone. Plus, she said her leg was hurting her last night, so I thought she should sleep as long as possible."

He was standing in front of the tiny grandmother now. She was gazing up at him with a gentle smile on her face. She glanced up at the clouds. "Yes, we're going to get some thunderstorms. No wonder Marley's leg is bothering her. And as for you, calm down. I was young once." Then, she winked at him.

"No, seriously, Eula Mae, nothing happened," Sebastian insisted as he followed her into the house.

"I think you're protesting too much," was her sage response.

Sebastian sighed. He was not getting anywhere with this stubborn octogenarian.

CHAPTER NINETEEN

IT RAINED FOR a solid forty-eight hours, but little damage was done to Port Domingo. Meanwhile Marley concentrated on getting some things straightened out, starting with Mrs. O' Neal. That remarkably smart lady had said she'd understood why Marley had suddenly been unable to speak to her when she'd phoned with the happy news that she'd located Chrissie's relatives. The situation was a stressful one all around. Before they got off the phone, they'd set up a time for Mrs. O'Neal to bring Belle Jackson to Marley's house so they could all sit down for a nice chat. Marley was looking forward to it.

Today the weather was wonderful, and earlier, she, Sebastian and Bastian had gone to Claude Benson's farm to pick up Bastian's puppy, whom Bastian had named Chewbacca. Marley had to admit the beautiful golden retriever pup did slightly resemble the character from the movies. Sebastian quipped that he hoped the name didn't portend what the puppy was going to do to the furniture.

With Claude's advice on what a puppy needed to stay healthy, they'd made a list and gone to a pet supermarket in Pensacola and stocked up. An appointment with a veterinarian was in the near future.

Now, Marley was smiling at Sebastian and Bastian as they rolled around with the dog on the lawn. The energetic Chewbacca was wearing the humans out. Sebastian gestured for her to join them on the grass. But she shook her head. She was perfectly happy sitting on a lounge chair, legs stretched out, sipping iced tea, in her shorts and a cropped top, while wearing a huge pair of sunglasses.

After a few more minutes, Sebastian grabbed the pup up and held him under an arm and walked over to her, with Bastian following close behind.

Apparently, Sebastian had been talking to Bastian while they'd been playing on the lawn because Bastian walked up to Marley with a serious expression on his face. "Marley?" he asked. "Daddy says you want to marry him. Is that true?"

He gave his dad a suspicious look. "He's joking, right? Because *I'm* going to marry you."

Marley had to sit up and pull her sunglasses off to digest that announcement. She swung her legs off the lounge chair and tried to wipe the surprised expression off her face. This was news to her. She knew Bastian loved her. But she never guessed he had marital intentions. He'd told Sebastian he was going to marry Chrissie one day. But, she also realized that when little boys set their hearts on someone, they were serious and their feelings had to be taken into consideration. She therefore looked him straight in the eyes, and said, "I'm flattered that you want to marry me, Bastian. What woman wouldn't be? But, as you know, your father's old and someone needs to take care of him. While you're still very young and strong and have many years ahead of you. You and Chrissie. You two could have a wonderful future together. While your dad and I will be old and silver-haired."

She hoped her facial expression was believably sad.

Bastian's expression was grave as he contemplated what she'd said. He moved closer to her and took her hand in his. Then, he spontaneously threw his arms around her neck. She bent down to receive his hug. He ended with a loud smack to her cheek. "Okay, but you'll still make me oatmeal cookies? And play songs on the guitar?"

Marley gave him an equally grave nod. "Of course. We'll be living together and I could sing you to sleep every night."

He kissed her again when he heard that. Smiling now, he regarded his dad. "Okay, you can marry my Marley."

Sebastian laughed. "Thank you, son."

Sebastian handed Chewbacca to Bastian. "You two go play while I talk to Marley."

Bastian gathered Chewbacca in his arms and happily walked away with his new puppy. Sebastian pulled Marley to her feet and planted a kiss on her that told her exactly how pleased he was to have that obstacle behind him. Or so she assumed.

When they parted, she smiled up at him. "You've got to make it clear to Bastian that he can only have one wife at a time. I thought he said he was going to marry Chrissie."

Sebastian smiled. "I reminded him about

that, and he said he could marry you, then Chrissie when she grew up."

"What about him growing up? Did he think I was going to marry a five-year-old?"

"I'm not sure he'd figured that out yet," Sebastian said, laughter in his brown eyes. "Besides, he's going to be six next month."

Marley kept her own humor under control. Bastian was close by and she didn't want him to think they were laughing at his expense. She peered over at him, her heart full of love for him. "I'm so proud of him. He's his own person and isn't afraid to fight for what he wants."

Sebastian nodded, smiling in his son's direction. "We've done a good job so far."

Marley was touched that he'd included her in that statement.

Sebastian was standing with his arm draped around her shoulders. Both observed Bastian and Chewbacca gamboling on the lawn for a few minutes, then Sebastian said, "It's time we got formally engaged, don't you think?"

She stared up at him, her eyes suddenly misty. "You do?"

He knelt before her, right there on the lawn in his backyard. He reached into his shorts pocket and retrieved a beautiful diamond solitaire engagement ring in a platinum setting.

Marley's hand was trembling as he slipped the ring onto her finger. It fit perfectly.

They were gazing into one another's eyes. "It's been burning a hole in my pocket for a few days now. Marley, my love, the woman of my dreams, will you marry me and be my wife, my one and only for the rest of my life?"

Marley didn't have to think about it. She'd been waiting for this moment all her life, it seemed.

"Yes. If it were possible, I'd marry you right now!" she exclaimed and pulled him to his feet. She threw her arms around his neck and kissed him with every ounce of emotion she was feeling at that transformative moment. Because she felt as if she would never be the same. She'd reached a level of happiness unknown to her before now.

SEBASTIAN WAS ENJOYING their celebratory kiss when he felt someone tugging on the leg of his shorts. He reluctantly drew away from Marley and looked down into his son's upturned face. "Dad, what are you doing to my Marley? She can't breathe!"

He and Marley burst into giggles. "It's just a kiss, buddy."

"Well, let go of her."

Bastian took Marley by the hand and led her back over to the lounge chair and made her sit down. He stood vigil by her side, his eyes casting warning glares at Sebastian, who stayed in the same spot and smiled at his son's behavior.

"Are you okay, Marley?" Bastian asked, concerned.

Marley reclined on the chair and put her feet up. She placed the back of her hand on her head as though she might swoon. Sebastian smiled. She was such an actress. "I'm okay, baby. I just need to rest."

Bastian aimed another warning glance at his dad, obviously reminding him to behave himself, and went back to play with Chewbacca.

In Bastian's absence, Marley grinned at Sebastian. "He's so sweet."

"He's not going on the honeymoon," Sebastian said seriously. Then, he pulled a lounge chair up beside hers and stretched out. They held hands while watching Bastian play with Chewbacca.

"So," he said after a quiet moment. "When and where do you want to get married? Please say as soon as possible. Otherwise, I'm game for whatever it is you want. A quiet garden wedding, a big church to-do, maybe a destination wedding?"

She was watching him with an enigmatic smile on her face. He looked deeper into her eyes. No, he couldn't even guess what she had in that admittedly complex mind of hers.

"I always wanted to get married outdoors with a choir singing as I walked down the aisle on Daddy's arm. And after Father Rodriguez declares us husband and wife, I want the choir to sing 'As' by Stevie Wonder." Then, she started singing the song and his heart melted.

"I can get with that," he said softly and gently squeezed her hand.

She beamed at him. And Bastian chose that moment to launch himself into his father's lap, puppy and all.

Sebastian hugged his son and Chewbacca eagerly licked his face. Sebastian laughed. "Two rambunctious boys in the house now. I have no idea how I'm going to handle all the energy bouncing around these walls."

A COUPLE OF days later, Sebastian stopped by his parents' house to pick up Bastian after a long workday. His parents' house was a huge bungalow-style place with plantation shutters on the wide windows and porches in the front and back. He often thought that they'd brought a little of Cuba with them to Port Domingo. The yard was dotted with banana and mango trees among the other flowers that were native to Florida like black-eyed Susans edging the front porch and Carolina jessamine climbing the trellises on either side of the front porch. After the recent rains, the plants looked vibrant and bursting with life.

His parents were sitting on the porch when he arrived. He didn't see Bastian anywhere. He bent and kissed his mother's cheek. She smelled of honeysuckle. And her cheek was silky smooth. She peered up at him with a smile. "Buenas noches, hijo."

Sebastian smiled. The sun was going down, so he supposed it was the evening. "Buenas noches, Mama, como estas?"

"Estoy bien," she said. Then, she lapsed into English. "Your son informed me you gave Marley a ring. I suppose you were waiting for a special occasion to tell us you are engaged."

She was using her formal voice, so Sebastian knew she was slightly angry with him. His father didn't even glance in his direction, so he guessed he was upset also. His father was not confrontational. He often demurred to whatever his wife wanted to do. But he couldn't say that was because his mother had his father whipped, or if that was simply his father's personality. His mother never made unreasonable demands on his father that he knew of, so maybe their way of doing things worked for them. His father probably simply subscribed to the adage, Happy Wife, Happy Life.

Sebastian sat down in the rocking chair between his parents. "Yes, I proposed and she said yes. We were waiting to announce it at a gathering for both families. Bastian's birthday is coming up, so we thought maybe we'd do it then since everyone would be at the party."

His mother deigned to smile at him. He knew she adored Marley and had been hoping he and Marley would finally awaken to the possibility of a life together. She, Auntie

Nevaeh and Eula Mae had thrown enough hints over the years.

She took a deep breath and clapped her hands delightedly.

"I'm so happy for you, son. We both are!"

His father was smiling, too, but didn't say a word. He did look him directly in the eyes, though, and mouth, "Way to go."

Sebastian laughed softly. His parents were odd, but lovable.

"Thank you," he said. "I'm very lucky. I could have stayed silent and risked losing her, but I spoke up and won her. I still can't believe my luck."

"It's not all luck," his mother assured him. "It's mostly love. You two have always loved one another. This is a natural progression of that love. An always kind of love that transcends friendship and physical love. Sometimes young people don't realize that when two people marry—two people who truly love each other—they fall more in love with each other the longer they are together. It becomes something spiritual. That's what your father and I have."

"Si," said his father. "What your mother said."

Sebastian wanted to chuckle but held his hilarity in check. His dad didn't say much, but when he did, it meant a lot to him.

"Another thing," his mother said, her smile gone. "It's come to our attention that you fired Augustin."

Sebastian grimaced. "He asked for it."

His father nodded grimly. This time, since the subject was Augustin and the business, Sebastian supposed, his father was ready to hold forth.

His father cleared his throat. "Your mother and I could never understand why you took to the business and Augustin never did. But parents can rarely predict how a child will turn out.

"We hoped that family would mean more to him. That tradition would win out. However, your mother and I are happy to let Augustin go and discover whatever it is he wants out of life.

"Give him a good severance payment. He's earned that. And since he's a member of the family, he'll get a quarterly dividend check. We hope that'll give him a good start at whatever it is he wants to do."

Sebastian breathed a sigh of relief. He'd

figured he was in for a dressing-down by his parents for firing Augustin. But, apparently, they had noticed Augustin was dissatisfied with his life as a fisherman all along.

"Okay," he said quietly. "It'll be done as you say."

His parents smiled sadly at him. They might be willing to let Augustin go, but they were not really happy about it.

Bastian put in an appearance then and threw himself into Sebastian's arms. "Daddy!"

Sebastian kissed his son's cheek. He heard a soft bark and looked down to see Chewbacca coming out of the house, also.

The little dog gazed up at Sebastian and whined. Sebastian bent and picked him up too and was rewarded with several enthusiastic licks to his face.

"Let's go home, boys," he said. "Thank your grandparents for watching over you."

"Thanks, Abuela, Abuelo," chimed Bastian.

Woof, barked Chewbacca, and they all laughed.

CHAPTER TWENTY

IT WAS ON a Saturday morning that Mrs. O'Neal brought Belle Jackson to Marley's home. When Marley opened the door, she gasped in surprise. No one had mentioned that Chrissie would be among the visitors. But there she was smiling widely, dimples showing in those chubby cheeks, looking exceptionally cute in her summery short-pants outfit and sneakers.

Marley flung the door open, fell to one knee in her jeans, and Chrissie ran into her outstretched arms. "Miss Syminette!" Chrissie cried joyfully. "I've missed you so much!"

Tears came to Marley's eyes. "I've missed you, too, baby girl."

While she hugged Chrissie, she glanced at her other two visitors, who were both dressed in jeans and blouses appropriate for the warm weather. "Thank you," she said. "Thank you for bringing Chrissie. Please, come in."

She rose and closed the door after the two ladies were inside. While Chrissie held her right hand, Mrs. O'Neal, an attractive, stout, African American in her midfifties with a beautifully cut and layered bob and warm brown eyes, introduced her to Belle Jackson.

"Marley, this is Chrissie's grandmother. Belle, this is Marley Syminette, the wonderful woman who was instrumental in finding you and your son."

Belle, tall, fit and with auburn box braids down her back, had the same golden brown complexion as her granddaughter. Marley could see now that Chrissie had double-dimple genes. Not only had her mom, Aisha, had dimples, but her paternal grandmother sported them, also. Belle grinned, displaying her own. "Miss Syminette, I've heard nothing but good things about you. It's my pleasure to finally meet you."

"It's my pleasure to meet you, too. And please call me Marley," Marley said, hugging Chrissie to her side. Chrissie had wrapped her arms around Marley's waist and didn't seem in any hurry to let go.

Belle laughed. "I'd be happy to if you'll call me Belle."

Marley ushered them into the living room, where they all sat down. Chrissie remained by her side on the sofa while Mrs. O'Neal sat across from them in an armchair. Belle sat with her and Chrissie on the sofa. She and Belle turned to face one another.

"Lovely house," Belle commented, taking a moment to look around. "And this neighborhood is so peaceful and quiet."

"It's one of the oldest in town," Marley said. "My grandparents lived in this area for over fifty years. My grandmother…"

"Miss Eula Mae!" Chrissie exclaimed.

Marley grinned, delighted that Chrissie's affection for Eula Mae was so strong. "She lives next door," Marley explained to Belle. "Chrissie got to know her quite well when she'd come over here on Saturdays for our hair day."

"Oh, yes, Chrissie's foster mother said that you washed and styled Chrissie's hair twice a month." Belle smiled warmly at her, and to Marley's surprise, tears came to her eyes. "I want to thank you for that. Baby girl has mounds of hair and in the hands of someone who has no idea what to do with it, it would have been a disaster."

They all laughed at that, especially Chrissie, who also got a kick out of preening a little. Marley noted that her hair was expertly braided with some slack at the edges, which she was thankful for. Too-tight braids could damage the hair's edges, making it fall out and possibly never grow back.

She reached out and gently touched Chrissie's hair. "Whoever did these braids did a great job."

"Oh, I did," Belle said, looking pleased. "My grandmother taught me how to braid when I was around eight."

Marley knew then that she and Belle were going to be friends.

They talked about Chrissie's year in her class. Belle wanted to know everything she could tell her. Most of all Belle wanted to hear about Aisha.

"I liked her a lot," Belle said. "I wondered what happened to her. And Khalid, Chrissie's dad, searched for her. To think she was just down the road from us! When Mrs. O'Neal gave me her diary, I couldn't help reading it. It tore me up to find out she believed she would be rejected if she told us about the pregnancy. Khalid loved her. He hasn't been in a relationship since she disappeared. I think he's afraid to get involved with anyone."

She took a deep breath, released it and continued. "This has given us so much closure. He's relieved to know what happened to Aisha but so sad that she's no longer with us. He's flying home as we speak to meet Chrissie." She paused to take her cell phone out of her shoulder bag and clicked on the screen to awaken it. Then she went to the gallery and showed Marley photos of her son, Khalid.

Marley smiled. There were those dimples again, the skin tone and beautiful eyes. There was no mistaking that Chrissie belonged with Khalid and Belle. This thought both delighted and saddened her. Chrissie was where she belonged, but Marley would never stop regretting the missed opportunity of becoming her mother.

"They resemble each other quite a lot," she commented with a smile.

"You should have seen Khalid when he was Chrissie's age. The resemblance was more profound then."

Belle was smiling and there was a faraway look in her eyes as she remembered her son's childhood.

Marley warmed even more to her. She felt comfortable enough to ask an important question.

"Belle, I know you and I have just met, but I was wondering if perhaps Chrissie could somehow stay in our circle of friends and family here in Port Domingo. There are so many people here who love her. Her best friend is the son of my fiancé, Sebastian Contreras. His son, Bastian, was in my kindergarten class, too. And my grandmother misses her so much. Would you consider allowing her to come to family functions like Thanksgiving or birthday parties, those kinds of things? Or if you ever need a babysitter. You're just down the road from us. I'd be happy to babysit sometime."

Belle was staring at her with an expression of wonder on her face. Her mouth made the perfect O. "As a matter of fact, Marley, your request fits right in with what I was going to ask you!"

Marley waited in suspense, her eyes meeting Belle's.

"Marley, as I understand it, Chrissie doesn't have a godmother. I realize it's a little late for that. She's far from being an infant, when we'd usually decide these things, but would you consider becoming her godmother?"

Marley couldn't control herself, she hugged Belle. Belle, laughing, hugged her back. Chrissie cheered, and Mrs. O'Neal with tears in her eyes did a little dance in Marley's living room.

"I wish all of my cases ended this way," she exclaimed.

Marley let go of Belle. "Yes, Belle, I'd love to be Chrissie's godmother."

"Then it's done. You are officially Chrissie's godmother," Belle pronounced as though they were in a court of law.

Chrissie hugged Marley around the waist. "Yay! I can call you Godmother now."

SEBASTIAN THOUGHT HE and Marley were going to have a quiet, romantic Saturday night alone. If *alone* meant with his son and puppy sleeping down the hall.

She'd told him about becoming Chrissie's godmother and how happy that had made her. Now, he was recounting his conversation with his parents about Augustin's firing. How he was so relieved they had understood and was willing to let Augustin go find himself. He'd made the mistake of telling her what he and

Augustin had said word for word on that fated phone conversation. She'd turned to stare at him. "Wait, um, he actually said he wasn't coming to our wedding?"

"Those were his words," Sebastian innocently reiterated.

She stared at him as though he'd just grown another head. *Horrified* would be the word to describe her expression. "Babe," she said softly. "That won't do. Augustin must come to our wedding. He's family. He's your only brother. The only sibling you'll ever have. For the sake of Bastian and any future children we might have, I beg of you to make it up with him. Get him to come to our wedding."

Sebastian couldn't have been more shocked if someone had shot him with a police-issue stun gun. "Have you not been paying attention to Augustin his whole life? He's unsatisfied with his lot so he wants to make the rest of us miserable. He shirked his duty as a captain and showed no remorse. Why should I lower myself and make nice with him? He should be the one to apologize for being a total jerk."

Marley was nodding yes, as though she agreed with him. But, obviously, her mind was made up. "Don't do it for Augustin. Do it for Bastian."

"What has Bastian got to do with it?" he asked, confused.

"Bastian and any children you and I might have," she said, a determined look in her eyes. "The most important thing about kids that I've learned in my years as a teacher is this— they pay attention to everything the adults who raise them do. We are their examples. If you can't get along with your brother, maybe one day, Bastian will decide that he doesn't have to make the effort to get along with his siblings. 'Daddy doesn't like Uncle Augustin, so why should I like these pests?' And he *will* think they're pests. He'll be years older than them and there's nothing more annoying than kid brothers, as you can attest."

Sebastian sighed. He hated it when she proved her point so easily. He had, of course, been unaware that Bastian had been watching when he'd slipped the engagement ring onto Marley's finger the other day. But, Bastian had noticed and told his grandparents about it. How many other things had Bastian been soaking up about his behavior over the years? It was definitely food for thought.

Marley stopped talking and just gazed into his eyes, pleading.

"I'll try," he promised.

On Monday, midday, he went to Augustin's apartment. He knew his brother was probably sleeping in since he had nowhere else to be. Sure enough, Augustin came to the door wiping sleep from his eyes. When he saw it was Sebastian, he twisted his lips in a smirk. "What do you want?"

Sebastian stepped inside and closed the door. "Marley thinks if you and I don't make up and you don't come to our wedding, Bastian will be a rotten older brother to his siblings. You and I are obviously bad examples for him to follow."

Augustin frowned. "Say what?"

"You heard me."

"I did hear you, I just have no idea what to make of it. Marley really knows how to turn the screws, doesn't she? She's got you jumping through hoops already, doing Her Majesty's bidding. That's ridiculous, thinking we're going to adversely affect Bastian's relationship with his not-even-born-yet brothers and sisters. That girl's crazy."

"So, you don't think if you and I had made

more of an effort to get along that we'd have a better relationship, and you wouldn't even think of missing our wedding?"

Augustin looked nonplussed. "I haven't even had my coffee yet and you're posing metaphorical questions."

"Why do you hate me so much?" Sebastian asked. "What did I do that was so wrong? All I ever wanted was to be a good example for you by working hard, making the family business a success. We all wanted you to be a part of that, Augustin. We genuinely tried our best."

Augustin turned away and walked into the kitchen, where he started opening cabinets and withdrawing items to make coffee. Sebastian followed and simply sat down at the tiny table in the kitchen.

"I don't hate you," Augustin said as he measured ground coffee. "I might be slightly jealous of you. You always seemed to do everything required of you so easily. Dad told me once that he didn't worry about the business and could relax in his retirement because he knew you would handle it. I don't think he realized what those words did to me. I began to wonder why I was even here.

I wasn't needed. I was superfluous, just an extra son that would always be in his older brother's shadow."

Sebastian wasn't sure what to say to that. It was the first time Augustin had completely bared his soul to him. He did understand how Augustin felt, though. As if no matter what he did, he would never be good enough. So, he'd quit trying.

Sebastian stood and smiled at his brother. Augustin met his eyes as he started talking. "That is so untrue. You're needed and wanted, Augustin. But I learned something recently, and that is, sometimes you have to let go and let others live their own lives. I fought you so hard about being more invested in the business, but I should have been listening to what *you* wanted out of life. What do you want out of life, Augustin?"

Augustin stopped and met his brother's eyes. "You won't laugh?"

"I swear I won't," Sebastian answered.

"I did a little modeling the last time I was in Miami, and ever since I've been getting calls from agents who want to represent me."

Sebastian wasn't surprised. His brother had the looks and build of a movie idol. He had no idea Augustin had ever considered a career based on his appearance, though.

"So you're thinking of accepting some of those calls and seeing what pans out?"

Augustin relaxed more after he knew he wasn't going to be ridiculed for his confession. "Yeah, maybe."

Sebastian smiled back. "Cool. I wish you the best. And I do believe Bastian would take it personally if you and I don't work this out. He loves his uncle."

Augustin laughed. "I love him, too."

"Then you'll be at our wedding?"

"Marley's a witch—she's cast a spell over all of us. But, you know, that girl does have a lot of sense. Yes, I'll be at the wedding."

They gave each other manly hugs with pats on the back to seal their newfound understanding. Sebastian turned to leave. "And you're going to be one of the groomsmen. So you'll have to wear a suit."

"Aw, man," Augustin grumbled. But he was smiling.

MARLEY AND SEBASTIAN were married at the biggest pavilion in the city park in downtown Port Domingo. Father Rodrigo officiated. It was a beautiful October day: the temperature was seventy-five degrees and the sky was a beautiful shade of blue and there were no clouds.

Marley's father walked her down the aisle—a slip-free red carpet rolled out between rows of seats that had been festively decorated. She wore a delicate tulle dress in ivory with a modest bodice and spaghetti straps. The floaty skirt fell to her ankles and she was wearing strappy ivory sandals. Her hair was wild and free, the curls falling down her back. The only jewelry she wore was a pair of pearl earrings and her engagement ring. The seats were filled with over two hundred guests. Before Marley and her father strolled down the aisle, Chrissie, the flower girl, tossed rose petals in the path. Bastian was the ring bearer and Chewbacca, who was leash trained by now, led his human.

Already standing on the stage was Sebastian in a gray morning suit and Italian loafers. Beside him were his best man, Miguel, and his groomsmen, Augustin and Torin, who was on leave from the air force. Across from them stood Marley's maid of honor, Tandi, her matron of honor, Bonita Faye, and her bridesmaid, Kaye Johnson. In the front row were their parents and Eula Mae with her date, Daichi. Akira sat beside his grandfather.

They had withdrawn their offer for the fishery, saying that they couldn't improve upon it. But they were thinking of expanding the inn with Mr. Mason's enthusiastic agreement.

At last, Marley and Sebastian stood before one another, their eyes locked. Father Rodriguez intoned, "We are gathered here today to unite Marley Nesta Syminette and Sebastian Antonio Contreras in holy matrimony. A union most of you knew was inevitable."

Laughter from the assemblage. Father Rodriguez's face was lit with humor and love. "I've known both of them since they were children, and I have to confess, even I knew this day was inevitable."

When he got to the kissing part, Marley fairly floated into Sebastian's arms. He held her in his strong embrace and they kissed. Eula Mae shouted, "Hallelujah!"

Indeed, Marley thought, *praise God*. She smiled up at Sebastian when they parted. "I love you. This has been the most perfect day of my life."

"Wait until the honeymoon," he whispered in her ear, which made her blush.

Thunderous applause erupted, then the choir consisting of at least fifty men and women, led by Kaye Johnson, began singing "As" by Stevie Wonder. "As around the sun the earth knows she's revolving…"

Sebastian carried Marley back down the aisle, and she took the opportunity to look into the faces of some their guests and loved ones. Mrs. O'Neal was there, as was Belle Jackson with her son, Khalid. He was quite the celebrity in this area and she'd noticed several people surreptitiously snapping his photo with their cell phones.

"Do you think we can sneak off?" Sebastian asked as he carried her. "My pickup is parked not far from here."

"And miss the reception?" she asked. "It promises to be the party of the year."

SEBASTIAN HELD MARLEY firmly in his arms as they danced for the first time as husband and wife, to the song "You Are the Best Thing" by Ray LaMontagne. He'd picked it because the lyrics said everything he wanted to say on this day. That she was the best thing that had ever happened to him. She made life so much more beautiful than it would be without her. And theirs was a love that would last forever.

For the reception, they had changed out of their more restrictive formal wear and now were in comfortable clothing. After the first song was over, Marley cued the DJ with a wink. "Despacito" by Luis Fonsi featuring Daddy Yankee began to play, and he remembered the night at Diego and Sandy's anniversary party when they had gotten off the dance floor because they thought the song was too risqué for a nonmarried couple.

His Marley looked at him now, and said, "We're married. We can legally dance to this. But not too suggestively. There are children present."

Sebastian threw his head back in laughter and pulled her securely into his arms.

Other couples joined them on the dance floor of the town civic center, and soon there was a crowd doing the salsa. Even Eula Mae and Daichi were out there simply holding one another, their cheeks pressed together. Smiles on their faces.

"Your grandmother and Daichi," Sebastian

said close to Marley's ear. "Who would have thought it?"

Marley smiled up at him. "Never underestimate a Syminette woman, my dear husband."

* * * * *

Get 4 FREE REWARDS!

We'll send you 2 FREE Books plus 2 FREE Mystery Gifts.

FREE Value Over **$20**

Both the **Love Inspired®** and **Love Inspired® Suspense** series feature compelling novels filled with inspirational romance, faith, forgiveness, and hope.

YES! Please send me 2 FREE novels from the Love Inspired or Love Inspired Suspense series and my 2 FREE gifts (gifts are worth about $10 retail). After receiving them, if I don't wish to receive any more books, I can return the shipping statement marked "cancel." If I don't cancel, I will receive 6 brand-new Love Inspired Larger-Print books or Love Inspired Suspense Larger-Print books every month and be billed just $5.99 each in the U.S. or $6.24 each in Canada. That is a savings of at least 17% off the cover price. It's quite a bargain! Shipping and handling is just 50¢ per book in the U.S. and $1.25 per book in Canada.* I understand that accepting the 2 free books and gifts places me under no obligation to buy anything. I can always return a shipment and cancel at any time. The free books and gifts are mine to keep no matter what I decide.

Choose one: ☐ **Love Inspired Larger-Print** (122/322 IDN GNWC) ☐ **Love Inspired Suspense Larger-Print** (107/307 IDN GNWN)

Name (please print)

Address   Apt. #

City   State/Province   Zip/Postal Code

Email: Please check this box ☐ if you would like to receive newsletters and promotional emails from Harlequin Enterprises ULC and its affiliates. You can unsubscribe anytime.

Mail to the Harlequin Reader Service:
IN U.S.A.: P.O. Box 1341, Buffalo, NY 14240-8531
IN CANADA: P.O. Box 603, Fort Erie, Ontario L2A 5X3

Want to try 2 free books from another series! Call 1-800-873-8635 or visit www.ReaderService.com.

*Terms and prices subject to change without notice. Prices do not include sales taxes, which will be charged (if applicable) based on your state or country of residence. Canadian residents will be charged applicable taxes. Offer not valid in Quebec. This offer is limited to one order per household. Books received may not be as shown. Not valid for current subscribers to the Love Inspired or Love Inspired Suspense series. All orders subject to approval. Credit or debit balances in a customer's account(s) may be offset by any other outstanding balance owed by or to the customer. Please allow 4 to 6 weeks for delivery. Offer available while quantities last.

Your Privacy—Your information is being collected by Harlequin Enterprises ULC, operating as Harlequin Reader Service. For a complete summary of the information we collect, how we use this information and to whom it is disclosed, please visit our privacy notice located at corporate.harlequin.com/privacy-notice. From time to time we may also exchange your personal information with reputable third parties. If you wish to opt out of this sharing of your personal information, please visit readerservice.com/consumerchoice or call 1-800-873-8635. **Notice to California Residents**—Under California law, you have specific rights to control and access your data. For more information on these rights and how to exercise them, visit corporate.harlequin.com/california-privacy.

LIRLIS22

COUNTRY LEGACY COLLECTION

Cowboys, adventure and romance await you in this new collection! Enjoy superb reading all year long with books by bestselling authors like Diana Palmer, Sasha Summers and Marie Ferrarella!

#427 THE BRONC RIDER'S TWIN SURPRISE
Bachelor Cowboys • by Lisa Childs

After weeks of searching for his runaway wife, rodeo rider Dusty Haven gets a double shock when he finally finds her. Not only is Melanie Shepard living at his family's ranch—she's pregnant with their twins!

#428 HER COWBOY WEDDING DATE
Three Springs, Texas • by Cari Lynn Webb

Widow Tess Palmer believes a perfect wedding beckons a perfect life. Roping cowboy Carter Sloan in to plan her cousin's big day might be a mistake—unless she realizes this best man might be the best man for her.

#429 AN ALASKAN FAMILY FOUND
A Northern Lights Novel • by Beth Carpenter

Single dad Caleb DeBoer hires Gen Rockwell to work on his peony farm for the summer. When she moves her daughters to the farm, the two families become close—but a startling secret threatens everything.

#430 THE RUNAWAY RANCHER
Kansas Cowboys • by Leigh Riker

Gabe Morgan found sanctuary as a cowboy in Barren, Kansas. But he can't reveal his true identity—even as he falls for local librarian Sophie Crane. How can he be honest with Sophie when he's lying about everything else?

Visit
ReaderService.com
Today!

**As a valued member of the
Harlequin Reader Service,
you'll find these benefits and more at
ReaderService.com:**

- Try 2 free books from any series
- Access risk-free special offers
- View your account history & manage payments
- Browse the latest Bonus Bucks catalog

Don't miss out!

If you want to stay up-to-date on the latest at the Harlequin Reader Service and enjoy more content, make sure you've signed up for our monthly News & Notes email newsletter. Sign up online at ReaderService.com or by calling Customer Service at 1-800-873-8635.

RS20